praise for GUARDIAN

"I couldn't put it down!! *Guardian* grabbed me from page one and didn't let me go! This romantic suspense is SO good. The reader is off to a fast paced adventure with plenty of suspense, danger, corruption, overcoming the past and a sweet romance."

JEANNE, GOODREADS

"A thrilling page-turner that's hard to put down. This is a clean, Christian fiction in which the characters discuss their faith and trust in God or their struggles to believe."

RD, GOODREADS

"*Guardian* is a fast paced WITSEC type of story. Plenty of movement, action, and a little bit of romance thrown in for a change of pace from all the action. It fits nicely into this series and definitely held my attention."

KELLY, GOODREADS

"I really enjoyed this story by a new to me author. Faith-filled, lots of suspense and quite a few surprises. I am really loving this series so much."

DANA, GOODREADS

GUARDIAN

HEROES OF RENEGADE

GUARDIAN

JENNIFER CHASTAIN

Guardian
Heroes of Renegade: Book 4 | The Brave

Print ISBN: 978-1-966463-80-1

For more information about Jennifer Chastain please access the author's website at www.jenniferchastain.com.
Published in the United States of America.
Cover Design: Sunrise Media Group LLC

The name of the Lord is a strong tower; the righteous man
runs into it and is safe.

PROVERBS 18:10 ESV

ONE

IT HAD EITHER BEEN A COLOSSAL MISTAKE VOLunteering to assist with the annual Fourth of July Renegade Days or a brilliant idea. Right now, Aubrey Richardson was leaning toward the former. She stared at the to-do list on her desk and sighed at the enormity of her effort to give back to the community that had been her safe space for the last six years.

In Renegade, she was simply Aubrey, assistant for the US Marshals Service. This city had become her home, her lifeline, and she owed them the best Renegade Days festival she could organize.

Yet lately, the memories she'd worked so hard to box away seemed determined to break out, taunting her and putting her on edge. Just one of the reasons for the plate of homemade brownies, baked fresh this morning, currently sitting on her desk.

She gave herself a mental shake to banish the nightmare of her childhood. *Focus, girl.*

Old-fashioned stagecoach? Check. Band of outlaws recruited

from the local community theater group? Check. Costumes and horses secured? Check and check.

Only two days until the festival, and everything was falling into line—except she hadn't heard from Judge Stephen Mullinax in three days.

She'd specifically asked him to participate since not only was he a fixture around town and a dear friend of hers, but he also looked the part. Salt-and-pepper hair. Full mustache and beard. That beat-up Stetson he wore whenever he was outside. The judge looked as if he'd stepped out of an old-timey black-and-white photograph from the Wild West. All he needed was a duster and a six-shooter strapped to his side.

She glanced down at her phone one last time before she logged in to work at the US Marshals office.

No messages. No voicemails.

Aubrey had formed a close bond with Stephen after she moved to Renegade six years ago. They'd known each other for years, and he'd looked out for her in a lot of ways, but over the last few years, they'd really gotten to know each other.

These days, he was the closest thing she had to a father figure. After her testimony at a high-profile murder trial had sent her and her family into hiding, her relationship with her parents had become strained, to say the least. Her presence put them in danger, and it had caused a rift. Six years ago, she'd left them to their life in witness protection and moved here to Renegade.

A tall figure opened the door of the Renegade branch of the US Marshals Service, his face obscured by the bright sunlight streaming through the glass windows behind him as he stepped in from the wainscoted hallway of the federal courthouse.

She raised a hand to her eyes, trying to determine if this was a friend or someone more sinister.

She shifted closer to the monitor, one hand on the office phone, one finger on the concealed panic button, ready. Oh, good grief!

Her imagination was getting out of control. It was twenty years since her world had been shaken. The man she had testified against was in prison, and he was never getting out.

"Hey, Aubrey. What's up?"

She squeaked and placed her hand over her heart. "Goodness, Liam. You scared the ever-lovin' wits out of me!"

Liam was the newest member of the US Marshals team in Renegade. Over six feet tall, with expertly styled dark-brown hair, he could charm the worst offender with his blue eyes and that easygoing smile. Even though he'd only been in town a few weeks, he was already one of the people she was comfortable confiding in.

"Guilty conscience." Liam laughed.

All the tension in her back and shoulders released. She sipped the now-cold coffee she'd picked up earlier from the Beanery. "You're in early this morning."

He leaned against the reception desk, a grin on his face. "Yeah, thought I'd come in and take care of some paperwork for my group of protectees." He'd pushed the sleeves of his dress shirt up his forearms.

His gaze locked on the platter of homemade brownies she'd baked earlier this morning. A few weeks ago, Liam had met one of the local firefighters, Samantha Williams. Now that she wasn't his protected witness, they were dating, and Liam's niece and Sam's sister--both in their teens—were best friends. Aubrey loved their new little family, but as far as baking goodies went, Sam was a bit of a disaster. She approached baking the way she approached a training burn—full commitment, lots of optimism, and a willingness to call for backup when things got smoky. She'd once set a pan on the counter and announced, "Good news: Nothing caught fire. Bad news: I'm not sure they're legally brownies."

Aubrey smiled as she picked up the plate. "Would you like a brownie?"

Truthfully, she was saving them for the return of Deputy US

Marshal Ethan Butler, but there was no sense in wasting them. Ethan probably wouldn't eat them anyway. The man was a health nut, usually, with no room for any "fun" food. Though lately, he had been acting out of character, so she was hoping the treats—if he actually indulged—would cheer him up.

"I made them this morning for Butler." She set the plate on the desk and pushed it closer.

"All those for Butler?" He quirked one eyebrow.

"Maybe." She cleared her throat and looked away. "But I have a feeling my efforts will be rebuffed, so you go ahead." Nothing she did seemed to break through Butler's gruff exterior. Maybe she should quit trying.

"Well now, you don't have to twist my arm."

She laughed and watched as he ate the brownie in two bites, wondering how Sam thought he was attractive. To Aubrey, he was more of an annoying brother, but maybe she worked with too many alpha males with guns and badges.

"What?" He wiped away the crumbs with a napkin.

Aubrey shook her head, then waved away the thought. "Never mind. There's a fresh pot of coffee on the credenza." She opened a tab on her computer and clocked in.

"What would this office do without you, Aubrey?" He wandered over to fill an official US Marshals mug with coffee and held it up in a salute.

"Starve. And probably have better dental checkups." She scanned her email, checking for any urgent messages. Nothing. "Anything new with your protectees?"

"Nope. All safe and secure." Liam leaned both forearms on her monitor, his blue eyes intense. "Look, I know I'm the new guy around here, but what's up with Butler?"

Ethan Butler was the one person in this office who seemed immune to her sunny disposition. She'd seen him with his elderly neighbor at the grocery store, witnessed his kindness toward animals. In those rare moments, he'd let down his guard and flash a brief smile. And yet here, he rarely talked to her or any of the others on the team unless it was necessary.

Always the protector, Ethan stepped into danger without a second thought. Between chasing fugitives and his talk of kayaking rapids and tearing across Renegade's mountain trails on his dirt bike—when he did mention personal stuff—it seemed clear that adrenaline wasn't just a rush for him, it was fuel. Given they worked together, he was someone she shouldn't want . . . but couldn't stop thinking about. Infuriating man.

Aubrey rearranged the already neat files on her desk. "I don't know what you mean."

"Oh, come on. All he does is growl at everyone in the office, especially you."

She rested her chin on her fist and sighed. "I don't get it. Most people like me. I mean, I'm easy enough to get along with, right?"

Liam smirked. "You're Little Miss Sunshine to his thundercloud."

"I suppose some people like to be miserable."

"Maybe, but I don't think that's the reason." He glanced over his shoulder, then came around the desk and sat in the extra chair beside her. "Do you think he's in trouble?" He motioned her closer. "I mean, after all, he was suspended."

As the office administrative assistant, she was privy to a lot of personal information. But Ethan's sudden removal from the office two weeks ago didn't make sense to her.

One day he was out visiting their witnesses, and the next day he was gone.

A few weeks back, he'd been on a short administrative leave following a shooting. That was standard procedure when a weapon was discharged by an agent. This suspension had been something entirely different, and it just didn't make any sense to her. Had it been anyone else, maybe. But Ethan?

She stood and grabbed the stack of files from her desk. "I don't know, but something *odd* has been going on lately, both around town and in the office." Goosebumps rose on her arms, and it wasn't the air-conditioned office.

"That's what I'm talking about." He leaned back and crossed his arms over his chest. "Look, I'm just trying to figure out what's going on. From what I've seen, Butler does everything by the book, so a suspension doesn't make any sense."

"And all this tension since he's been gone isn't good for the team." Aubrey nibbled on a brownie. "Butler should be back either today or tomorrow, from what little information I've been given."

"Good. When he shows up, I really need him to fill me in on whether he's discovered more about this shadow syndicate since Dr. Torres was killed. I know he was looking into it, but I haven't heard anything."

She sighed. "I wish I could tell you, but the man is a closed book. The only thing I really know about him is that he transferred from a much larger field office two years ago. Denver, I think."

Did Liam really think Ethan would tell him what he was working on? Especially if it was sensitive.

They should probably quit gossiping about the guy, but Aubrey was the first person to admit she wasn't perfect. Ethan was just so difficult to figure out.

"That's what he told me. Denver." Liam crossed his arms and watched her under hooded eyes.

She opened the file cabinet and stuffed the folders inside. She'd figure out where they were supposed to go later. "In the two years that he's been here, this is how he is. With everyone. Even Supervisor Howard."

"Maybe that was the reason for his suspension. Insubordination." Liam followed her over to the filing cabinets.

Aubrey shook her head. "I don't think that's why he was suspended." She slammed the drawer shut, then sat down behind the desk and shrugged. "The paperwork I saw said that he was suspended for an unintentional and improper discharge of a firearm while on assignment."

"You're kidding me."

"I wish I was."

Liam frowned. "I can't see Butler being careless so soon after he was cleared for a different shooting. The guy is meticulous."

"I know, right? It doesn't make sense. He's one of the best marshals out there." She looked around the office area, hoping no one else could hear them. "There has to be something else, some logical explanation as to why he's been suspended."

"You're right." Liam held up his hands. "If Ethan wants to tell us, he will. But when he does arrive, can you let him know I'd like to sit down and talk with him?" Liam picked up a flyer for Renegade Days from her desk and glanced at it. "Or is that asking you to risk your life?" He smirked and sat on the edge of her desk, his back to the door.

Didn't the guy have any work to do?

"You have no idea." She took his empty mug back to the credenza. "I just wish I knew what his problem is. Renegade's not that bad, is it?" She sighed. "Maybe he needs to get out of Renegade for a bit—take a couple of days and go kayaking. Go visit his friends or family somewhere else."

Someone cleared their throat behind them. "Who needs to get out of Renegade?"

Heat rose up Aubrey's neck as she and Liam looked at each other.

Busted. When would she learn to keep her opinions to herself? She knew better than to talk about a coworker. Every coherent thought in her head stalled, and she slowly glanced up at the man in question.

Ethan's mouth turned down in a grimace, his eyebrows practically touching. Shoot. Mad and *gorgeous.*

Aubrey shot Liam a death glare, but Liam's smile only grew wider, if that was even possible.

"You do, my friend." Liam stood and slapped Ethan's back. "I'm hoping you took your shot to get out of town and into the great outdoors, work out some of that tension you carry."

Ethan's gaze moved between Aubrey and Liam, his eyes shooting sparks, and Aubrey glanced back at her keyboard. "Don't you two have some work to do? Someone else to annoy?"

She looked up and saw him shrug off Liam's hand. "And you"—he turned his dark-blue eyes on Aubrey, his gaze polar-ice-cap cold—"shouldn't gossip."

Was it hot in here? She stood and leaned on her desk, smiled sweetly at him.

Ethan's frown deepened.

Liam snorted, and Ethan's gaze drifted to his coworker. Liam coughed into his hand and stood.

Aubrey bit her lower lip and cleared her throat. "Anyway, welcome back! I made these this morning. Care for a brownie?"

She held out the plate, along with a napkin. Who knew they were destined to be apology brownies?

Ethan stared at her for another long moment before Liam grabbed a napkin and loaded it with two chocolate squares.

"Don't mind if I do." Liam held up the brownies in a salute. "You make the best brownies of anyone I know." He leaned closer. "Just don't tell Sam I said that, or she'll have my hide."

Aubrey laughed, and it felt good to release some of the tension from the past week. She made an X over her chest. "Promise."

"My girlfriend has many talents, but baking isn't one of them." He started to walk back to his office, stopped and pivoted. "Don't tell her I said that either."

Liam whistled on his way back into the old office building, the jaunty tune echoing off the marble floors.

Aubrey shook her head and sat down, staring at the open email inbox on her computer screen. Nothing new.

She felt Ethan's gaze on her, and she looked up into those mesmerizing blue eyes of his. He was a handsome man, if you could get past his grumpy exterior. Short brown hair a little long in the front, and a smattering of freckles.

She gave herself a mental shake. "Something else I can help you with, Deputy Marshal Butler?" She pasted on a smile. She'd kill him with kindness.

If it didn't kill her first.

"Uh, no. Thanks for the brownie." Ethan grabbed one of the bigger squares and headed back to his office, his footsteps drifting away.

Huh. Will wonders never cease?

Aubrey checked her phone one last time. She moved her to-do list into the file folder marked Robbery Reenactment.

It looked like she needed to make a personal visit to Judge Mullinax.

Thankfully, she didn't need to understand Ethan Butler in order to make this year's Renegade Days a success.

Ethan closed the door to his office and leaned against it, staring at the brownie in his hand. Aubrey and her baked goods.

It was better than thinking about the past few months though.

He needed to check in with Sebastian Carlsson, his good friend and the US marshal in charge of the Denver office. They'd met while on assignment over ten years ago, and he was one of the few people Ethan completely trusted.

A few months ago, Detective Michael Martinelli and a private investigator named Luca Saxon had shared with Ethan that they suspected local businessman Roger Rousseau was in the middle of a criminal organization operating in Renegade. But without evidence, neither could do anything about it. Ethan had started to dig into Roger Rousseau, and all too quickly, the threats had begun.

Ethan had put in a request for surveillance on Roger and a warrant to look into the guy's financials, but he'd been turned down. The same day, his elderly neighbor had been roughed up by two men who'd told her that Ethan should back off from looking into Rousseau. And she'd told Ethan that one of the men had been wearing a silver star like his.

After that, Ethan had been forced to come up with a more radical plan. If someone in the office was working for the Shadow Syndicate, he had to keep his investigation under the radar. And do it in a way that kept the people around him safe.

He and Carlsson had devised a ruse to throw off whoever was leaking information to the Shadow Syndicate. They'd agreed to set things up to make it look like Ethan was suspended for improper use of a firearm, to give him the chance to investigate without anyone knowing. He'd spent the past two weeks following Rousseau and trying to unearth the evidence they needed.

Ethan dialed his friend's number.

"Carlsson."

"It's me." Ethan closed the office door and sat behind his desk. Morning light filtered through the double-paned glass, a few dust motes floating in the air.

"What did you find out tailing Rousseau on his trip?"

Ethan ran his free hand through his hair. "Nothing."

He studied his usually tidy office, and a shiver of apprehension raced up his spine. A fine white dust covered his desk and bookshelves. Strange. Two weeks out of the office shouldn't have produced that much dust.

"Martinelli and Saxon were so sure Rousseau's involved in the syndicate."

"I know. I still think he is." Ethan exhaled. "Look, I know we were supposed to connect this morning, but I don't think I should talk about this now."

"Hang on." Muted sounds bled through the line. "You at the office?" Carlsson asked.

"Yeah. Let me get back to you later this afternoon." Ethan disconnected the call.

He fired off an email to private investigator Luca Saxon, asking to meet, and sent the same email to Detective Martinelli.

An automated response came from Luca. *I'm out of town right now. If this is an urgent matter, please contact Detective Martinelli of the Renegade Police Department.* The email included Martinelli's number.

Muted laughter from the reception area drifted down the hallway, and he popped a corner of brownie in his mouth and groaned in appreciation, savoring the rich, chocolatey flavor.

Ethan called Martinelli's number, but the call went to voicemail. "You've reached Detective Martinelli of the Renegade PD. I am unavailable for the next two weeks. If this is a police matter, please contact my lieutenant."

He leaned back in his chair and stared at his phone. What were the odds that both were unavailable?

He closed his laptop with more force than necessary. Everything was messed up, and now his coworkers assumed that he was in trouble with the Marshals. The fewer people involved in this investigation, the better he'd be able to narrow down who was working against them.

He brushed a stray cat hair off his pant leg and grimaced. He'd stopped by his elderly neighbor's house to check on her two spoiled felines. He should've known better than to wear dark dress slacks.

He didn't want to interact with anyone in the office today. Too much weighed on his mind—too much confusing information he'd gathered that didn't make sense. He was convinced Roger Rousseau had to be working with the syndicate, but he just couldn't prove it. Yet. He'd followed the guy during his trip to Denver and, afterward, questioned the shady guy Roger had met with.

No dice.

No one would talk, and Ethan still had no evidence. But the attack on his neighbor couldn't be ignored. Rousseau was connected somehow.

With a loud exhale, he massaged his temples, eyeing the remaining portion of the decadent brownie. Aubrey knew how to push his buttons, sure. But she also knew the way to his heart. He didn't dare tell her he had a sweet tooth that he tried not to indulge. If she continued baking, he'd be as big as a barn.

A small smile lifted his lips as he stared out the multipaned window. He'd never hear the end of it from Liam if he ate the rest of that brownie. Ethan shook his head. Liam seemed like the kind of guy who could easily become a friend. Ethan was reluctant to admit he missed the camaraderie of a close-knit team to lead.

But what he needed right now was silence and a solid lead to break open the case he'd been secretly assigned. Just when he thought he was getting close to ferreting out the mole, another clue surfaced linking his theory to another suspect. If he didn't know better, he'd wonder if there weren't multiple people in charge of the syndicate—or if power kept changing hands.

He raked his fingers through his hair. This was a case he really needed help with. A second set of eyes.

But could he trust Liam?

If he knew Liam a little better, had worked with him more than a few weeks, he might be able to get a better read on the guy. Maybe trust him.

Before his manufactured suspension, Ethan had been invited to join Liam for his weekly pickup game of basketball at the high school. Even invited to his house for a cookout with some of the other marshals. Ethan shook his head. Liam seemed to be a good deputy marshal. Hard-working. Dedicated. But after investing fifteen years into his own career as a marshal, it was easier for Ethan to keep his own counsel than risk facing another career disaster.

He glanced at the brownie on his desk, debating whether to finish it. A knock on his door made him pause, his hand hovering over the baked treat. He cleared his throat. "Come in."

"You busy?" Aubrey stood in the doorway, her dark-auburn hair shimmering around her shoulders. Her deep-green blouse matched her eyes, and man, she was stunning. She held a stack of manila folders.

Ethan shook his head. "What's going on?"

She moved to stand in front of his desk. "Supervisor Howard wanted me to give these to you for review. Looks like we're getting more protectees in a few weeks."

"Thanks."

She placed the stack on his desk, and they locked eyes for a moment. He cleared his throat. "Something else I can help you with?"

She glanced away first. "Uh, no. Just making sure you have everything you need now that you're . . . uh, *back* and all." Aubrey tucked a strand of hair behind her ear.

"Thanks."

"Sure." She gave him a small smile. "I'll see you later, then."

"Yeah."

Butler, you are an idiot.

"Aubrey, wait up." He stood, and she slowly pivoted toward him. He pointed at the brownie. "Thanks again for making the brownies. They're really good."

A smile lit up her face. "Thanks. I tried a new recipe. Less sugar."

"Well, they're great."

They stood there awkwardly, staring at each other. The air shifted and sizzled until the moment was broken by his phone ringing.

Ethan cleared his throat. "Sorry, I have to get that."

She gave him a little wave. Most days, he might go so far as to wish they weren't coworkers so he could ask her out on a proper date. But dating a coworker was a bad idea. He needed to keep her at arm's length.

He glanced at the caller ID and answered, a small smile forming. "Mrs. Hanover, what can I do for you?"

His elderly next-door neighbor was sweet and a little nosy, but he enjoyed their nightly talks. She treated him like a grandson and was the one person in town who had made him feel welcome after his transfer from Denver.

"Oh, Ethan. I'm so sorry I missed you this morning. The girls were glad to see you though. They're always so pleasant after you visit. When did you get back?"

"Late last night." He cradled the phone between his ear and shoulder and opened his laptop, scanning through the documents he'd sent himself. "I didn't want to wake you up, so I just left the cat treats on the front porch."

"Oh, that's so sweet."

If he didn't get control of this phone call, she would go on for hours. He'd love to chat, but he was working on the biggest case of his life. "Is there a problem? Do the cats need to go to the vet?"

"Heavens, no." She laughed, almost a girlish giggle. "You're so thoughtful. No, this is something else."

He pinched the bridge of his nose. "Anything." He'd do anything at this moment to end this call, but his grandmother would tan his hide if he was rude.

"Yes, well," she said. "I don't know if you can or not, what with your schedule, but I need a huge favor."

Mrs. Hanover's sunny personality reminded him so much of his own grandmother, which made it difficult to refuse her requests. Not to mention his work had put her in danger. He didn't want to say yes purely out of guilt, but he was still going to help her. "Of course. What is it?"

"Could you watch Mittens and Simba for me while I'm away this week?"

He exhaled and a smile tugged at his mouth. He should've known this call would have something to do with her "girls."

This week wasn't good though. The cats would want extra attention. "I'd love to, but . . ."

"Oh, thank you, dear. They just adore you. I'm leaving tonight. My granddaughter is having a baby, and I want to be there to hold her."

Ethan shifted in his chair. He cleared his throat, forcing calmness into his voice. "Now how can I refuse that?"

Despite what she'd said, Ethan heard the fear in her tone, the tremor. The same fear he'd heard when she told him about the two masked men who'd shoved her around while she was loading groceries in her car. Ski masks, broad shoulders . . . and one idiot who hadn't bothered hiding he was a marshal.

Did the police follow up with her after? No.

The case had seemingly fallen through the cracks for lack of evidence.

A tight burn settled beneath Ethan's ribs. Mrs. Hanover had been scared enough the first time. No way was he putting her through a voice-ID lineup that would only drag her back into that moment and maybe paint a fresh target on her. He wouldn't take that risk with her. Not ever.

The old woman's voice wavered. "You're a good man, Ethan Butler. God has a special woman just for you."

He'd heard this tune multiple times from his neighbor. "As I told you, I'm content being single."

"Come now. Wouldn't you like to come home to a special someone every night?"

The question hit harder than it should have. Once, he'd thought he had that future. An engagement ring. A promise that should have been ironclad. Turned out he wasn't half as good at reading people as he was at tracking fugitives. If he were, he'd have seen the truth behind his fiancée's words and actions.

And he wouldn't be spending his evenings with an elderly neighbor who baked him casseroles out of pity.

"It's not good for a man to be alone," she continued gently. "Just be patient. God has the perfect woman prepared for you."

Perfect. That word scraped along a raw edge he kept buried deep. He'd chased perfect once. It hadn't ended well.

He cleared his throat. "What time are you leaving?"

"Around four."

"I'll drop by tonight after work, and I'll feed the cats and make sure they're taken care of while you're gone."

"Thank you, dear. I'm praying for you."

She disconnected the call before he could respond or even ask when she was returning.

He shook his head. Prayer. He hadn't been praying about the Roger Rousseau case. Who to bring in to help. Or even if he should. Which was the problem. He was forging ahead in his own strength, his own wisdom, without seeking the Lord's guidance.

The lapse was subtle. If he were honest with himself, ever since he'd been reassigned to Renegade, he'd neglected his relationship with the Lord. Instead of being thankful for the move, he'd allowed bitterness to creep into his daily interactions with his coworkers. He'd done this to himself. No wonder no one wanted to be around him.

A knock on his doorframe jolted him out of his thoughts.

"Glad to see you back in the saddle." Adam Montgomery towered over Ethan's six feet, two inches and looked like he needed to eat a huge plate of pasta. Montgomery had to be ten years younger than him. Shoot, most of the staff were younger than him. Ethan felt like a grandpa most days.

"Thanks." Ethan returned to the encrypted files he'd sent himself. The sound of leather squeaking pulled his concentration away from the monitor. "You're in early."

Adam leaned back in the chair. "Yeah. I thought you might want to know what happened these past two weeks."

"I already have the notes from last week's briefing." Ethan picked up the single sheet of paper and waved it at the kid.

Adam leaned forward, resting his forearms on his thighs. He glanced over his shoulder. "I'm going to close the door."

"Do whatever you want." This guy could be the office traitor for all he knew.

"Testy." Montgomery closed the door and resumed his seat. "Look, dude, I know a lot more than you think I do."

Ethan snorted. "Sure, kid."

Adam pulled the notepad that was sitting on the corner of the desk closer to himself and wrote on it.

YOUR OFFICE IS BUGGED.

All the breath froze in his lungs. Ethan pulled his chair closer to study the man in front of him. Montgomery had a lot of nerve, but he sat there unwavering. Ethan narrowed his eyes and responded on the notepad.

How do you know?

Adam shrugged. "Want to grab a coffee?"

"I could use the caffeine." He picked up the notepad and scribbled another message, then turned it around for Adam to read.

Adam stood and nodded. "Yeah, I need something to counteract all the sugar from Aubrey's brownies."

"Montgomery, you could eat an entire plate of brownies and still not gain an ounce." Ethan chuckled. "Let's go. I'm buying." Ethan locked his laptop. "I need a good, stiff black cup of coffee from the Beanery."

Outside the old courthouse that housed not only the federal

courts but also the US Marshals on the third floor and holding cells for prisoners in the basement, Ethan exhaled.

"What do you know?" Ethan stepped off the curb and turned to Adam.

"Not here. Let's get that coffee." Adam headed for the storefront with the dark-blue awning.

The rich aroma of roasted coffee beans greeted Ethan as he stepped across the threshold of the Beanery coffeehouse. Rich wood floors, small café tables, and wide picture windows added to the charm of the old building. Ethan inhaled and closed his eyes, willing the caffeine into his bloodstream, the fatigue and stress from the past few weeks weighing on him.

"Can I help you?" A barista with pink hair and a nose ring greeted him.

"Hey, Chloe." Ethan resisted the urge to ask for his usual drink. "I'll have a large black coffee with two shots of espresso, and my friend here will have . . ."

Adam stared at the petite woman, mesmerized. "Uh . . ." His Adam's apple bobbed up and down.

Ethan poked him in his ribs. "Speak up, man."

Adam leaned closer to Chloe. "I hope you won't think less of me, but I'll have one of those white chocolate mint iced coffees." He grinned.

Chloe shook her head. "Coming right up, gentlemen."

The whir of the machines made conversation impractical while they waited, but a few minutes later, Ethan paid for their coffees and pointed to a table in the far corner of the shop. "Let's sit and you can fill me in."

Adam grabbed the drinks from the far end of the counter and joined him. "While you were suspended, a tech team came into the offices and were supposedly upgrading the Wi-Fi, some of the phones, you know, that sort of thing."

"Go on." The jolt of coffee soured as it hit Ethan's stomach.

"But the thing is, they were only in your office."

All the customer chatter and noise faded into the background. "And that's your basis for thinking my office is bugged?"

"They replaced the Wi-Fi access point in your office and out front. That's it."

Son of a gun.

Ethan glanced around the shop. Nothing seemed out of place—just the normal, everyday activity of customers needing their coffee fix. *Think, man.* "Okay, thanks for letting me know." Ethan leaned his forearms on the table, gaze focused on his colleague. "Did you mention anything to Supervisor Howard about surveillance?"

Adam shook his head.

"Good." He wrapped his hands around the paper cup, the heat seeping through and almost burning his palms. "Did Aubrey know they were coming?"

"No. She was a little suspicious. Stalled them until Howard got into the office."

"Makes no sense."

Adam shrugged. "I'm just telling you what happened."

"But why bug my office?"

"And the entryway. Someone is fishing for info." Adam sipped his drink. "I had lunch with a Renegade PD detective friend of mine. He heard some gossip around town that Roger Rousseau might be involved in some shady stuff."

Ethan tried to play it off. "Like the syndicate people are talking about?" Seemed a bit coincidental that his coworker wanted to talk about the very thing Ethan was secretly working on. "What do you know about it?"

Adam sipped the last of his drink and tossed the cup into the trashcan by their table. "Nothing, really. It's just word-on-the-street type of chatter. But come on, it's the most interesting thing that's happened around town recently. Some shadow syndicate in Renegade, and witnesses like Torres getting murdered." Adam shrugged. "Your office was bugged for a reason. Is Rousseau really involved?"

"To determine that, I need evidence." Ethan paused a moment, considering his limited options. He didn't want to wonder if Adam was the dirty agent in the office. He'd never have believed that before now and wasn't inclined to think it just because the guy was astute enough to put some of the pieces together, but right now, everyone was a suspect.

"I can't tear apart the life of a guy like Roger Rousseau without cause," Ethan said. Judge Mullinax would never give him a warrant for wiretaps and surveillance without proof something was going on. "So let me know if you hear anything else, because I could definitely use the help."

"I know you were on a special assignment the last two weeks and not really suspended."

Ethan leaned back in his chair and crossed his arms. *This is bad.* "How did you find out?"

"Come on, man. You're a rule follower, and I've never seen you lose control. Word around the office is that it was misuse of a firearm. That's baloney." Adam shook his head. "Besides, it makes sense. I think you're onto something. There are too many inconsistencies in what's happening in town, witnesses and suspects like Torres and old Ralph Rousseau dying, and evidence disappearing. There's more to Roger than meets the eye. If he's a small player, maybe we can flip him for info on the big boss—whoever is in charge of the syndicate."

"I agree." Ethan stood, tossed his half-empty cup in the trash. "Come on, let's get back to the office." He'd need to do a sweep of his room for the bug, but with Adam on board, it felt like a fresh injection of energy into this case.

Adam nodded. "You got it. Thanks for the coffee."

"Anytime."

He paused in front of the three-story federal courthouse that housed multiple departments. Built in the neo-classical style of the early 1900s, the light-gray sandstone created an air of sophistication, while the dormer windows reflected the morning sun, almost blinding him. The old-fashioned globe lights at the entrance were yellowed with age, and an American flag fluttered in the breeze.

Adam stood off to the side, his gaze watchful. "I'll let you know if I hear anything else." He opened the reinforced glass door, and a blast of cold air washed out. "I have courtroom duty today." Adam slid his sunglasses onto the top of his head.

Ethan grinned. "Lucky you."

Adam's tall form passed through the metal detectors and then disappeared down the long hallway. Ethan rubbed the two-day stubble he hadn't bothered to shave before he came in this morning.

Even though Adam was a good guy and wanted to help Ethan with this case, there was no way he would let him. If life had taught him anything, it was that the fewer people involved, the better.

Otherwise, someone else was going to get hurt because of him.

TWO

AUBREY STARED AT THE OFFICE PHONE FOR A beat, indecision warring with a need to know. She hated bothering Stephen during the week, since his docket was typically full. She blew out a breath. Oh, for crying out loud. This was getting ridiculous.

She picked up the receiver and dialed the judge's office.

"Renegade Courthouse. Judge Stephen Mullinax's office."

Aubrey's stomach dropped at the sound of Claire Carnforth's greeting—she sounded stressed. Claire had been working for the judge for a couple of years now, and even though she was young, she kept him organized and on schedule. Aubrey checked the caller ID and verified she'd dialed the judge's direct line.

"Hello?" Claire said.

"Hey, sorry. It's Aubrey Richardson. Is the judge in?" *Please be in.* She really needed to speak with him about some last-minute changes to Renegade Days. Well, that and he hadn't returned any of her calls or texts. She couldn't remember many days since she moved to Renegade when he hadn't sent her a text or called to see how she was doing.

"No, he hasn't. He missed his eleven a.m. appointment. I'm worried."

"Me too." This wasn't like him. He was always punctual, and even though he had a busy schedule, he always made time for Aubrey. "When was the last time you heard from him?"

"He left work early on Monday. Said he had to meet someone at home. I even called his housekeeper yesterday when he never showed, and she said she was sure he'd be back soon. But where did he go?"

A sense of dread settled in Aubrey's stomach, but she forced herself to remain positive. "Thanks, Claire. I'm sure he's around somewhere. Maybe he got caught up in something sensitive and that's why he's out of contact."

"Yeah, sure, that has to be it." Hope clung to Claire's statement.

Aubrey prayed it was true. But all the what-ifs pummeled her best deflections. "Tell you what. I'll go to his house and check on him."

"Would you?"

"I'd be happy to do that." Aubrey grabbed her purse from her desk drawer and locked her computer. "If the judge contacts you while I'm out, will you let me know?"

"Not a problem. And thanks again, Aubrey."

"Anytime." She disconnected the call. She was going to have to take matters into her own hands. If Stephen wouldn't talk to her, she would ride over there and see him.

She poked her head in Liam's office. "Got a minute?"

He glanced up from a file he was reading and leaned back in his office chair. "I need a break from these files. What's on your mind?"

She tugged her purse higher on her shoulder. "I need you to cover the front desk while I'm gone. Maybe an hour."

"I'm intrigued."

"My life isn't a mystery, and it's not a case to be solved." Aubrey braced herself against the doorframe and fidgeted with the purse strap, hoping that didn't sound too harsh. Nothing about her needed to intrigue *anyone.* She exhaled. "Sorry. I'm going to swing by the judge's house on my lunch break. I'm part of the organizing committee for Renegade Days, and he's helping me."

Liam grinned and his dimple peeked through. "That's all you've been talking about for weeks now."

"I know." She felt heat climb up her neck. She'd lived in the shadows for so long. Helping with Renegade Days gave her a sense of purpose. A sense of belonging.

She tried to shrug off his comment. "I'm actually a little bit worried about the judge. He's not answering his phone."

Liam frowned. "He's a pretty busy guy. I'm sure he's just gotten caught up in something."

Maybe Liam was right. Maybe she needed to give this to the Lord, exercise a little faith. But it had been a long time since she had done that. Did she even know how?

Liam's easygoing smile returned. "Admit it. You're getting bored behind that desk, and you're looking for something to add excitement to your life."

She forced herself to smile. "I'm just trying to work on the Renegade Days festival. I've had enough excitement in my life, and it was overrated, thank you very much."

If only he knew. But nothing had happened to her since she moved here. The man she'd testified against was still in a federal prison, with no chance for parole. She'd trusted Judge Mullinax's judgment when he convinced her that uprooting her life and moving here was the best thing for her and her family.

Renegade was safe, and so was she.

"Really? You *want* things to be boring? That's an interesting take on a community festival that's the highlight of a lot of people's year." He leaned forward. "What about Butler? If you need an assist, I'm sure he'd be happy to help."

Aubrey snorted. "Hardly. Ethan and I should just agree to stay in our own corners." She should give up trying to win him over with brownies.

Liam laughed at her discomfort. "Butler is a good guy. He's a bit closed off, but he just needs the right person in his life to help him. Like Sam and me."

He thought Ethan needed a girlfriend? She snorted. "I don't think I'm the right woman for the job. It's awkward being around him."

"That's because he likes you."

"What are you, in sixth grade?" Aubrey shook her head. "Anyway, I still need to find the judge."

Liam frowned. "Now that you mention it, the judge is always around the coffee shop or charming the older ladies at the Mountain View Café. I haven't seen him."

She huffed out a breath. "Right? He loves a good cup of coffee and a fresh doughnut. Chatting with his gaggle of lady friends."

She paused a moment, choosing her words. "Here's the thing. We're having our final run-through of the stagecoach robbery tomorrow, and the judge is portraying the sheriff. I've got this bad feeling something is . . . off." Lately, he'd distanced himself whenever she wanted to talk or even meet up for breakfast on a Saturday morning. "I'm going to see if I can track him down."

Liam sat upright, his steady gaze searching hers. His deep-blue. eyes twinkled. "Maybe you should take Butler with you. You know, for backup."

"What? No!" She'd have swatted his arm if he were nearer, and he knew it.

Liam grinned. That rascal. Why was he pushing her toward Ethan? What a ridiculous idea. If she was into the whole tall, dark, and handsome-with-a-side-of-grump type of guy, Ethan was it. But in every way other than simple attraction, it was a bad idea. "Look, if I wanted to scare somebody away, I'd take Ethan."

Liam's smile faded. "I don't think you should go alone." He closed his laptop and locked his desk.

"It's just a visit to an old friend. Nothing is going to happen."

Liam leaned against the desk. "I don't know, Aubrey." He rubbed his chin with his knuckles. "Like you said, this entire situation feels off. Let me go with you."

"I tell you what." She grabbed her cell phone out of her oversized bag. "I'll call Jenna and have her meet me there."

"I'll have the police meet you out there."

She opened her mouth, but Liam cut her off. "Please? For my peace of mind."

"Fine."

Liam followed her outside into the bright July sunshine. Even though it was the middle of summer, the mountain range to the west ensured that the town had moderate temperatures, not blazing hot like the Southern states. In some ways, she missed her small hometown in North Carolina. But days like this, when the sun was shining, the humidity was low, and a soft breeze swirled around her . . . Yeah, she liked this part of the country.

She unlocked her SUV, started the engine, and rolled down the window. Liam rested his palms on the roof and leaned in, examining the interior of her vehicle. He whistled. "Nice ride. Is it new?"

"Yep. Picked it up a couple of weeks ago. With the cold winters, I needed a dependable car. My old two-door Honda Accord was on its last legs."

She didn't mention that the judge had helped her with a huge down payment. If her coworkers knew about his generosity, it would raise some red flags. They might get the wrong idea about her relationship with him.

"That car was, what? Almost thirty years old?"

She nodded and patted the steering wheel. "Look, I'll be fine."

"Sometimes people surprise us." He quirked one eyebrow, tapped the roof with his knuckles, and stepped back. "So be careful."

"I'm sure it's my overactive imagination and he decided to take a couple of personal days." She held up her phone. "I have my cell phone, and I'm calling Jenna now. Watch my desk."

"Yes, ma'am." Liam gave her a mock salute.

She drove away, blowing out a sigh. She didn't have time for overprotective-big-brother vibes. She'd been on her own for a long time. But that was just the way Liam was—with everyone.

There was no way it meant he'd noticed something about her that he was trying to figure out. After all, if it were obvious, Ethan would have seen through her a long time ago.

She left the hustle of the crowded city behind for the relative peace of the newer developments at the outskirts of the city limits, navigating out of downtown Renegade and going west into the suburbs near the Renegade Mountain range.

This town was a sanctuary for her. Here, she was accepted, no questions asked. She had a job she loved, close friends, a sense of belonging. No one saw her as the girl whose sister had been murdered. She had a good life here. She enjoyed spending time with Stephen at his house. He always had company, and when he was on vacation, she would house-sit and make herself at home, make use of his in-ground pool.

She exhaled and called Jenna. When her friend picked up, Aubrey said, "Hey, girl, what are you doing right now?"

Jenna was a librarian at Renegade Mountain Elementary School. They'd met several years ago when both had volunteered to help with props and costumes at the local children's theater. They'd bonded over their shared love of coffee and books. This year, Aubrey had recruited Jenna to assist with the Renegade Days festival costumes.

"Hello to you too." A crash sounded, and some mumbling bled through the line.

"You okay?" Aubrey admired the passing scenery. The houses were becoming larger, and the green spaces increased the farther she drove away from the city. She loved getting out of the city, away from the noise, the summer heat.

"Depends on what you mean by 'okay,'" Jenna said.

Aubrey frowned. "That doesn't sound good. Where are you?"

Jenna sounded out of breath. "Ooh, I think I pulled a muscle. I thought you were supposed to help me get all these costumes out and labeled."

"That was today?" A small smile tilted her lips. Aubrey loved the organizing, just not all the other stuff. She'd rather delegate, but she wanted to be there for Jenna.

"You know it was today."

"And that's why you're my right-hand woman, keeping me on track."

"You're laying it on kind of thick, aren't you? You totally forgot to take the morning off work. Hang on." Muffled voices filtered through the speaker. "Okay, I'm back. As I was saying . . ."

"I'm sorry, and something has come up. I'm heading over to the judge's house." Aubrey braked at the red light.

A soft breeze floated through her open windows, and she lifted her hair off the back of her neck. Her face felt flushed. Despite what she'd told Liam, she wasn't going to ask Jenna to drop what she was doing and come with her. Aubrey had been keeping herself safe for years.

"Mullinax is locked in as the sheriff in the reenactment, right?"

Aubrey hummed her response.

"Aubrey?" That sounded like the exact tone Jenna would use with her third graders if they were too loud in the library.

She licked her dry lips. "Yeah?"

"What's wrong? You've kind of been off since the conversation at Bible study last week when we talked about favorite childhood memories."

She should've deflected before now. "You are really nosy, you know that?"

Jenna laughed. "I know when something is bothering my bestie."

"I don't know if I should tell you . . ." Aubrey bit the inside of her cheek.

"You know you can tell me anything, right?" Jenna softened her tone, her voice barely audible above the hum of the tires. "You haven't been your normal, cheerful self."

"Yeah?"

"Yep."

This short drive was turning out to be one of the longest of her life. Next week was the anniversary of her sister's death. Her knuckles turned white as she gripped the steering wheel.

She pulled up to an intersection and sat as the opposing traffic moved through the streets, an almost ballet-like choreography. "I'm worried about my friend."

Aubrey fought the tears that formed at the corners of her eyes. She swiped under them and glanced in the rearview mirror. Odd. That same black sedan had been behind her when she left the courthouse parking lot.

Goosebumps formed on her arms.

Ridiculous. She was safe. *It's nothing.*

Aubrey cleared her throat. "I know, but I'd rather not talk about it."

Jenna continued, "At first I thought maybe you just don't have many happy childhood memories. But the more I think on it, the more I wonder if you experienced a traumatic event when you were young. And maybe you're scared."

Aubrey swallowed back all the fear. "I don't think it's any of your business."

Everything Jenna said was true. With every question, Jenna

probed and pushed, picking at the fragile scabs that had formed over her heart.

"Honey . . ." Jenna's voice softened. "I understand if you don't want to talk about it, but I hope you know I'm here if you do."

Aubrey's breath caught and her vision dimmed around the edges. She'd kept her life carefully hidden, never revealing who she really was.

The car behind her honked, and her entire body jerked forward when she pressed the accelerator too hard. She had to focus on her breathing. Get this situation under control.

"Aubrey?"

"I'm still here." She glanced down at the speedometer and backed off on the gas. One thing she didn't need was a speeding ticket.

A bead of sweat trickled down her back, and she reached over to turn on the car's AC. Sweet, blessed cool air washed over her skin, and she released all the breath in her lungs.

Aubrey forced a lightness into her voice. "It seems like you have me all figured out."

"Maybe because we've been hanging out ever since you came to Renegade. I know you."

"Hmm." Surely if Jenna knew that associating with Aubrey potentially put her in danger from the man Aubrey had sent to prison, then she'd run away as fast as her legs would take her. "How so?"

"You love to help but won't let anyone help you, which was why I was surprised you asked me to help with Renegade Days."

The silence lengthened between them, like the mountain shadows at dusk. Mysterious and a little murky. Usually, silence between them was comforting. The peaceful rest of two people who loved and trusted each other. But right now, it seemed to foreshadow something. A storm Aubrey wasn't going to be able to hide from.

Aubrey cleared her throat. "I would argue the point, but I'm a little concerned about the judge."

"I get it. Change of subject." Jenna's tone reflected hurt and betrayal.

"I'll explain as much as I can later." Aubrey hated keeping her friend out of the loop, but the less Jenna knew of her past, the better.

She glanced at the digital clock on her dash. "Look, I'm almost to the judge's house. How about I grab some lunch for both of us on the way back and we can talk?"

"I could really go for a turkey Reuben from Schwartz's Deli."

"You got it."

Traffic thinned the farther away from the city she traveled, the area greener, more densely populated with cottonwood, quaking aspen, chokecherry, and Rocky Mountain maple trees. She relaxed her grip on the steering wheel as she and Jenna went over the last few details about Renegade Days.

Aubrey hated to admit it, but her friend was close to the truth. Too close.

What if she showed Jenna even more of the real Aubrey?

But years in WITSEC kept her from revealing too much. She would always be in danger as long as Finn Donovan was alive.

She'd always figured people didn't want to hear about her childhood trauma. She kept all those experiences buried deep, hoping no one would unearth them. But maybe, just maybe, they might like her and not look at her with pity.

Aubrey punched in the code to Stephen's front gate. "I just pulled into the judge's driveway."

"Be careful."

"I will. But stay on the line with me." Aubrey exited her vehicle and walked up the front steps. She paused at the top. "That's odd."

"What is?"

Aubrey frowned and studied the front of the house, forgetting for a moment that Jenna was still on the phone. "The judge's front door is open."

"Maybe one of the staff forgot to close it."

"Maybe." Sure, he lived in a gated community, but the judge still locked his doors.

She pushed the door open with her foot and stood inside the cavernous foyer. She pulled the phone away from her ear. "Hello? Judge Mullinax? Stephen? Anybody home?"

The hairs on the back of her neck stood up, and she whirled around and saw the chaos. The open drawers. The blood splatter on the walls and floor.

"Aubrey? What's going on?"

"Someone ransacked the judge's house." Her voice was a strained whisper. Pictures had been ripped off the walls, curtains had been pulled off the rods, the material puddling in front of the floor-to-ceiling windows, and the furniture was shredded.

And his housekeeper lay in a pool of blood.

Aubrey's mouth went dry. "I don't think I'm going to be able to bring you that sandwich."

Ethan shoved his chair back and pinched the bridge of his nose. All the information he had gathered the past two weeks as he followed Roger Rousseau around Denver amounted to nothing but a pile of unrelated clues. He hadn't caught Rousseau doing anything illegal. At least, not yet.

Even the guy he'd questioned, Rousseau's associate, a man he'd identified as Draven Frost, didn't have anything concrete. It was all just hearsay. Nothing made sense no matter what angle he looked at it from. The members of the syndicate were sneaky. Every contact, each piece of evidence and information, was unrelated. It was how they'd gone on unchecked for so long, infiltrating every part of this city.

And trying to pull it all apart was driving him absolutely nuts.

He studied the bug he and Adam had found in his office. There had to be some small detail, some seemingly inconsequential fact he was overlooking. He grabbed some tweezers, dropped the bug into an evidence bag, and locked it in his desk. He needed to send it off to forensics for testing.

He sat up, pulled the file closer. Perhaps . . .

The ping from an instant message popped up on his screen, and he groaned. Daniel Howard, the supervising deputy US marshal in the Renegade office.

Howard

Welcome back. Meet me in my office in 5.

Ethan

Will do.

Howard wasn't typically big on pleasantries, so that wasn't unusual. But a request like this was.

A shaft of sunlight streamed through the blinds, and the brownie he'd eaten earlier sat like a lump of gooey dough in his stomach. Ethan hadn't made time to develop friendships other than with his elderly neighbor, although maybe Aubrey could be an exception. Only because she wouldn't leave him alone, which was annoying, but man, he sure enjoyed sparring with her—heaven help him.

He shook his head. He had a job to do. He had to find out who was behind the Shadow Syndicate, end of story. He didn't need to get involved or bring anyone into his sphere of influence.

People who got close to him ended up dead.

Ethan didn't want a repeat performance from two years ago, when he lost almost his entire team.

After briefing Carlsson in Denver yesterday before he left, this summons didn't bode well.

Even though he'd been instructed not to tell Howard anything, keeping information from a fellow marshal chafed. But orders were orders, and he needed to get in there. Pretend he was contrite for an offense he hadn't committed. Howard could be the mole, after all. But Ethan had the guy pretty low on his list of potential suspects.

He grabbed a small notebook and pen off the corner of his slightly dusty desk. Aubrey should've sent housekeeping in here to dust. But then, in the past, he'd chewed her out for entering his office while he was out. Yeah, probably why no one had set foot in his office while he was "suspended."

Howard's office was at the end of the long, narrow hallway, facing the Renegade Mountain range. As the supervisor here in Renegade, Howard had a corner office with the best view in the entire building.

Every step on the polished marble echoed down the third-floor hall. Ethan stopped in front of Howard's office and knocked on the heavy wooden door.

"Come on in." Howard waved him inside. "If you don't mind, close the door, please."

Oh boy, this couldn't be good.

Ethan sat in one of the leather guest chairs facing Howard's desk. Howard continued to stare at his laptop, and Ethan restrained himself from shifting in his seat.

"Reporting, per your request." His heart thundered in his chest, and he focused on breathing.

Howard tapped a few keys on his laptop, his focus on whatever document was in front of him, before he finally glanced up. "I see you're back from your suspension."

"I'm eager to get back to work." Ethan shrugged off his exhaustion like an old shirt. He simply needed to get through the next few hours, then he could go home and dig through his files again. Sleep in his own bed.

Howard steepled his fingers under his chin. "If I can be honest with you, this suspension doesn't look good on your record."

"I agree. I'll try not to let it happen again."

"Help me understand what really happened, Butler." Howard leaned forward—an attempt to intimidate him, no doubt.

Ethan met his gaze. "An unfortunate series of events. A mistake on my part."

"No, I don't think that's it." Howard reclined again and picked up a pen, twirling it between his fingers. "My gut is telling me this was a setup. What happened to you, Butler? You've always been a straight shooter."

God, I don't want to lie. Give me the words.

Ethan held up his open palms. "I'm an open book. I follow the rules."

Howard barked out a laugh. "That's why it makes no sense. I hear you were out of town for most of your suspension. Taking a vacation?"

Ethan tried not to wince. "With all due respect, sir, I checked with the Marshals office in Denver and they approved my travel. I was able to do some hiking. Clear my head."

Although, it had been anything but a vacation. Red herrings, clues leading to dead ends, mysterious messages. Roger Rousseau was connected to something huge, and Ethan couldn't put his finger on what it was—or what might be gearing up to happen. He just knew that whatever illegal activity it was needed to be stopped or prevented.

Howard narrowed his eyes. "Hmm. Yes."

Ethan pulled a copy of the approval email out of his notebook and handed it to Howard. "If I recall, this approval was forwarded to you. Even though I was suspended, I was given permission to leave town."

Howard scanned the sheet of paper. "Yes, I remember now. Please make sure that Aubrey puts this in your personnel file." Howard pushed it back with one finger as if it was contaminated.

For some reason, Howard didn't like him. Ever since Ethan had transferred here, they'd butted heads. If only this guy knew he was on a list of potential moles, he probably wouldn't be so smug.

"Sure." Ethan placed the email in his notebook and stood. "If that's all?"

"Actually, I need a few more minutes of your time." Howard pointed to the chair Ethan had just vacated.

Ethan sank back into the seat and swallowed his rising anger.

"I'm a little concerned about you." Howard pulled a file folder from his drawer and placed it on top of the desk. He removed a sheet of paper. "About you and your career. First, you were put on standard administrative leave for a shooting you were involved in a few weeks ago. Now you have an infraction on your service record for a so-called mistake. In the two years that you've been assigned to this office, you have been a strictly by-the-book type of marshal. No infractions. That's why I'm so concerned. We've mapped out some action points for you to follow." He blew out a breath and tapped the paper with a finger. "We'll need you to sign off on the action plan."

"If I can explain . . ."

Howard held up one hand. "Let me finish. You're a good marshal—one of the best I've had the opportunity to work with in a long time."

That was a surprise. "Thank you."

"You might want to hold off thanking me until after you hear this." Howard pinned him with a stare. "My observation is that I haven't seen your usual focus. Your peers genuinely respect you, but being a lone wolf can be deadly in this type of work."

Howard leaned back in his chair. "Is there something I can help you with? A personal issue bothering you? If you don't want to confide in me, there has to be someone else in our office. The agency has professional counseling services. Butler, you're one of the best, and we all need help at times. It's nothing to be ashamed of."

Howard had no clue the stress Ethan was under working this special assignment. But Ethan didn't need a thunderbolt from the Lord to verify the truth of his supervisor's words. Stress was no excuse for rebuffing help from others on his team. A wave of conviction rolled over him.

Ethan nodded. "I can assure you that I'll do a better job."

Howard's mouth opened, as if he didn't quite know what to make of Ethan's humility. "I know you will. We're a team here, and when one of us hurts, we all do."

Howard wanted to discuss Ethan's pain? Perhaps he was digging, trying to get Ethan to reveal his assignment. Did Howard suspect he was investigating the Shadow Syndicate? There was no way. Carlsson only used a secure phone line when he contacted Ethan. But if their suspicions were right and someone at the office was connected to the criminal group, that meant Ethan couldn't trust anyone.

He shook his head. "Thank you, I appreciate the offer, but I'd rather not talk about it right now." He clenched his jaw, and tension settled across his shoulders.

"You don't have to talk to me about it. But get some help for that anger of yours. Losing people is part of the job. It's never easy, but it happens, and as much as we don't want to believe it, it does affect our job performance." Howard held up his hand and leaned back. "I know we don't have a close relationship, but I think you need to find someone to confide in."

"Understood."

Sitting down with someone who understood him and his quirks sounded all well and good, but when he couldn't trust anyone, what was the point in taking the risk?

"Just don't carry it alone, Butler. It gets heavy fast in this job."

Ethan shifted in his seat. "I'll make the call."

"Yes, you will." Howard slid the sheet back into the folder and clicked his mouse. "Otherwise, the next suspension won't be temporary. We're talking career-level consequences."

Ethan's jaw clenched. He didn't need a lecture; he needed answers.

The printer kicked on. Howard collected the pages and handed them across the desk. "Approved counselors in the Renegade area."

Ethan stared at the list, the names reading like accusations. "Fine. I'll look."

Stay calm. He wants a reaction.

"Not look. Schedule." Howard's tone hardened. "I expect confirmation."

Ethan lifted a brow. "And if I don't?"

"Then I will be recommending you be removed from fugitive apprehension. We can't afford to have distracted team leaders in the field."

Heat flushed under Ethan's collar. The silence pressed in, and the weight of the investigation hollowed his lungs.

Lord, help me. He bit the inside of his cheek and forced himself to think through the consequences. Peace edged in and he maintained eye contact. "With respect, this doesn't warrant removal."

A muscle twitched in Howard's jaw. "Don't think I won't bench you." He leaned forward. "You're usually a rule follower. They've got you on something else, don't they?"

Bile rose in Ethan's throat. He kept his face neutral. "I have no idea what you mean."

He fixed his gaze just past Howard's ear. He hated lying—but why was his supervisor pushing this hard?

Howard leaned back, shoving the file into his drawer. "Very well. Make the call or you'll be removed from fugitive apprehension, Deputy Marshal Butler."

Ethan stood, fighting the urge to slam the office door on the way out. Not today. Not with eyes on him.

Now wasn't the time to lose his cool. He needed to keep building his case. When he and Adam had pulled a listening device from the wall socket last night, he'd considered alerting the rest of the Renegade team, but until he knew who'd planted it, that stayed between him and Adam—and Carlsson.

But what was Howard up to? Was it just his ego? Possibly.

From what Ethan understood, Howard had clawed his way to this position, stepping on other people's hopes and ambitions to get where he was today. He seemed to know Ethan was on a special assignment, which meant he wanted Ethan to spill so he knew what was going on.

Problem was, that would be too much of a risk. There were other forces at work here in Renegade, and Ethan intended to discover who was behind the crime wave without Howard's ego messing things up.

No, he couldn't confide in anyone right now.

He didn't wait for the elevator but took the stairs instead.

Outside of the courthouse, he called Carlsson. "It's Butler. We need to talk."

THREE

AUBREY DRUMMED HER FINGERTIPS ON THE steering wheel, holding on tight but not going anywhere. Her gaze fixed on the open door of Stephen's three-story mansion.

Leaves skittered across the paved drive, the manicured lawn a perfect backdrop against the clear blue sky. Sunlight streamed through the canopy of trees and heated the inside of her SUV.

It would be a gorgeous day if there wasn't a dead woman inside the house.

She glanced at the clock on her dashboard. Liam had said he would get the police to come to the house. *Come on. What's taking them so long?*

Aubrey glanced at her phone and sighed. Just when she'd finally found a place to put down roots, somewhere where she wasn't constantly looking over her shoulder, tragedy occurred.

A bead of sweat trickled down her back, and she shivered.

Please, God, let him be safe.

She really didn't expect an audible response. It had been a long time since she'd spoken with the Lord. And an even longer time since she'd felt His presence in her life.

A tap on her car window startled Aubrey out of her musings, and she jerked away from the door. Heart pounding out of her chest, she closed her eyes for a beat and held her breath.

When she opened them again, she exhaled at the sight of one of Renegade's finest standing at her door, a concerned look on his face. Aubrey cracked the window open, and a soft mountain breeze lifted the ends of her hair, rushing across her cheeks and cooling her skin.

"Ma'am? Are you okay?" His name tag read *Ferguson*, and his tactical belt creaked as he rested his hands on his trim waist.

"Yeah, I'm fine." She gave him a wobbly smile and pointed to the big house. "You might want to get the crime-scene techs, because Judge Mullinax's housekeeper is in there, lying in a pool of blood in the entry between the kitchen and dining room."

Bile rose up her throat, and she forced back the sour taste.

Officer Ferguson stepped back, hand on his gun holster, looking imposing with his uniform and short hair. "Ma'am, can you get out of your vehicle, please."

That wasn't a question.

Hands shaking, she unbuckled her seat belt, then glanced around the driveway as two more cruisers stopped behind her vehicle. An ambulance skidded to a stop behind the patrol cars, lights flashing, and a pair of EMTs in matching navy uniforms emerged carrying medical bags.

"Slowly, please."

She nodded and exited her SUV and almost collapsed against the side panel.

"Driver's license, please."

"I need to reach into my car and get my purse." This guy looked like he was a powder keg ready to explode, with his red face and defensive stance.

"Fine, no fast movements."

She nodded and reached in to grab her purse. Slowly, she unzipped her bag and pulled out her wallet with her ID.

He held his hand out, and she placed her Colorado driver's license in his outstretched hand. "I'm Aubrey Richardson. I work for the US Marshals."

He glanced at her ID, then back at her. Nodded once. "I'm going to call this in. Be back in a minute."

Where could she go? The officers had purposefully blocked her in. If she'd been trying to hide the body, she certainly wouldn't have hung around and waited until the cops showed up. She would've called 911 on her way out of town.

She crossed her arms and leaned against the driver's door. A patch of clouds had obscured the sun, throwing her in a pocket of shade, and she rubbed her hands up and down her arms to ward off the chill.

"Well, you are who you say you are." Officer Ferguson handed Aubrey her driver's license.

She resisted rolling her eyes. Of course she was who she said she was. She came by her red hair honestly, and not out of a bottle.

Aubrey tucked the license in her skirt pocket. "So I can leave?" She glanced over his shoulder to see a plainclothes detective walking toward them. Great.

"Thanks, Ferguson, I'll take it from here."

Aubrey narrowed her eyes. She knew this detective. She would have to be vigilant, as he tended to be overzealous.

"Ms. Richardson, I'm Detective Joseph Murphy." He had to be in his mid-forties, the start of a dad-bod evident, a little squishy around the middle. His receding hairline accentuated his beady green eyes. He held out his hand and they shook. *Eww.* His palm was sweaty, and she forced herself not to wipe her hand down her skirt.

She willed her racing heart to slow down. Deep breaths. "I think we've met before, when you testified in federal court last year."

"Ah, yes, I remember now. That drug case." Murphy clapped his hands and glanced over her shoulder. "This shouldn't take long. Can I ask you a few questions?"

"Sure, go right ahead."

"What were you doing out here at Judge Mullinax's house in the middle of the day?"

Easy question, she had this. "The judge has agreed to portray the original sheriff in the Renegade Days reenactment tomorrow. He wasn't answering my phone calls or texts, so I decided to come and check on him."

A smile curved his lips. "Is that what you kids are calling it these days?"

Her blood pounded in her ears, and her hands fisted at her side. "Excuse me? What are you implying?"

"Oh, come on now, Ms. Richardson." Detective Murphy circled her car, his gait slow and his words condescending. "Why on earth would an attractive single woman leave her office in the middle of the day if not to, well, *you know* . . ." He let the implication hang in the air between them, like a sour smell wafting on the breeze.

"Just say it." She tossed the terse words back at him.

He leaned in, his coffee-scented breath fanning her face. "You know very well what I'm saying. You were having an affair with the judge."

She barked out a laugh because that was the most ridiculous thing she'd ever heard. "Give me a break. He's old enough to be my grandfather."

"Some women like older men." Detective Murphy rocked back on his heels, a smug smile on his smarmy face.

"I know. I've met all the women who like *this* older man. I'm not one of them." She shook her head. "You're unbelievable. I wish the judge was my grandfather. He's the kindest, most helpful man I know."

"That's not what I've been hearing around town."

She crossed her arms. "Do tell."

"From what I've heard, you come out to his house quite a bit. You've been seen around town with the judge, having coffee or enjoying a meal together. I've even heard that you house-sit for him when he's on vacation."

Of course. The first responder–law enforcement gossip mill was worse than Aubrey and Liam in the office.

"All true." She lifted her chin. "Because we're *friends.*"

"Did this start off as friendship and morph into more? Because I have to ask myself why. Why would this beautiful young woman want to hang around an older man? Is it his money? His connections?"

God, I know I haven't asked for anything in a long time, but I could use some help here.

She exhaled and counted to five. What did this have to do with a dead housekeeper?

Murphy raised his brows. "Well?"

"You've already made up your mind that I'm guilty of your disgusting insinuations. But I would never harm the judge. Or his housekeeper. He helped me when I first came to Renegade."

"Oh, I'm sure he did." His nasty comment fueled her anger, but she forced herself not to react.

Man, this guy was relentless—and he was going to twist everything she said into something sordid.

"A woman is dead, Detective." Aubrey choked out her response, and all her good intentions failed her. She wouldn't cry. At least, not yet. "Does this conversation have a point?"

He only smirked.

"Is there anything else I can help you with?" Aubrey clenched her fists at her side.

"The crime-scene unit needs to check you for gunshot residue before you leave."

Aubrey shrugged. "Perfect. They won't find anything."

"We'll see about that."

The detective stepped away, and the tight band around Aubrey's chest loosened. She grabbed her cell phone and called Jenna.

"Are you okay?" Jenna's panicked tone didn't help calm Aubrey's jangled nerves.

"The police are here and questioning me like I did something."

"Did they find Judge Mullinax?"

"No. Just his dead housekeeper." Aubrey pinched the bridge of her nose.

Jenna inhaled sharply. "Oh, have mercy. I'm so sorry you had to see that, Aubrey."

"Me too." She stifled a sob. "I-I bent down to check her pulse and she was cold." Aubrey closed her eyes as she relived the scene. "This detective thinks Judge Mullinax and I were . . . ah . . . *more* than friends." Just saying those words felt as if someone had stabbed her in the heart.

Jenna mumbled under her breath. "Oh, for pity's sake, the man was old enough to be your grandpa. Listen, just stay put. I'm calling the Marshals office. Maybe one of the guys can come get you."

"Thanks, Jenna." Aubrey sniffed.

"No worries," Jenna said. "There's no way you should even be a suspect."

"I know. Crazy, huh?"

"It'll be okay." Jenna kept Aubrey on the line while she called the Marshals office.

Aubrey leaned against her car. A wave of dizziness washed over her, and she grabbed the door for balance.

It better be okay, although the detective seemed to think this was an open-and-shut case, with her as the primary suspect.

"Aubrey?" Jenna asked.

"Yeah. I'm still here."

"I talked to Liam, and he's bringing another marshal with him to drive your vehicle back."

Relief washed over Aubrey, and the tightness in her chest loosened. "Thank you. And Jenna?"

"Yeah."

"Pray for me."

"You know I will." Jenna began to pray, and a calmness washed over Aubrey, a feeling of security that she hadn't experienced in a long time.

"Excuse me, Ms. Richardson?" One of the crime-scene unit technicians tapped her on the shoulder, and she whirled around.

"Yes?" She muffled the phone against her shoulder.

"I'm sorry, but we need to check your hands for gunshot residue." He pulled on a pair of gloves.

She nodded. "Hey, Jenna, let me call you back." She disconnected the call and dropped the phone in her bag.

The crime-scene tech opened a kit and had her place both palms on a tacky sheet of paper. "That's all I need. Thank you."

"Sure, no problem."

But it was a problem. A huge problem. She glanced over and noticed the detective staring at her. What was with him, and why did he think she was the guilty party? Stephen's sweet housekeeper didn't deserve to be murdered. It had nothing to do with her.

And where was Stephen, anyway?

Ethan sat in front of his laptop, not quite sure what to make of his meeting with Howard. He scanned the list of therapist names and shoved away the offending piece of paper.

"This is a load of . . . manure." He really wanted to swear at the paper. At the names, at the world in general. But swearing never solved any problem, big or small.

Help, Lord. Get a handle on my temper.

He got up and paced his office in front of the open door—wanting so much to go back and confront Howard, and yet, at the same time, he knew he needed to lay low, play it cool.

During his conversation with Carlsson, they'd both agreed that this was the best course of action. For now. Right up until the time when he could spring his information on the individuals who were members of the syndicate.

Stress, high anxiety, and danger were all part of being a marshal. It was something he'd lived with for a lot of years. It wasn't like he needed a therapist to help him.

He knew how to do his job.

"You won't believe what happened to me this afternoon!" Aubrey's voice seemed to infiltrate the office halls. Normally, she was the glue that held the office together, not the one causing a stir. She was the one who soothed and calmed scared individuals who had been relocated here after entering WITSEC for the first time.

Now, though, a cabinet drawer slammed shut, along with an office door. The sound of one excited voice in the lobby area of the Marshals office drew Ethan's attention away from his work.

He strode back to his desk and pushed the laptop closed. Conflicting evidence still bothered him, but he'd have to look at it later, when he wasn't so distracted.

The outrage in Aubrey's voice yanked his attention off the case file faster than any alarm. ". . . and then they took my fingerprints, Emma. Like I'm the one who killed that poor woman!"

He stepped into the reception area and saw half the office clustered around Aubrey's workstation. She sat behind her desk, dark-rimmed glasses a sharp contrast to all that deep-auburn hair cascading down her back.

Deputy Marshal Jodi Glover propped a hip on the corner of her desk, arms folded, expression dark. Deputy Marshal Emma Kennedy, fresh from court security, still in her blazer with her badge clipped to her lapel, leaned over the reception desk, eyes wide. Deputy Marshal Nick Stanton, former military sniper, hovered at the edge of the group, massive shoulders blocking part of the aisle, jaw set in that permanent don't-mess-with-my-people line.

"Can you believe it?" Aubrey sat at her desk, gesturing wildly with her free hand. "They marched me right past the bullpen. Everyone staring at me like I was wearing handcuffs."

Ethan stood just out of line of sight and listened. He eased closer, keeping to the wall. He shouldn't be listening to her conversation with someone else—again—but as soon as Aubrey mentioned a dead body and fingerprints, that raised his curiosity. Raised all his instincts, if he was honest.

Perhaps if he hadn't been so intent on proving he didn't need anyone and pushing away all the suspects in the office, Aubrey might actually confide in him. But that required a level of friendliness he hadn't practiced in a long time.

Emma's voice drifted over the low hum of the office. "They actually booked you into the system?"

Aubrey exhaled hard. "I know it's procedure, but that detective—grrr. I'd like to give him a piece of my mind."

Jodi muttered, "Name and badge number, and I'll give Internal Affairs a piece of my mind."

Nick said nothing. He just planted his feet behind Aubrey's chair like a silent sentry, arms folded over his chest. His gaze flicked to the door, then the windows, then the elevator, a slow, practiced scan that said the soldier in him never really shut off.

Ethan leaned against the doorjamb with his arms crossed. "Don't give away too much of that mind of yours." He pitched his voice just loud enough to carry. "We need it here in the office."

She shrieked and practically launched out of her chair.

Emma jumped. Nick's only reaction was a slight tightening at the corners of his eyes, like he'd just recalculated Ethan's threat level from *annoying* to *mildly irritating*.

Aubrey closed her eyes for a beat, then fixed her gaze on him. "What are you doing sneaking up on me like that, Deputy Marshal Butler?" Her voice was a low hiss.

He stepped in, closer than he probably should have, and he had to give her credit—she didn't retreat an inch. "I could hear your conversation all the way down the hall." He kept his tone dry. "Some of us have to work, you know."

"Some of us were detained this afternoon," she shot back. "So excuse me if I need a minute to vent."

Emma cleared her throat. "Uh, Aubrey? Maybe call one of us next time before you spontaneously combust."

"Breathe, Sunshine," Nick said quietly.

She sucked in a breath. Then another. Her shoulders lowered.

"Better?" Ethan asked, softer this time.

Aubrey nodded once. She reclaimed her chair, grounding herself with a hand on the desktop. "Thanks, guys."

Ethan scanned the circle of faces—Jodi simmering, Emma worried, Nick unreadable as stone—and clapped his palm lightly against the doorframe. "All right, everyone, back to work."

Emma leaned in and gave Aubrey a quick hug. "Call if you need anything tonight. Okay?"

Aubrey shook out her hands and gave her a tight smile. "Thanks."

Ethan moved off the doorway toward her, part of him glad she hadn't broken, part of him wishing he knew how to make her feel safe enough to talk to him.

He held out his hand. "Don't be mad, but I overheard you saying something about being detained by the police." He sat on the edge of her desk. "Let me help. Let *us* help. Start from the beginning and catch me up."

She propped her chin on her closed fist. "I went out to Judge Mullinax's house to check on him."

She looked up at him with those big green eyes of hers, and he was mesmerized by her intensity. Her gaze dropped again as she shuffled a few papers into file folders, but anxiety radiated off her in waves.

Ethan said, "What happened?"

She paused a moment before answering. "I found Stephen's housekeeper, Mrs. Silano. Dead."

"I'm sorry." He wanted to offer some type of comfort but wasn't sure how much she'd accept from him. Instead, he lightly touched the back of her hand. It was a brief touch, featherlight, not enough to give her the wrong idea about his intentions. Best to keep this professional.

"Thank you." Tears shimmered in her eyes.

"After the police showed up, what happened next?"

She inhaled. "Detective Murphy questioned me. Asked me about my relationship with the judge like I'm having some kind of disgusting affair with him. And then I had to be tested for gunshot residue. *Then* they took me downtown and booked me. Liam had to follow me to the precinct before he could bring me back here, even though it was out of his way."

Ethan knew Detective Murphy at the Renegade PD. The man had a reputation. "I've had a few run-ins with Murphy."

"Then you know how he is?"

Ethan nodded. "Let me know if you need any moral support if he comes around. Okay?"

Murphy could be a loose cannon. Always jumping to conclusions. Trying to solve cases in as little time as possible. He was like a bulldozer, running over anyone who got in his path.

She nodded. "Actually, that would be really helpful. Thank you."

Before he could respond, her computer beeped with an incoming message. She woke the computer with the mouse and opened the IM. "It's from Liam. He went back out, doing whatever he has going on, after he dropped me off."

"May I?" He gestured toward the screen.

Aubrey scooted back from the desk, and he read the IM over her shoulder.

Liam

Montgomery got a notification that some kids are reposting a video of a downed aircraft. Here's the link. Pull it up and begin recording. Tried calling but Butler didn't answer.

Shoot. He'd left his phone in his office.

Ethan said, "Message Liam back for me."

She nodded, typing.

Aubrey

Where are you? Ethan is here.

Liam

We're on the way back to the office.

She clicked on the hyperlink Liam had sent. The link opened a posted video on her computer. Once they'd watched it, he'd have her download and save it.

"Look at that." She pointed to the screen, at a downed plane in a remote mountain area. Ponderosa pines rose at an angle from the side of the mountain, while jagged boulders covered part of the barren hillside.

A couple of teens, from probably fourteen to seventeen, climbed over the debris field. Multiple pine trees had been snapped in half from the impact. The nose of the plane looked like an accordion. Debris and tree limbs partially hid the open door.

"This was a recent crash, from the look of the branches and the skid pattern on the ground." Ethan frowned. Where was this? He could barely identify the emblem on the tail. But he knew what that symbol meant.

"Is that what I think it is?" Aubrey asked.

Ethan leaned closer to the screen. "Yeah." Man, she smelled good. Like sunshine and sweet lemons. But that wasn't the point right now. "It looks like an old US Marshals symbol." His hands gripped the back of her office chair. "Send me the link to the video."

"You got it."

"Where's Howard?"

She shrugged. "I don't know. He sent me a message saying he had a working lunch, but he left before I did and hasn't returned yet."

"Call and let him know about the plane wreckage." Ethan watched for clues in the surrounding terrain while she snatched up the phone and dialed, listening. Nothing stood out in the video. "Any response from Howard?"

"The call went straight to voicemail." She replaced the receiver in the cradle.

"Keep trying him, please."

Roberts and Montgomery sprinted through the office door, eyes wide, panic written across their faces. Adam held a pastry bag from the Pie's the Limit and tossed it on the desk.

"Did you see it?" Liam glanced between Ethan, Aubrey, and Adam.

"Yeah, we saw it," Aubrey said.

Ethan said, "The plane might be one used by the Marshals. How did you find out about the post?"

"Some teenagers were in the coffee shop, talking loudly about a prison transport plane that crashed," Liam said. "We asked them some questions, but they didn't know who the kids were that found the plane. Said that the video popped up on their feed."

"How can we be sure it's a Marshals transport plane?" Adam looked as confused as Ethan felt. "And we have no idea when the video was recorded. The post is from a few days ago, and it seems like it was live at the time."

Ethan didn't like being behind and having to catch up. "There's a partial US Marshals emblem on the tail, but we're going to have to do some research. It looks outdated."

"Okay then. Maybe it's not ours." Adam grabbed a giant chocolate chip cookie out of the bag. "Decommissioned, probably. Whatever it is, tragic that it crashed and all."

"I'm pretty sure it's a Marshals transport plane, and it could still be in service." Liam clapped Adam on the back. "It's one of the smaller planes that's used to transport high-value targets, I think."

"But that still doesn't tell us who was on the plane, where they were going, or why they were being transported." Adam brushed some crumbs off his shirt front. "Or if it was even official business."

Ethan pointed to the computer screen. "The US Marshals office in DC is supposed to inform us whenever there's a transport headed our way. We typically receive an encrypted email, and I haven't seen anything this week."

"So then how can it be ours?" Aubrey asked.

"Procedures weren't followed, which makes me suspicious. But it isn't out of the question that it was a real transport." Ethan forced the words out, his jaw tight. "The Marshals are the best at keeping prisoner identities a secret, and I have a gut feeling this wasn't an ordinary transport. We need to find out who was on that plane and where they were headed."

On the screen, the teenagers crawled all over the plane, touching surfaces, contaminating whatever evidence was left. The environment would have washed away a lot of forensics too. This was going to be tough to figure out.

"At least there aren't any bodies," Aubrey said.

"Yet," Ethan and Adam responded at the same time.

Aubrey's face drained of all color. "Yeah, of course." She closed her eyes for a moment, exhaled, and turned to look at Ethan. "So what are you going to do?"

"First, we contact the DC office and see if they can help us figure out the destination for this plane and who requested it for their operation. Roberts and Montgomery, see if you can track down those kids from their social media accounts and ask them some questions."

Adam swallowed his bite of cookie. "On it, boss."

Liam and Adam headed down the hall, and Ethan turned back to Aubrey, who sat in front of her screen with her gaze glued to the days-old post, her lips tightened in a flat line. "Aubrey, see if you can find a location attached to this video. Keep trying Howard's phone. I'll look for a landmark. I've hiked these mountains. We need to know where the plane went down."

"Are we in danger?" Her voice was a whisper as she swiveled in her chair and stared at him, her eyes wide with fear and uncertainty. "I mean, if there was a dangerous fugitive on that plane, they could have escaped. Or someone could be in real danger."

He reached out, wanting to offer some bit of comfort, but instead shoved his hand in his pocket. "Let's save the worry for when we know for sure there's something to worry about."

"Right." Aubrey nodded once, then returned to the tasks he'd assigned her.

Ethan sat in his office and pulled up the post. The kids were climbing all over the wreckage, the wings, and even sitting in the cockpit. There was no one else in there—so where had the passengers gone?

They had to find those kids and that plane. Only problem was, he had no idea what he was looking at or even where this plane could be.

It was smaller than their typical prison transport. The kids had zoomed in on a pair of discarded manacles, so someone was being moved on that plane. Not broken, the cuffs were simply open and lying on the floor. Someone on the plane had released the prisoner? A few blood splatters covered some of the seats, but nothing to indicate that anyone was seriously hurt.

Where were the passengers and the pilot? The bodies?

He only prayed they could find out what was going on before anyone else was injured. Or worse.

FOUR

BY THE NEXT MORNING, THE ENTIRE OFFICE buzzed with a low, restless current. Yesterday's chaos, beginning with the judge's disappearance and ending with the investigation into the downed plane, still clung to Aubrey's nerves. She sagged against her chair and massaged her temples as a dull ache crept up the back of her skull.

She'd only been here an hour.

While she was waiting for the Marshals office in Washington, DC, to send her the list of prison transports that had been scheduled this past month, next on her to-do list was to contact the Marshals office in Denver. Although she didn't think they would be any help, she picked up the receiver and dialed the number anyway. Someone had to have an answer.

"US Marshals Service, Denver. How can I help you?"

"This is Aubrey Richardson from the Renegade office."

"Aubrey! It's so good to hear from you. This is Marissa Logan. What can I do for you?"

Finally, someone she knew who might be able to help. She'd met Marissa a couple of years ago when they'd had mandatory training for some new office systems. A few years younger than Aubrey, Marissa had paired up with her during the hands-on sessions.

Aubrey exhaled. "Do you know anything about a transport plane bound for Renegade or leaving the area recently that's unaccounted for?"

"Let me check." The sound of computer keys clicking in the background bled through the line. "No, sorry. We haven't had any transfers for Renegade in over a month. Why?"

Oh, this wasn't good. Aubrey forced a calmness she didn't feel. "We received a message about a social media post featuring a downed plane. It looks like the aircraft belonged to the Marshals, but we never received any information about a prison transport plane heading this way."

"Oh my. That's scary," Marissa said.

"I'm praying that it's not one of the Marshals' prisoner transports."

"Me too," Marissa said. "I'll call if I have any information for you."

"Thank you." Aubrey hung up the receiver as Howard strolled into the office from the hallway.

"Richardson, where is everyone?" He glared at her as if it was her responsibility to keep the deputies in line.

"Supervisor Howard." She forced herself to smile, her jaw locked in place. She wouldn't give him the satisfaction of letting him see how much she disliked being called by her last name. She wasn't one of the dudes in this office.

"Deputy Marshal Butler is in his office, working to find some information on a downed plane that was reported earlier today. He assigned Deputy Marshals Montgomery and Roberts to work leads in the field."

"Why wasn't I called immediately about this plane crash? I had to find out about it from the police chief."

"Supervisor Howard, I tried calling your phone several times. I sent multiple texts and left you a voicemail message."

Just then, his phone beeped, and Howard grunted as he glanced at the screen. "Huh. Well, what do you know? I'll check in with Butler." His gaze lifted again, and he pinned Aubrey with a steely look. "I heard about your run-in with the local PD yesterday. The optics aren't great for our office—you being such good *friends* with the judge, and now there's a dead woman and a murder investigation."

"Sir." Heat rose up Aubrey's neck. "It's not what you think . . ."

He held up a hand. "Maybe not, but the Renegade PD chief told me everything." Sympathy softened his gaze. "I know you and Mullinax have history and he's a big part of your life, but for everyone's sake, please stay away until we figure out what's going on. The police will find the judge, so you don't need to worry. They'll locate him as part of their ongoing murder investigation."

She nodded. "Fine."

As much as she didn't like it, Howard was right. She had to let the police do their job. She bit her tongue to keep herself from saying something she shouldn't. Where would she be if she got fired?

Aubrey waited until Howard's footsteps echoed down the hallway and then a door slammed. She exhaled.

Why would someone kill the judge's housekeeper, sweet Mrs. Silano? And where was the judge? For the second time today, she prayed for the judge's safe return and for the killer to be caught.

The office door swung open as Liam and Adam entered.

"You'll never guess what we found out." Adam sipped from a bottle of water, a half-eaten doughnut in hand. This guy was a bottomless pit.

She rested her chin on her closed fist, trying to regain her composure with this constant revolving door of people. "I have no idea, but I'm sure you're going to tell me."

"Those kids are locals. They all go to Renegade South High School," Liam said. "They have some kind of hiking club, and they also like to visit abandoned mines, houses, and wreckages. That sort of thing. They record what they find and post it online."

"Wait. So they discovered the plane while out hiking?"

"They sure did," Adam said. "Sort of."

Liam shifted his weight. "What Adam is trying to say is that we talked to the kids, but they couldn't remember the exact location of the crash. They gave us a general area to search."

"Hang on a second. Let's get Howard and Ethan out here. I'm sure they'll want to know." Aubrey buzzed Howard's phone.

"I'm a little busy, Aubrey."

"Sorry, sir." She made herself smile. "But this is important. Liam and Adam are back and have some information you might want to hear." She sent an instant message that said the same to Ethan.

Howard and Ethan appeared in the hallway, striding over to stand in front of her like two towering pines.

Howard said, "Okay, tell me what's going on."

Adam and Liam took turns explaining everything they'd learned about the teenagers and their discovery.

Ethan frowned. "How did no one know what they were doing? And why didn't the parents report the crash?"

Adam sat on the edge of her desk, as if Aubrey needed him in her personal space. "It seems our young adventurers didn't divulge all their secrets. They simply posted the video footage days later. The kids explained away the crash by telling their parents it was an old plane they'd found and there were no victims on board anyway. The parents are more than willing to let them go out unsupervised since they're experienced hikers."

Liam said, "I guess they thought they could become TikTok famous."

Aubrey shook her head. "Obviously, they weren't thinking. Maybe the kids thought the police already knew about the plane."

"It's possible. From what we could tell, the plane looks to be in bad shape." Ethan turned to Liam. "When was the video posted, and how long has it been since they discovered the plane?"

"The kids we talked to said they found the plane about three days ago and then posted the recorded footage yesterday," Liam said.

A sliver of fear coiled low in Aubrey's stomach.

Nonsense. The man she'd testified against was sitting in a federal prison far from here. There was no way he was ever getting out. Over the years, she'd learned she couldn't freak out over every escaped prisoner, and thankfully, it didn't happen often. Still, the trauma from her past haunted her at inopportune times.

"Did you uncover anything about that plane yet?" Howard asked.

Aubrey shook her head. "I called the Washington office and am waiting on confirmation from them about any recent or upcoming prisoner transports." She flipped through her notes, frustration tightening her voice. "I just got off the phone with the Denver office, and no one there seems to know anything either. What we *do* know is this—there haven't been any scheduled prisoner transfers in the last two weeks." She looked up. "I'm still waiting for additional information. Either this was a flight so classified it didn't hit the usual channels . . ."

"Or something went wrong." Howard's gaze bounced among the group. "Here's what we're going to do. Montgomery, Roberts, track down the parents. I want consent to pull cell phone data and see which towers their phones pinged off. The kids couldn't give us an exact location, but maybe their phones can narrow it down. See if they can retrace their steps, show us where they *think* the wreckage might be." He turned toward Ethan. "I want you to work on finding Judge Mullinax. I received a phone call, and the

DOJ now wants us to investigate his disappearance, since Judge Mullinax has a high-profile case on the docket."

"Got it." Ethan nodded.

The room stilled, everyone unwilling to voice what was on their minds. Adam broke the uncomfortable silence. "So, where does that leave us?"

Liam snorted. "It's not good, that's for sure."

"A downed airplane. Possibly some missing prisoners," Ethan said. "And a missing judge."

"If there are missing prisoners, we have an even bigger problem on our hands," Howard said. "This will be a publicity nightmare once the story gets some traction. We need to find the plane before that happens."

Aubrey's stomach churned. "So, um, what are we going to do?"

"I'm sure there will be phone calls from reporters," Howard said. "You've been here long enough, Aubrey, to know how to handle those types of things. Follow office protocol."

Yeah, she had. She didn't like to keep the truth from the public. But sometimes, informing the general public of the entire truth would only make the outcome worse.

"All right." Howard clapped his hands once. "You all have your assignments. Report back here by four this afternoon."

Everyone dispersed except Ethan. He sat on the edge of her desk, and she tried not to fidget in her seat. His intense stare caused goosebumps to pebble on her skin. What was with these guys and sitting on her desk?

She finally broke his gaze and turned back to her monitor. "What do you want, Ethan?"

Out of the corner of her eye, she could see him still staring at her. Ethan said, "You okay?"

Aubrey opened her mouth to tell him she was fine, but no words came out.

She didn't know how much longer she could keep up this

facade. Her breath rate increased, and her chest felt as if a huge, flat stone pressed on her. She closed her eyes for a moment, tried to slow down her breathing.

Ethan moved closer, his presence calming her frazzled nerves. He touched her shoulder.

She slowly raised her gaze to meet his and recognized his determination to protect people. To guard her from outside forces. "Is there something you need to tell me, Aubrey?"

"About the dead woman at the judge's house that the police think I killed, or about the downed plane?" They didn't have anything else to talk about right now.

A half smirk tilted his lips. "If you think of anything that can help with the judge's disappearance, please tell me immediately."

She hated that Ethan could read her so well. If she wasn't careful, he'd dig up all kinds of secrets.

His hand left her shoulder. "I'll do my best to figure out where the judge is, and you'll be the first to know what I find."

So Ethan did have a heart. "I appreciate that."

He grabbed a pen from the pencil holder. "I just don't want you to get your hopes up, in case I don't have good news."

"I understand." She looked at the page in front of her, afraid to meet his gaze. Afraid she'd give away more information than she was comfortable with, just in case it helped find Stephen. "I'll feel better once you find the judge."

He didn't leave. "I know you're scared and that you and the judge were close."

You have no idea.

"I'm going to do my best to find him."

She forced a smile. "I know you will."

"Could you contact Renegade PD? Tell them I'm heading out to the judge's place. I don't want to step on anyone's toes, but since Mullinax is a federal judge, this falls into our jurisdiction." He dropped the pen back in her holder, looking more unsure than she'd have expected.

She nodded. "You got it."

"Thanks." Ethan strode out of the office, his posture rigid.

She bit her lower lip. She was safe here in Renegade. Perhaps if she repeated that mantra enough times, she'd believe it.

Judge Mullinax had assured her when she moved here six years ago that nothing bad would happen. Now his housekeeper was dead, and he was missing.

Maybe that was a promise the judge shouldn't have made.

Ethan let out a low whistle as he traveled through the judge's gated community outside of Renegade. Tall oaks spread their branches across the road, creating an intricate weave of shadows on the asphalt. Two- and three-story homes that looked like something out of a Hollywood movie stood as silent sentinels on either side of the wide street.

Each home was surrounded by an iron fence, a call box in front of each gate. Immaculately manicured lawns peeked through the fence posts, while expensive luxury vehicles zoomed down the street.

How did a federal judge afford to buy a house on this side of town?

Ethan stopped his older-model F-150 pickup in front of the judge's house. A patrol car sat in the judge's drive, along with an older Camry, and a uniformed police officer stood watch at the gate.

Ethan rolled his window down.

"Can I help you?" The guy had heavy brows and a square jaw.

"Ethan Butler, Deputy US Marshal. I'm here to check on Judge Mullinax's house."

"Identification?"

Ethan pulled his wallet from his back pocket and opened it to show the officer his federal ID.

The officer handed it back. "Thank you, Deputy Marshal Butler. Just drive around to the front door. I'll let them know you're on your way. The detective is waiting for you."

A moment later, the gate opened on silent casters. The driveway was at least a hundred feet long, making it difficult for someone to access the house and kill the housekeeper. Maple and oak trees created a verdant canopy over the drive. The houses in this neighborhood were old money, probably built by the town founders, who'd struck gold a century or two ago. Ancient history to most. But the judge reaped the benefits.

Ethan parked his truck just to the side of the double front door and behind the police cruiser. The house was even more impressive up close.

After exiting his truck, he did a little reconnaissance, checking the windows, the manicured shrubs.

He inspected the camera attached to the doorframe. It was still intact. Hopefully, there would be some footage from the previous day he could review.

The crime-scene tape blocking off the entrance had been removed. The only visible evidence that this had been an active crime scene was a smattering of dried blood smeared on the steps.

He raised his hand to knock on the door, but it opened before he had a chance to announce his presence.

Ethan stared at Detective Murphy from Renegade PD.

Murphy crossed his arms. "Well, well, well. If it isn't Deputy Marshal Butler. What can I do for you?"

This guy was a piece of work. And that was putting it mildly. Ethan had to bite back his response. He needed Murphy's cooperation. "Mind if I come in, look around?"

Murphy looked over his shoulder and shrugged. "Suit yourself. Not sure what you'll find. The crime scene unit went over this place with a fine-tooth comb. We cleaned up the scene already." He stepped back into the foyer but blocked Ethan's further entry into the house.

"Look, Murphy, I'm just trying to figure out where the judge disappeared to. It's a federal investigation."

Murphy snorted. "Good luck finding him."

Ethan leaned against the entry door. "We need to work together on this case. Right now, all I want to do is check the security camera footage."

They stared at each other for a few moments, the air thick with tension. Murphy started walking. "Right this way."

He led Ethan down a back hallway, the house eerily quiet. The heavy scent of disinfectant clung to the air, and Ethan sneezed. They entered a small room where four screens covered one wall. A security room?

"The judge had all four entrances covered." Murphy flipped a switch, and the monitors flickered to life. He pointed to the one screen with a solid black image. "This is the front-door camera, mudroom, patio, and the garage. You can see from the time stamp when they all went dark. Here's the crazy thing." Murphy squeezed the back of his neck. "The blamed thing was working fine up until about five a.m. yesterday. After that, all the footage is blank."

"That's odd." To say the least.

"Here, I'll show you." Murphy pressed a button, and the footage replayed until the cameras blacked out.

A flash caught Ethan's eye. "Hang on a second. Rewind that section of the tape."

Murphy replayed the video, and Ethan pointed to the screen. "There. Did you see that flash? Can you rewind and then play it in slow motion?"

Murphy shrugged. "Sure."

The same image flashed across the screen, only this time it looked like a concentrated beam of light.

"Back it up and pause the image." Ethan frowned. "That's not a headlight, because the headlight of a car couldn't penetrate all the trees and shrubs in the backyard."

Murphy leaned closer. "Huh. Well, what about that. So what is it?"

"I've heard about this technique. How old would you say the cameras are? At least ten years old?"

"Yeah, that's about right. Why?"

Ethan tapped the image. "Because if they are, then the judge's cameras could've been easily disabled using a laser tag gun. Just point it at the camera eye, pull the trigger, and poof, no evidence. You've now taken out the surveillance camera."

"That explains a lot."

A sliver of apprehension set Ethan's senses on edge. This wasn't just some random killing. This had been planned.

Murphy led the way back into the main part of the house.

Ethan said, "I take it there weren't any fingerprints either. Nothing to give a clear indication of who could've killed Mrs. Silano."

"Nope." Murphy shoved his hands into his pockets. "Single shot to the chest."

"You'll let me know if you find anything?"

"Absolutely. Same goes for you." Murphy extended his hand, and Ethan had no choice but to shake it.

"Thanks. I'll be in touch."

Murphy said, "You do that."

Ethan slid his sunglasses on and stood on the top step, surveying the neighborhood, or at least what he could see of it. There was a house across the street and another one to the left of the judge's house that might hold potential.

He drove to the closest home and pressed the call button.

A woman answered. "Name, please."

Ethan showed his federal ID. "I'm Deputy US Marshal Ethan

Butler. I'm investigating the disappearance of Judge Mullinax. Do you have a few minutes to answer some questions?"

"Sure." The speaker crackled.

The gate slid open, and he drove to the front of a stately colonial-style mansion. He itched just thinking about the cost to run these places.

Standing in front of the door, he noticed a small camera that lined up with the driveway. Perfect.

"You mentioned that Judge Mullinax is missing? How can I help you?"

He jerked upright and pivoted to find an older woman in a short kimono, leaning against the doorframe, her perfectly made-up face devoid of any wrinkles, a martini glass in one hand.

She studied him from head to toe, a small smirk on her face. "Something I can help you with, cowboy?"

Holy smokes. Her sultry voice was an invitation he was *not* interested in. He cleared his throat and pulled out his ID again. "Excuse me, ma'am."

"Please, not ma'am. I'm not ancient yet. It's Melanie Calder."

He nodded once. "Ms. Calder, I'm sure you heard about Judge Mullinax's housekeeper."

Her blue eyes widened. "Yes, it was quite a shock. A lovely woman. She could make a mean boeuf bourguignon."

What did he say to that? His stomach rumbled at the thought of a home-cooked meal. "Yes, well, have you talked to the Judge this week?"

She opened the door wider. "It's too hot out here to talk. Come on inside."

Why did he feel as if she were a spider waiting to pounce on an unsuspecting insect? He stepped inside the darkened foyer and closed the door.

"Can I interest you in something cool to drink?" She tossed the question over her shoulder as she moved toward a seating area.

"I'm fine, thank you." The sooner he got out of here, the better.

She sat and crossed her legs, and he had to glance away. "So, what were you saying about Judge Mullinax being missing?"

"When was the last time you saw him or spoke to him?"

"That's right." Her painted lips tilted up in a smile that Ethan was sure charmed the men. "Let's see . . . the last time we spoke was this past weekend. Our community typically celebrates the Fourth with a big cookout and party at his place the weekend before. He asked me to bring a dessert."

Ethan was pretty sure that wasn't the only item on the menu. "So that was when? Saturday? Sunday?"

"Sunday afternoon." She leaned forward and placed the glass on the table.

"Did you notice anything or anyone suspicious? Strange cars? You've probably already told the police what you saw, but I'd love to hear it firsthand." He gave her a polite smile.

"No, can't say that I did." Melanie leaned back against the loveseat cushion. "This is a quiet neighborhood, and we pay for the added security. But I did see him and his little protégé, Aubrey, arguing."

"Did you happen to hear what it was about?" This woman could simply be stirring up trouble, but it might be a lead he had to follow.

"He was always fussing at her as if she were a kid. Maybe his kid." She smirked, taking a drink from her glass. "Anyway, none of my business."

Ethan stood, unsure this was anything more than a woman causing trouble if she was insinuating Aubrey might be the judge's daughter. If he heard the same from anyone else, he would look into it. "I'd like to inspect your door camera and the footage, if that's all right with you."

"This way, Deputy Marshal." She walked toward the back of the house and inclined her head. "Coming?"

Unfortunately, yes, he had to follow her. She opened a small door to reveal a closet-sized space with multiple monitors, a desk, and a chair. "This is the setup my husband insisted on. Although I don't know why."

"Do you mind if I check the files on the computer?"

"Go right ahead."

Ethan rewound the digital file from yesterday and sighed. Figured. Just some blurry images of cars passing by.

The judge's car left his driveway around four p.m. on Sunday, and then nothing after that.

He fast-forwarded to yesterday. Nothing showed on the monitor until an SUV pulled up to the judge's house around noon. He'd recognize that car anywhere. Aubrey's. "Mind if I make a copy of this file?"

"Feel free."

He quickly copied the file onto a thumb drive and shoved it into his pocket. "Thank you again, Ms. Calder."

He shouldered past his hostess, and her steps followed close behind him. He stopped at the door and handed her one of his business cards. "If you or your husband have any other information, please feel free to contact me."

She took the card and studied it for a moment, twirling it between her long fingers, their nails painted a garish red. "I'll do just that."

He slid out the door and tilted his head back to the sky. *Man oh man.*

Sitting behind the wheel, Ethan exhaled, thankful he wasn't that person any longer. Were there temptations? Sure. Every day. But he'd been redeemed and cleansed.

He tapped the Bluetooth on his steering wheel.

"Montgomery."

"I'm on my way back to the office. I was able to get some footage of the judge's driveway from a neighbor's house across the street. I want you to check it out."

"Sure thing." Montgomery hung up before Ethan could respond.

Ethan frowned at the abrupt click. Probably nothing. Montgomery wasn't exactly a conversationalist.

Still, unease traced along his nerves as the office came into view.

Footage was good. Footage was progress. Unless it showed something they weren't ready to see.

Whoever thought they could intimidate a judge in Ethan's jurisdiction was about to find out redemption didn't make a man soft.

It made him relentless.

FIVE

AUBREY PULLED INTO A PARKING SPACE BEHIND St. Mark's Community Center. The old church had been converted into a wedding venue that now had a two-year waiting list. She sighed. She would love to get married in the historic place of worship.

Sunlight highlighted the old stained-glass windows depicting the life of Christ. The black metal steeple shimmered, and the white wooden structure welcomed all who passed through the arched door, the church standing open and welcoming as it had for generations.

Aubrey stifled a yawn, her body heavy with fatigue but her nerves humming just beneath the surface. Sleep had eluded her again, sending her into the kitchen sometime after midnight to bake cookies she'd hoped might quiet her racing thoughts. But the silence of the house had only made them louder.

She grabbed the container of fresh oatmeal chocolate chip cookies she'd made this morning as a peace offering for the Renegade Days volunteers. After yesterday's excitement, she'd planned to take a personal day to focus solely on making sure everything was ready for tomorrow's reenactment. But the search for the downed Marshals prisoner transport refused to stay neatly contained at the office.

Responsibility pulled her in two directions. The town depended on her presence here, and the unanswered questions about the judge and the plane tugged at her conscience. Tomorrow was the reenactment, and she needed to make sure everything and everyone was ready, even if the judge wasn't able to make it. After that, she could focus back on her work keeping the office running.

She stopped at the door that led to the fellowship hall behind the main church building, bringing the sweet aroma of cookies with her into the building. But the acrid scent of burning gasoline from outside overpowered the baked goods.

A dark cloud obscured the sun on the other side of the structure. Only, it wasn't a thundercloud. It was a black cloud of smoke coming up from behind the building—over by the front parking lot.

Aubrey threw open the door. "Everybody out—now! There's a fire out front!"

All activity stopped as the volunteers focused their attention on her.

She waved at the door. "Move quickly!"

The handful of volunteers scrambled for the exit, leaving behind racks of costumes tagged with reenactors' names. Costumes could be replaced, but not people. Aubrey called emergency services while propping open the door with her hip.

"911, what's your emergency?"

"We have a fire in front of St. Mark's Community Center." Volunteers brushed past Aubrey, their wide-eyed gazes filled with panic as they stumbled out of the historic building.

"Is anyone injured?"

"I don't know. We're trying to clear the building now, just in case."

"Get outside and away from the structure. I'm sending fire, police, and medics."

"Thank you." Aubrey coughed as the acrid smoke in the air tickled her throat.

"Aubrey!" Jenna grabbed her in a tight hug. "Thank God you're okay."

"You too." She stepped back. "Come on, let's head over to the rendezvous point."

Aubrey and Jenna walked across the parking lot and saw the rest of the volunteers standing under a box elder maple. Aubrey looked around. "Is everyone out?"

Jenna began counting heads. "I think everyone is accounted for."

"What about the costumes?"

"I think as long as the building doesn't catch fire, we'll be fine."

Aubrey sagged against her car. *Thank You, God.* A black cloud of smoke drifted toward the crowd, and everyone began to cough.

"Get back. Move toward the ballfield behind us!" Aubrey yelled.

Smoke thickened and the wail of sirens could be heard in the distance.

One of the volunteers, an elderly man, ran around from the front of the building, waving his hands. "There's a car out front, and it's on fire!"

Aubrey didn't like the sound of this. She had to make sure no one else was in front. The air was bad enough back here.

She pulled up the front of her T-shirt to cover her mouth and ran across the parking lot, around the community center building. As she inched closer to the front of the building, the crackle of burning metal and the sharp pop of exploding glass pulled her toward the vehicle engulfed in flames about twenty yards away.

A black sports car with a government license plate on the front.

"No. It can't be." A ball of dread traveled up her throat, and she swallowed back her fear. She'd recognize that car and license plate anywhere.

It belonged to Judge Mullinax.

Two fire engines swung into the parking lot in front and pulled to a halt near the fire hydrant. Firefighters jumped down from every door on the trucks and ran in different directions. A couple unrolled the hoses attached to the sides of the vehicles. With practiced motion, they began extinguishing the fire, comforting Aubrey with their professionalism.

Police cruisers pulled over to block off the street, their blue lights flashing, while passersby stopped to watch. The loud diesel engines and shouts from the firefighters filled the air.

Aubrey ran back to where Jenna stood with the rest of the volunteers, now along the side of the building. They'd followed her to see the car? She'd have to shout over the noise, or Jenna would never hear her. "I think that's the judge's car!"

What if he was in there? She started toward it again.

"Stay back. You can't go over there." Jenna tried to drag her away from the burning vehicle.

Aubrey managed to spot a figure in the vehicle and gasped. "There's someone in the car." Terror paralyzed her legs. She yelled to the firefighters, "You have to get them out!"

A young police officer came over to them. "Ma'am, you can't stay here. You both need to move back behind the community center."

A sob burst through. *Oh dear God, no.* "Someone is in that car."

The putrid stench of burning flesh singed her nostrils as the officer forcibly walked her away from the burning car.

Alongside the community center, Aubrey stared at the firefighters and officers as they contained the fire and kept the crowd and reporters away from the scene.

"That's the judge's car, Jenna." And he'd been missing for days. "I'd recognize it anywhere."

A wave of nausea hit her, and she had to rush over to the shrubs to expel the little bit of breakfast she'd eaten earlier.

Jenna rested a hand on her back. "Here. Take a sip of this." She handed Aubrey a water bottle.

Aubrey took a swig to rinse out her mouth. "Thanks." She wiped her lips with the back of her hand.

Jenna wrinkled her nose at the odor hanging over the area and pulled her T-shirt neck up to cover her mouth and nostrils.

"Do they know . . . ?" Aubrey couldn't voice her fears. This felt like her nightmare was coming back to life in the place she had come to for safety and refuge from the memories. "It's Stephen's car, isn't it?" Every word scratched against her raw throat.

"Yeah. It's the judge's car." Jenna glanced away for a moment. "I recognize it."

Aubrey's knees started to give way, and her friend caught her. "They'll figure it out, Aubrey." Jenna's voice gentled, but her grip didn't as she shook Aubrey hard enough to break through the haze. "You need to focus right now. Keep it together."

Her eyes unfocused, Aubrey slowly nodded. Jenna helped her sit on the curb, and Aubrey gulped a big lungful of air.

Jenna squatted in front of her, her sooty face filled with concern. "Aubrey, we don't know if it was him in the car." Jenna coughed into her hand.

"Who else would it be?"

What would she do without the judge? He was like a second father to her now that they'd lived near each other for six years. But even before that, he had been guiding her, helping her when no one else had believed she was in danger all those years ago, before her family had gone into WITSEC. Ashes floated on the breeze and landed on her lap, and she quickly brushed them away.

A shadow loomed over her and she looked up, shielding her eyes as she squinted in the bright light. Unshed tears clouded her vision, but she had no trouble recognizing the man extending a hand to her. "Ethan."

She hesitated for a moment before grabbing it, letting him help her up. She dusted off some grass clippings from her backside and grimaced. She must look a mess. "Thank you."

Those deep-blue eyes of his filled with compassion. He nodded once. "You two ladies okay? I can have an EMT check you out."

She didn't know what to say.

His gaze lingered on Aubrey. "Let's get you over to the paramedics, just to be safe." Ethan waved his hand, and they walked over to the ambulance.

"Riley, can you check out Ms. Stockton?"

"I'm fine, Ethan. Just sucked in a bit of smoke," Jenna told him.

"Let me check your lungs." Riley smiled and held out his hand. "Right this way."

They watched him lead Jenna over to the ambulance. Aubrey rubbed her hands up and down her arms. Why was she so cold in the middle of the day? "I'm not hurt."

Ethan wrapped a blanket around her shoulders, and she jumped. He held up his hands. "It's just me."

"Sorry." She clutched the blanket around herself. "That is the judge's car, right?"

"We ran the plates, and it matches what he has on file with the DMV." He didn't look at her, which wasn't a good sign.

"There was someone in the car." She forced herself to look at Ethan, but he was partially turned away. She grabbed his arm. "Tell me the truth." That came out a little more forceful than she wanted. She loosened her grip as he faced her. "Please, I have to know."

His jaw tensed as his gaze bored into her. "We'll have to confirm with DNA testing, but it's likely it is the judge's body in the car."

Aubrey closed her eyes for a moment and felt a tear escape. She inhaled and straightened, forcing herself to accept this news that knocked her world off its axis.

She wiped away the tear and faced Ethan. "Thank you for telling me."

He nodded and stuck his hands in the pockets of his black dress slacks, the wind mussing his hair, his focus on the burnt-out car. "You're welcome," he said quietly, the words nearly carried away by the breeze.

The weight of everything—the fire, the judge, the violence of it all—pressed against Aubrey's chest until breathing felt like work.

"How can this even be real?" Her voice cracked as she gestured toward the charred wreckage.

Ethan glanced over at the controlled chaos in front of the community center. "I'm really sorry about the judge."

She folded her arms around herself, bracing against the ache rising in her chest. Her throat was raw from the smoke. Or the tears. Or both.

A medic passed them and pressed a water bottle into her hand. Ethan said, "Thanks, Mack."

The brown-haired young man nodded and passed on to someone else.

Aubrey twisted the cap and took a long drink, the coolness easing the raw sting. "Can I tell you something?" She met Ethan's concerned gaze.

"Yeah."

"You're probably wondering why I'm falling apart over a judge who wasn't even related to me."

He shook his head slightly. "Two dead bodies in two days would shake anyone."

She managed a weak smile. "He was like a father to me. He helped me get on my feet—helped me find work, stability." Her voice caught. "Renegade was supposed to be my safe place. He made sure it was. Stephen and I have been family for a long time."

"I had no idea."

"Most people don't."

She placed the bottle against her warm skin and sighed. She really needed to get out of here and figure out what they were going to do tomorrow. But how was she supposed to do anything when she could barely breathe with this new reality?

Her friend was gone. Her stabilizing force. The one person whom she trusted with her life.

And someone had murdered him.

Ethan surveyed the area in front of the community center that had just turned into a crime scene. Thankfully, the old brick structure had withstood the nearby fire. A few streaks of dark smoke covered the walkway leading to the front, but the building stood. Like a beacon in the night—strong, confident. Faithful. Like the Lord's goodness and faithfulness. When the world wanted to overwhelm, God was there.

Water puddled in the street, a news station van arrived on scene, and a reporter and cameraman interviewed people in the crowd. This whole situation was a big mess. The boss had sent him over here after talking to some of the judge's neighbors. How in the world had Mullinax's body ended up in a burning vehicle?

Ethan glanced over his shoulder at Aubrey as she sat on the curb, Jenna next to her.

Aubrey looked lost, vulnerable. Her green eyes unfocused.

A pang of sympathy hit him in the gut. But if he started caring about another woman, he'd probably end up hurting her, just like he had with his fiancée. So focused on his work that she'd turned to someone else. But that had been over two years ago, and thank the Lord, he'd changed.

A forensic pathologist from the local coroner's office had arrived in one of their vans to take away the body. Bystanders still crowded the area, trying to capture footage with their phones. The crime-scene unit searched for evidence around the car, placing number tents next to possible items of forensic value.

Ethan walked over to stand near Aubrey and Jenna and watched as the water ran down the street under their feet. The smell of smoke still lingered in the air.

One of the EMTs, Mack Jenkins, kneeled in front of Aubrey, and Jenna wandered away to speak with an older couple.

The medic was young, slim, and had dark hair and eyes. She shook her head at something he said. Mack glanced at Ethan, then said to her, "Smoke inhalation is nothing to mess around with."

She started to shake her head again.

Ethan went to her side and crouched. "What is it, Mack?" The young man was Rowan Wallace's half brother, but Ethan didn't know him in the same way he was familiar with Rowan or his buddy Luca. "She's fine, right?"

"Someone needs to stay with her, ideally." Mack looked back at Aubrey. "If you won't see a doctor, you'll need to sign a form. And don't be alone. Just in case. Because a swollen throat can close suddenly, and it's pretty scary."

Sounded like the kid knew what he was talking about.

But Aubrey said nothing. She looked absolutely exhausted.

"Right. Of course. Thanks, Mack." Ethan studied the growing crowd of onlookers but didn't see Jenna. If anyone was going to stay with Aubrey, it would be her best friend.

The EMT returned to the ambulance and talked with a group of local firefighters, probably waiting for the all-clear signal.

Aubrey sat with her arms wrapped about herself. She needed protection and someone to take care of her. He was out of practice at taking care of someone else's needs. A ball of dread swirled in his stomach.

An unmarked sedan rolled to a stop in front of the police barricade. Detective Murphy climbed out.

No way was he talking to Aubrey right now.

Ethan got up and met Murphy by the car.

"Butler." Murphy studied what he could see of the burned vehicle. "What happened?"

"That's what we're trying to figure out."

Murphy leaned closer and took a photo of the license plate. "This is Judge Mullinax's car, right?"

"Yeah. Not sure how it got here or where he was for the last four days, but I'm investigating."

Murphy pocketed his phone. "I'm thinking this is linked to his housekeeper's murder."

"That's my assumption too."

Murphy smirked. "Well, looks like we might have to actually collaborate on this. You know, rather than just saying we will." He barked a laugh.

Ethan didn't want to collaborate with this guy on anything. "Right." He glanced over at Aubrey again, an air of dejection hanging around her. He clapped Murphy on the back. "If you'll excuse me a moment."

Ethan wasn't the type of guy to fall over himself for a woman's attention. Although he and Aubrey butted heads daily, their outlooks were just different. She always looked for the positives in whatever situation she found herself in. Him? Well, let's just say he expected the worst.

But seeing her like this, exposed and shaken, ignited a protective resolve he'd kept buried beneath a badge and office protocol.

"You ready to head on home?" Ethan asked.

Aubrey stood. "More than ready."

"Let me get Jenna to take you home." He looked around the area in front of the church. "Where is she?"

"I think she's checking on the other volunteers." Aubrey searched the crowd and waved Jenna over. "I'm fine, Ethan. Besides, we still have to get the remaining costumes ready for the reenactment. That is, if there's going to be one."

She wanted to keep working on that today?

"I'll make a deal with you. You let me take you home after you take care of the costumes, and I'll buy you dinner. Make sure you rest. Jenna can sleep over at your place and make sure you're all right."

Aubrey smirked, a little of her old fire returning. "That's not much of a compromise. That sounds way more like you getting what you want."

Yeah, peace of mind. "Humor me. I'll be here when you're ready to go."

"Fine. I'm too exhausted to argue." Aubrey walked toward the back of the community center building and met Jenna at the corner, their heads coming together as they immediately began to chat with each other.

He was heading back to the scene at the front of the building when a local Renegade officer ran up to him.

"Hey, Deputy Marshal! Wait up a second!"

Ethan turned to the guy. "What can I do to help you, Officer?" He still needed to take Aubrey home and run by Mrs. Hanover's place to check on her cats. After that, he was gonna call it a day—and get back to working on the plane investigation.

The young officer ran a hand through his hair. "Captain Bennett from the FD said you need to come look at what we found."

Ethan nodded. "Lead the way."

He sidestepped a maze of fire hoses and puddles on the ground until they reached the end of the block. Several local police vehicles were parked under a canopy of shade trees, along with the coroner's van.

The forensic pathologist from the coroner's office zipped up the body bag and began loading the remains into her vehicle. She nodded once and pushed the gurney into the van, then locked the wheels and slammed the door.

Ethan took a quick detour to her, flashing his silver star badge. "Hey, Doc. Any idea what might've killed the judge?"

"Too early to tell." She shook her head. "But I'll go out on a limb and say it likely wasn't the burning vehicle."

"How do you know?" That was pretty specific, even if it was a guess.

She stripped off her gloves and stuffed them inside her jacket pocket. "Probably because he had a gaping head wound." She spun around and got in the van. "The Marshals office will be the first to receive my report, since Mullinax was a federal judge. We'll send a copy to local PD too."

"Thanks. I appreciate it." Ethan nodded.

She waved and sped off, leaving him standing there with the late-afternoon sun beating down on his back.

The officer came back over. "Sorry, Deputy Marshal, but that's not what the captain wanted you to see." He pointed to the judge's car. "Take a look inside."

A large square box, bright-orange paint peeking through the soot and grime, sat in a puddle of water on the back seat.

The black box from an airplane.

Someone clapped him on the shoulder.

"Good, you're here." One of the firefighters removed his helmet and pushed his Nomex hood down. "I'm Cole Bennett, captain of Station 3."

They shook hands. "Good to meet you." Ethan stared at the box and then looked over at the captain. "Is that what I think it is?"

"Yep. A flight recorder," the captain said. "Know a plane that's missing one?"

Ethan blinked.

"Are you serious? I didn't think you'd actually know."

Ethan shook his head. "Yeah, welcome to my day."

Why on earth would a flight recorder be sitting in the judge's car? The thing looked pretty banged up, with one corner smashed in, sitting precariously on half of a mounting bracket.

"We thought you might want to see it."

They both studied the recording device. Black stripes covered the surface in an uneven pattern.

"What do you think, Captain?" Ethan asked.

Bennett nodded. "From where I'm standing, it looks like this might've been doused with some kind of accelerant."

"We'll need to call this discovery in to the FAA. NTSB. Whoever. Find out what plane it belongs to." He knew of exactly one missing plane in Renegade. Was this really the black box for the downed Marshals plane? It connected the judge's death with the stolen plane.

"Forensics can tell us what kind of accelerant was used," Bennett said.

"Murphy! Over here!" Ethan waved the detective over to the car.

The detective jogged over. "What's up?"

"Back seat."

Murphy used his phone as a flashlight to get a better look at the burnt interior of the car and whistled. "We need CSU to document this." He looked around. "Hey! Miller! We need you."

The tech came over and carefully pointed his camera at the black box, taking several pictures.

Detective Murphy said, "Let's log it in as evidence, and then we'll send it off to the NTSB for processing."

The tech asked a couple of firefighters to help him remove the device from the judge's vehicle and take it to the crime-scene van.

"Thanks." When Murphy nodded, Ethan walked away, pulling out his phone.

Liam answered his call quickly.

"Roberts, any word on the location of that plane?"

"The parents wouldn't allow us to interview their kids. Adam and I narrowed it down to somewhere on Renegade Mountain's west side, but when they were talking about where they were, it seemed like they got turned around and weren't exactly sure. We just need another day to download some more satellite shots, and then we can start to search on foot."

"Good work. After the reenactment tomorrow, let's meet back at the Marshals office."

"You got it."

Ethan disconnected the call and wandered to the community center. He poked his head in the back door of the fellowship hall. "You ladies ready to leave?"

"Let me grab my purse," Jenna said.

"Aubrey?" She still looked exhausted, but that was no surprise.

Aubrey nodded. "I'm ready."

The two of them walked in silence to his truck. Jenna followed them out to the parking lot, and Ethan watched as she unlocked her car and started her engine.

He assisted Aubrey into the passenger seat of his truck. She didn't argue. Didn't joke. Just stared straight ahead as he shut the door for her. Quiet wasn't unusual for Aubrey, but *this* quiet was different.

Ethan turned the key, and the engine roared to life. "Penny for your thoughts?"

"You don't want to know."

He backed out of the lot. "Maybe I do. Maybe I care."

Aubrey stared at him for a moment and then sagged against the seat. "I don't want to talk right now."

He let it go because he had plenty to think about. The road hummed beneath the tires, his thoughts colliding faster than he could sort them. Fire accelerants, a federal judge dead in a burning car, a plane crash on Renegade Mountain.

After a couple of miles of driving generally toward downtown, he cleared his throat. "We recovered a black box. From the back of the judge's car."

She stiffened. "What?"

"It could be from the plane." He reached over and turned down the radio. "It fits."

Her head snapped toward him, fear flashing in her eyes. "You think it's connected to his death? A missing federal plane?"

"It's possible that nothing about the past couple of days was random violence." He paused. "Where were you before the fire department showed up?"

She exhaled, rubbing her forehead. "I couldn't sleep, so I baked cookies for the retirement home. I'd already booked today off for the preparation, so I went to the community center since I ditched my Renegade Days responsibilities yesterday to go find the judge. I needed to make sure everything was organized and ready for tomorrow."

His stomach chose that moment to growl.

She glanced at him, a tired smile tugging at her mouth. "You hungry?"

"Starving," he admitted. "Chinese sound good?"

"Comfort food sounds perfect."

"I'll order once we get to your place." He handed her his phone. "Punch in your address."

Twenty minutes later, he parked his truck in front of her house and walked her up to her door, scanning the street out of habit while she disarmed the alarm.

"Come on in. Make yourself at home." She dropped her purse on a bench by the door.

Ethan slid off his sports coat and hung it on a hook above the bench. "What do you want to eat?"

She toed off her shoes. "Surprise me. I don't eat squid or octopus."

"Good. Neither do I." He pulled out his phone and ordered, wondering if there was somewhere secure he could put his duty weapon. "Should be here in about twenty minutes."

She dropped into an overstuffed couch in her living room, and he sat next to her, close but still giving her space. She let out a short, brittle laugh. Then it broke apart.

"Of course this would happen. The one time I convince a federal judge to help with the reenactment, he ends up dead in a burning car." She scrubbed at her face. "It's my fault."

"No." The word came out sharper than he intended. He softened his tone, trying to figure out how to tell her this couldn't be her fault. "I'm sorry about the judge. I know he meant a lot to you."

She nodded, swallowing hard. "Yeah. He did."

Mullinax was the kind of judge who looked past what was handed to him and asked *why*. Ethan had worked cases with him before. Smart. Fair. Relentless. Losing him felt personal.

"But this isn't on you." Ethan leaned forward, forearms braced on his knees. "And it's not about the reenactment."

She looked at him, really looked. "Then what is it about?"

"The housekeeper," he said. "And whatever she knew, or whatever Mullinax figured out after she died. That's at least one possibility."

Her breathing slowed. "You think the two deaths are connected?"

"I'm fairly certain they are." He met her gaze. "Two deaths. One quiet, one loud. That's escalation. Someone was trying to shut a door, and when that didn't work, they set a fire big enough for everyone to see."

Aubrey straightened. The self-blame drained from her expression, replaced by something steadier. Sharper. "So the fire was a warning?"

"Yes, I think so." He didn't hesitate. "And the black box being in his car? That's not a coincidence either. Someone wants us chasing the wrong thread, or they want us pulling on the right one before we're ready."

She let out a slow breath. "Then they picked the wrong people."

A corner of his mouth lifted. “That’s what I was thinking as well.”

Silence extended between them. A few cars passed by out front, the rumble of their engines muted. Aubrey stood up and paced the length of the room, and Ethan took the chance to look at the simple landscape above her fireplace. A mountain scene. It looked peaceful.

He looked at her and saw the tension in her movements. “What’s wrong?”

“I’m about to go crazy with all the what-ifs.” Aubrey pivoted toward him. “I can’t think about the judge’s death right now. I need to focus on something else. Like the reenactment.”

“I don’t think that’s important right now.”

She stopped in front of him. “Please, humor me. I need to think about something else.” A multitude of emotions paraded across her features. Fear. Hope. Longing. Determination.

He was starting to worry about her. The car fire. Learning about the judge’s death. Could she really handle all this? “What’s going on in that fascinating mind of yours?”

“I don’t know.” Aubrey plopped onto the couch next to him. “The judge was going to portray Sheriff Samuel Dennison.”

“That does create a dilemma for tomorrow.”

“Yeah . . .” She drew the word out, then gasped and gave his arm a light punch. “Wait. Why didn’t I think of this sooner?”

He did not like the sound of this. “What?”

“You.”

“Me what?” He narrowed his eyes.

“You’d be perfect. You and the judge are about the same height and build. Put a fake mustache on you, and no one would notice the difference.”

“Whoa. Whoa, whoa, whoa. I’m not an actor . . .”

“No, but you’re perfect for the role. All you have to do is ride a horse and then cut off the stagecoach's progress in front of the old bank and trust, and voilà! Problem solved!"

"No, Aubrey." His voice was a low grumble.

"Please, Ethan?" She clasped her hands and placed them under her chin. "I promise, this is an emergency. You're my only hope . . ."

"Do not quote *Star Wars* to me." Proof it was far too risky to open up to people at work—even about entertainment.

"It's your weakness." She didn't even pretend innocence. "Everyone has seen the calendar on the wall in your office. And your Luke Skywalker mug."

"That's not fair. You're using the Force against me!" The corner of his mouth twitched, despite everything they'd just talked about. He turned toward the window, regrouping. Figuring out how to say . . . Did he want to say no?

Being the town's original sheriff. Riding a horse in the reenactment.

Sounded like every little boy's dream.

"Aubrey . . ."

"You know you want to ride that horse," she singsonged. "Wear the hat . . ."

Now that he thought about it . . .

Oh man, did he ever. He hadn't ridden a horse since he moved to Renegade. He glanced at her one more time. "Okay, I'll think about it."

"Thank you!" She leaned over and pecked him on the cheek.

He sat frozen to the seat, his tongue unable to form the words he wanted to say. Heat rose up his neck, and he finally forced himself to stand.

"I said I'll think about it. I didn't agree to do it." His words were gruffer than he intended, and he forced himself to smile at her enthusiasm.

Truth was, right now he'd do anything for her. If only to be near her for a few more minutes. Her presence gave him a reprieve from everything else going on and all the unanswered questions he had.

"*Yet*. You haven't agreed to portray the sheriff *yet*." She stood and headed to the kitchen. "What do you want to drink with your dinner?"

"Water is fine."

Oh brother, what had he gotten himself into? Her sunny personality was starting to wear him down. Make him wish for things that could never be.

He needed to get out of here. Get back to the office. But it seemed his good sense had left him once Aubrey turned to him.

Yeah, he was probably going to regret getting involved. Staying for dinner. Saying yes to being the sheriff.

It seemed far too much like falling down a slippery slope he was never going to get back up.

But did he even want to?

SIX

MORNING SUN SLANTED THROUGH THE BLINDS as Aubrey paced the length of her living room. Ten steps from wall to wall. She glanced at her smartwatch. Again. Where was Ethan?

A band tightened around her chest, making it difficult to breathe. They only had two hours before the reenactment began, and she wanted to arrive early to go over her checklist one last time.

A wide shaft of sunlight illuminated the small but tidy bungalow. She'd carefully chosen each eclectic piece of decor. A yard sale lamp that had simply needed a new shade. The overstuffed couch that she'd reupholstered to fit her more relaxed vibe. What had Ethan thought of her place?

She checked her lipstick in the silver-framed foyer mirror and set her tote bag by the door. *Come on, Ethan. Where are you?*

As if she'd summoned him, the doorbell rang, and she dashed to the front door.

Remembering personal safety at the last second, she checked

the peephole first. All the air in her lungs expelled at the sight of him, and that steel band loosened.

She swung open the door and was greeted with a vision of Ethan dressed as the sheriff of Renegade from 1885. Boots, cowboy hat, dungarees, and a plaid shirt, along with the holster for his revolver, situated on his right hip.

Aubrey nearly swallowed her tongue.

Mercy. She hadn't thought she liked the cowboy look, but on him? He was devastatingly handsome.

She gave herself a mental shake and pulled him inside the foyer. Which was probably a very bad idea. Her stomach performed a couple of backflips as his gaze intensified, searching hers, then inspected her from head to toe.

But he was her coworker, and he was simply helping her out today.

"Good. You wore comfortable clothes." He shut the door behind him, and she retreated a step.

"Hey." She crossed and recrossed her arms, not quite looking him in the eye. "You're late."

"Let's start over." Ethan placed two fingers on the brim of his hat. "Howdy, ma'am." He rested his hands on his gun belt. "I heard you were the little lady that needed protection in this here town."

"Oh, for pity's sake." She shook her head and tried to hold back her grin. "You're really hamming it up this morning."

Which was so not Ethan. Where was the serious deputy US marshal she'd gotten used to these past two years? Instead, this easygoing, teasing cowboy stood in front of her.

And she kind of liked it.

He removed a toothpick he'd been chewing on from his mouth. "Just trying to give the townsfolk a good show."

She stuffed a water bottle in her bag and muttered, "Believe me, they'll get a show all right."

His eyes twinkled underneath the shadow of his hat. "Something bothering you?"

"Nope." She didn't dare tell him what she really thought. His larger-than-life presence filled the house. And was it hot in here? "You look great. You look the part."

He embodied exactly what she'd envisioned for this reenactment, right down to his scuffed cowboy boots. She liked him, quietly and inconveniently, and the cowboy costume only made it worse. But telling Ethan would inflate his ego, and she already had enough trouble pretending she hadn't noticed.

All her confession would earn her was more teasing, and her nerves were strung so tightly this morning, she'd probably snap in two, like an old rubber band. Ethan made her feel alive again, something that no man she'd ever met had accomplished.

She grabbed her tote, fumbling with the straps. "I'm ready. I need to help Jenna over at the assembly point."

"We'll be there in less than ten minutes." Ethan paused, then held out a hand and stopped her before she opened the door. "Hang on a second. I want to check a few things first."

He walked through the foyer and back to the kitchen, his sharp gaze assessing the small home.

"Everything locked up?" He headed toward the bedroom at the back of the house, his boots echoing on the hardwood floors.

"Yes," she shouted to his back. Craning her neck, she tried to follow his movements. Doorknobs rattled, and the sound of blinds closing set her nerves on edge.

He came back to the front room and checked the windows, finishing up with the side door.

She crossed her arms and leaned against the wall by the front door. "Satisfied?"

He stopped in front of her, and all the breath in her lungs was suspended. There was a look of concern—or was it confusion?—written on his face. He opened his mouth, then closed it, his lips set in a tight line. "Yeah."

They stood there, the space between them unmistakably charged, until Ethan finally cleared his throat. "Hang on a second."

She watched as he struggled to say something. "What's on your mind?"

He removed his hat and raked his fingers through his hair. "Did you get my text? I was late today because I was on the hunt for the downed plane. I met with Adam and Liam to go over some photos of the mountain, and I think we've narrowed down the approximate location of the plane."

Oh. "Okay." Well, if that didn't take all the starch out of her sails. She sagged against the wall. *Time to be grateful, Aubrey.* She cleared her throat. "I must have missed your message."

He nodded. "I just didn't want you to think I wasn't coming." The tension in the room increased, and his gaze drifted to the floor. "What I really want to know is"—Ethan's blue eyes drilled into her—"how are you really doing? I mean, dealing with the judge's death, finding his housekeeper, and all of that."

Aubrey exhaled. "I really don't want to talk about it right now, if that's okay."

Same as she hadn't wanted to talk about it last night. Thankfully, he'd been content to eat Chinese and make small talk.

"Sure. Whenever you're ready to talk, I'm available."

A satisfying warmth spread through her body at his concern. "Thank you. You don't know what that means to me. But I can't talk about Stephen and focus on the reenactment. I need to keep it together today."

"I get it. I really do." He touched her elbow.

The contact stole her breath for a brief second, and she hoped he didn't notice. This wasn't fear. This was far more dangerous to her heart. She glanced away first and pulled her sunglasses out of her tote. "Ready?"

"Yes, ma'am." Ethan jammed his hat back on his head and moved toward the door. "Let's get this show on the road."

This was the Ethan she was used to, that she was more comfortable with—the one who was all business. Best to keep her distance from the man who tore down her defenses until this day was over.

Aubrey turned to the door and watched as he inhaled deeply, the muscles in his back flexing. "Lead the way, Deputy Marshal."

He swung the door wide. "After you." A small smile graced his lips as he closed and locked the door behind her. "And that's Sheriff Samuel Dennison to you today, ma'am," he added in a thick Southern drawl as he touched the brim of his hat.

She shook her head and made her way to his truck.

They rode in silence, the earlier tension dissolving in the brilliant sunshine. Several streets had been blocked off to accommodate the reenactment. St. Mark's Community Center gleamed in the sunlight, casting a cool, sheltering shadow across the street, as if holding the space in quiet reserve.

Red, white, and blue pennants were strung above the street, and speakers blared music authentic to the time period. A crowd had already gathered, their excitement for the day's events rippling outward—bright, expectant, and unaware of the undercurrent beneath it all.

Aubrey smiled through the side window of the truck, watching the happy crowds milling around different vendor booths as the laughter of children floated on the breeze. All these spectators had no idea that the possibility of danger lurked here in their hometown.

Children held on tightly to brightly colored balloons that bobbed up and down in the warm breeze. The aromas of deep-fried corn dogs, funnel cakes, and popcorn made her stomach churn. She placed a hand over it and grimaced as her breakfast of yogurt, coffee, and fruit threatened to make a reappearance. *So nervous.*

"You okay over there, boss?" Ethan glanced her way as he parked in a designated spot for volunteers behind the historic church. "Do we need to grab you an antacid before this shindig starts?"

She swallowed. "No, I'll be fine. Thanks for offering."

Aubrey closed her eyes for a second and inhaled before unbuckling her seatbelt.

Ethan grasped her hand. "Before we get out of this truck and we're busy with our duties, I . . ."

"Yes?" Aubrey looked at him, something steady and certain passing between them.

"Just be careful out there. Okay?"

She tossed him a dazzling smile that he returned. "I will. I'll be fine. It's a beautiful day. What could go wrong?"

She said it because she wanted to believe it. She needed a quiet reassurance to hold on to, with all the work she'd poured into Renegade Days. *Lord, protect us all today.*

Ethan's gaze drifted out the window. "My concern is for your safety after what's happened the past couple of days."

"I know." Aubrey softened her response with a smile and squeezed his hand. She opened the truck door and slid out, then leaned in to grab her satchel. "Coming, Sheriff?" She slammed the door.

She bit the inside of her cheek as she listened to his laughter. She didn't want to think of all the possibilities of what could go wrong. Today, she was simply focused on providing an exciting event for the people of Renegade.

Jenna came out of the community center and jogged down the steps. "I'm glad you're here. I was worried." She bit her lower lip, then smiled and tucked her arm through Aubrey's. Then she lowered her voice. "I kind of thought he was going to bail on us after I gave him the costume this morning."

"Not a chance. We just had to go over some ground rules for today, is all." Aubrey forced herself to smile, pretending that professionalism was all there was between her and Ethan. "Look around you."

She motioned to the crowds gathering at the different food trucks and games. Lights were strung across the streets in a crisscross fashion for the street party later on tonight. Families laughed together, the children running through the crowds and wanting to pet the horses being used today.

Jenna frowned. "I don't see anything except families."

"Exactly. Everyone is enjoying themselves." Aubrey leaned in. "You wouldn't know it, but police and US marshals are here. You just won't be able to see them unless, God forbid, something happens."

"That's my prayer for today," Jenna said. "That things will be calm and go well."

Mine too. They strolled through the venue and stopped back in front of St. Mark's Community Center, where the cast and crew assembled.

The stagecoach robbery would take place here, in the open. The old First National Bank was situated across from the community center and had now been converted to a restaurant. Aubrey pulled her checklist out of her purse and began to recheck supplies, the sound system, and props.

"I just have this really bad feeling," Jenna said.

"Shush. It's going to be fine." Aubrey straightened the hat on one of the actors. "Ethan and his team are here."

If Aubrey repeated it often enough, maybe it would settle into truth. A whispered prayer that everything would be fine, that the reenactment would unfold the way it was meant to.

"You're right."

Aubrey said, "I know I am."

Jenna exhaled. "Let's pray for today's activities."

As they held hands in the shadow of the old church, Jenna

prayed for everyone's safety. Especially the actors and animals involved. Aubrey echoed her amen and they hugged.

Some of Aubrey's tension eased, but there was still that underlying doubt and fear. A sixth sense telling her to be on guard, that something was *off.*

This was the hard part. When things were going well, it was so easy to trust God and His provision and protection. But now? This was where her faith would be tested.

Trusting God when she didn't know what the future held.

The way she always wanted to.

Ethan sat astride the black mare and waited for his cue so they could get this done and get back to the office—and find that plane.

The sun beat down on the city of Renegade this morning. He removed his Stetson and wiped his damp head with a bandanna while a trickle of sweat rolled down his back. Wearing jeans, chaps, and a long-sleeve shirt didn't help his discomfort. He adjusted in the saddle, and his mare danced a bit, her hooves kicking up some dust.

Tilting his hat back, he scanned the crowd of spectators, looking for Aubrey. Standing on the old church steps, she was easy to spot, with her deep-auburn hair and large sunglasses. She waved, and he touched the brim of his hat in salute.

"Butler." Montgomery rode up on his mare, looking at ease in the saddle, and grinned as his gaze followed Ethan's. "See anything of interest?"

Ethan grunted. No way was he going to spill what he really thought about the office admin. "You look like you've done this a time or two before." Ethan scanned the gathered crowd, checking to make sure the marshals on duty were interspersed with the festivalgoers.

"Yeah." Montgomery adjusted the brim of his hat. "Every summer, I'd head to my uncle's ranch in Texas and help out with the cattle. It's where I learned to ride. You?"

"I've ridden a few times over the years." Ethan twisted in his seat to see the rest of his "posse." That was enough information for now. No use spilling his secrets to everyone in the office.

"What are you two discussing over here?" Liam sauntered over on his horse.

Montgomery smirked. "He's checking out our administrative assistant over there." Adam pointed with his chin to where Aubrey stood under an awning.

Ethan glared at them as they laughed. Hilarious. "I'm not checking her out." Okay, maybe he was, but he had no time in his life, either personal or professional, for a relationship. He had a plane to find and cats to feed. "You two about finished with your crowd surveillance?"

Liam held up his hands and returned to his place at the back of the group.

Ethan checked his watch. "It's almost go time." The horse skittered sideways. "I don't think this beast likes me."

"Aww, you just have to show her some love." Adam grinned and patted the side of his horse's neck, but then his smile faded. "Can I tell you something?"

"Sure." When was this thing supposed to start?

Adam leaned closer. "I've got a bad feeling about this event today." He exhaled and then straightened.

Ethan stiffened. "What do you mean?"

"I dunno." Adam shrugged. "Something just feels . . . *off*."

Ethan tilted his hat back on his head. "Yeah, I feel it too."

If he had his way, he'd cancel this entire shebang right now and sequester Aubrey until they could figure out what was going on and why the judge and Mrs. Silano had been killed. He hoped

Aubrey wasn't a target as well, but he couldn't be sure until he knew who had killed them and why.

The biggest item on his list was finding enough evidence of wrongdoing that he could apprehend Roger Rousseau and bring him in for questioning about the syndicate. And about the dirty marshal in his office.

"Well, what are going to do?" Adam asked.

His answer was automatic. "Pray."

Adam shifted in his saddle. "Look, I know you're a Christian. But seriously? How is that going to work?"

Ethan sent up a prayer for wisdom and then angled in his saddle to face the young deputy. "Let me ask you a question—have you prepared for this event?"

"Well, yeah, I suppose so."

"And you trust your horse."

Adam shrugged. "Sure. She's been trained."

"Exactly."

"I'm not sure I'm following you."

Ethan's gaze drifted to Aubrey one more time and then focused on his colleague. "It all comes down to trust. You trust the saddle won't fall off while riding, because the livery guys prepped the horses and tightened the cinches properly. You trust Aubrey to have planned this event down to the minute details. You trust me to direct you once this thing starts."

"Yeah, but I can see you."

"True. But what about unseen threats? We've discussed exigency plans, what would happen in an emergency, etc. Maybe nothing will happen, or maybe your horse will step in a small hole and break its ankle. So it comes down to trust again. Trusting each other. I trust the Lord with my safety every day. Do bad things happen, or could they happen? Sure. But I know that God's plan for my life is perfect. He doesn't want to see us harmed. But sometimes,

God does allow it. His definitions of harm and good don't look like ours."

Adam rested both hands on the saddle horn. "That's all good, but what about evil men?"

"There will always be evil men and women in this fallen world, and that's why we're here. To protect the innocent. We're a shield, a buffer. 'The Lord is my shield and buckler, my strong tower.' That's who God is. He's our refuge when times get tough. He wants us to come to Him, to rest and find strength in His presence."

Ethan leaned over his saddle horn and continued, "I know I haven't been the best example, but I'm trying to be the man God wants me to be. To trust Him in every aspect of my life, even this job. This career. I'm learning to lean on God more."

Liam called out from the back of the group, "Amen to that."

They all sat there for a minute, each one lost in their thoughts.

Ethan said, "I know I've given you a lot to mull over, Adam. But anytime you want to talk, I'm available."

His earpiece crackled to life. "Butler, the stagecoach is on at the edge of town. Get yourself and your crew ready."

"Roger that. In position." Ethan grinned at the others, realizing he was actually excited for this. "And now the fun begins."

He turned in the saddle and gave his posse the agreed-upon hand signal. Lining up the horses, he could feel the wave of anticipation in the air as a cloud of dust and clapping from the crowd announced the arrival of the main attraction.

The roar of the crowd and the echo of gunshots grew louder, as if they were riding a cresting wave on the ocean. The horse stomped her feet, and he patted her neck.

"Easy there, girl. It's almost go time."

The horse pricked her ears and snorted.

The red Wells Fargo stagecoach rumbled down the street, to the delight of the kids and adults in the crowd, while the "bandits" chased the coach, shooting their old-fashioned six-shooters into the air.

Crack.

Ethan flinched. That wasn't from the six-shooters.

Then suddenly, the whoops and hollers of joy turned ominous. Children's screams filled the air, and chaos erupted. Some of the crowd dispersed, others were frantic, running into the street, directly into the path of the stagecoach.

This wasn't part of the plan.

"Clear the streets!" Ethan yelled to his nearby team.

"What's going on?" Liam pulled back on the reins.

The marshals used their horses to corral frightened spectators off the street and onto the sidewalks.

Zip.

Ethan's head whipped around.

That was a sniper shot.

The stagecoach careened around a corner, taking the sharp curve with two of the antique wooden wheels high off the ground. Another rifle shot ripped through the air and whizzed past Ethan's head. He ducked low over his mare's neck, trying to keep her from running away.

"I'll get the lead horse!" Adam shouted over the chaos, charging ahead as if he were in a John Wayne Western. He grabbed the reins of the horses, which slowed and eventually stopped, their sides heaving and covered in sweat.

Another shot pinged past him.

Spectators were screaming, running for cover behind the old-fashioned props, entering shops, trying to escape the sniper's bullets.

Ethan pulled his horse alongside the stagecoach. The driver was slumped over the thin metal railing that surrounded the driver's box, a red stain covering his left shoulder and soaking through his blue-and-white-checkered shirt. "Hey, Mr. Petersen, can you hear me?"

Ethan climbed over to perch on the top of the stagecoach wheel and tied the reins around the wooden brake handle. Petersen was an expert horseman and had been driving the stagecoach for years. He knew how to handle a team of frightened horses.

"Stagecoach driver's been hit! Call it in—now!" Ethan shouted.

Petersen grunted. "Shot."

Whoever ended up coordinating what was sure to be a mess needed firsthand information to flow through official channels.

Montgomery nodded and pulled his phone out of his pocket. He contacted local PD, and moments later, radios crackled nearby. Ethan recognized the sound of a scene locking down.

Gunfire cracked through the air again. Dirt kicked up near Ethan's boots.

Liam sprinted toward them.

"Hang on," Ethan told Petersen, keeping his body between the man and the open street. "Help's coming."

More shots rang out, close enough that Ethan ducked instinctively. Liam grabbed Petersen under the arms, and together they hauled him off the seat and out of the line of fire.

Ethan's head stayed on a swivel, scanning rooftops and alleyways, but he couldn't spot the shooter—only the chaos left behind.

Another shot hit the dirt by his feet. Either the sniper was a really bad shot, or Ethan wasn't the primary target. These seemed like warnings. Or whoever was firing only wanted chaos.

"I'll get him to the medical tent." Liam placed Petersen's arm around his shoulder, and they disappeared behind a brick building.

Ethan removed his service pistol from his holster and flattened himself against the building. Multiple screams split the air, women and children were crying. *Oh, Lord, please help.*

"Ethan!"

He recognized that voice. Aubrey.

He grabbed his horse's reins and ran across the street, using the stagecoach and horse as a shield between himself and the shooter. He pulled the whole team to a stop. "Aubrey! Where are you?"

He found her and a man and woman with their young child, crouched behind a pile of boxes. The man held his frightened family and looked directly at Ethan. "What is going on?"

"I don't know, sir, but look." Ethan pointed to the street. Renegade PD and US Marshals swept the area, weapons drawn, escorting the crowd away from the stagecoach. "I think you'd be safer inside the store."

The man nodded and led his family to shelter.

Ethan exhaled. At least they were safe. Aubrey was still crouched against the building, her eyes closed.

He lightly touched her shoulder, and she flinched. "It's me. Ethan."

She opened those big green eyes, tears shimmering at the corners. "Hey."

"I'm going to get you out of here." Another bullet whizzed over their heads and shattered the glass behind them, and she screamed. That was too close. "Aubrey, we have to leave."

"No." Her plea was a strangled whisper.

He reholstered his weapon and gripped her shoulders. "Listen to me. We have to leave. We're in the direct line of fire. It's our only chance to survive."

More bullets splintered the wood behind them, closer to their heads, and she winced.

"Okay, on the count of three, follow me."

Aubrey nodded once.

"One . . . two . . . three . . . go!" He slapped the horse's flanks, grabbed Aubrey's cold hand, and dragged her behind the old mercantile. A flurry of bullets whizzed by, and he placed his hand on her back. They ended up in an alley and rested their backs against the cool brick, gasping for air.

His mare must've followed him, because there she stood, watching him, as if telling him that he could trust her.

He patted the side of her neck. "Hey, girl. I'm gonna need your help."

The horse whinnied and bobbed her head up and down as if she understood. Fear and gunpowder scented the air, along with smells of frightened animals.

"I've never ridden a horse before." Aubrey stood beside him, almost shrinking in stature. Fear rolled off her in waves, her hands balled into fists at her sides.

"Well, Sheba here is going to help us escape, aren't you, girl?"

The horse neighed softly and stamped her feet. She turned her head toward Aubrey and nudged her toward the saddle, and Aubrey gave a little squeak.

"I guess that's our cue to leave." Ethan mounted the horse and extended his hand to Aubrey.

She stared at his hand. "Where am I supposed to sit?"

"Behind me."

Aubrey opened her mouth to respond, but Ethan wiggled his fingers at her. "We don't have time to argue. Now, put your foot on top of my boot, and I'll hoist you up."

She tentatively put her hand in his and settled behind him, then clasped his waist in a death grip.

"Hey, ease up there, woman. You're going to suffocate me."

"Sorry." Aubrey's grip loosened, and she leaned into his back. Her perfume filled his senses, and he had to mentally school himself to focus.

Oh man, he was in trouble now. He'd sworn off women, but Aubrey was causing him to have second thoughts that maybe dating again was a possibility. But his highest priority was to get her out of harm's way and to safety.

He cleared his throat. "Hang on tight. And keep your head

down." He patted Sheba's neck and leaned forward. "Hey, girl. We're gonna need you to get us out of here."

Another gunshot split the air, and he dug his spurs into the horse's flanks. "Ya!"

The horse leaped forward, and he felt Aubrey bury her face in his back. He navigated through back alleys, bent low over the saddle, praying the entire time.

As soon as he got Aubrey settled, this was gonna stop. No more threats. Whoever was in charge of this chaos today would soon pay.

Ethan prayed they caught whoever was behind these attacks before someone else was hurt.

Or worse.

SEVEN

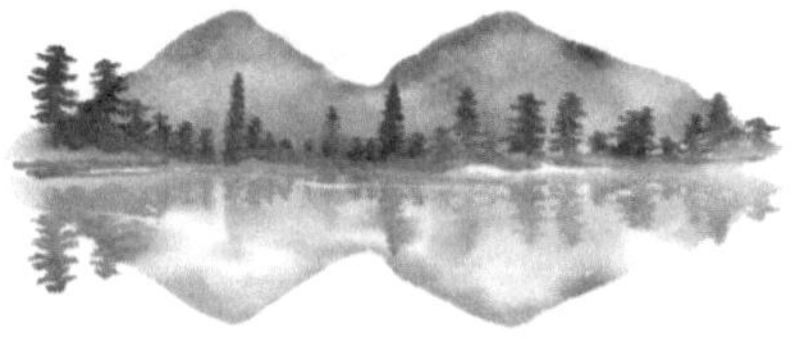

AUBREY KEPT HER EYES CLOSED THE ENTIRE ride back to safety, not wanting to look down. Bouncing up and down on that saddle, she felt as if a few of her fillings were knocked loose.

The noise and chaos of the crowd faded as they traveled farther from the reenactment. Gravel and dust from the horse's hooves flew into her nose and mouth.

One moment, everything had been going according to her plan, then the next, chaos had broken out as shots were fired at the crowd, sending groups of spectators screaming and running for the nearest cover. When Aubrey had crouched behind that barrel in front of the feedstore, she'd prayed like never before.

She'd been so scared she couldn't move, all the fear from years ago rushing back to the forefront.

And then, Ethan had shown up. *Thank You, God.*

They sped down back alleys and side streets all the way back to . . . not her house. Ethan helped her down, dismounted, and tied the horse's reins to the porch railing.

The lack of traffic was unnerving.

She glanced over her shoulder at the deserted street and climbed the porch stairs, each step heavier than the one before. Memories swirled in her mind. "Where are we?"

"One of the department's safe houses. The horse needs to rest, and this place has grass."

"So we're not here because we're in danger?" Just like years ago, before Donovan went to prison, she'd felt as if someone was tracking her.

"Don't know about you, but I was ready to get off the horse."

She smiled, even though he wasn't ruling out their being in danger. Maybe it was too early to know. She said, "Me too." Though holding on to him had been nice.

"This is the closest place I know of that the horse will be okay until someone can come and get her." Ethan touched her arm. "You okay?"

She stared at the door and gave him a tight smile, trying to tamp down the nightmare images flashing in her mind. "I must've lost my purse somewhere at the festival."

"We'll get a replacement for you. We can get into this place through the back. Come on." Ethan held out his hand and led her to the back door.

Her eyes clouded with tears. "I'm sorry. It's all my fault . . ." She sniffled and searched her pockets for a tissue. "At least, I can't help but think it is. This brings back a lot of memories. Sorry." She needed to get a handle on herself.

"Why are you sorry?" Ethan stilled her hands, holding them between his calloused ones. She glanced down at their intertwined hands. He had nice hands. Strong. Warm.

"Because until we know it wasn't my fault, the fact is, it could be. Even if I've believed I was safe since I moved to Renegade, there's still someone who wants to kill me. Twenty years ago, my testimony sent Finn Donovan, a hired killer, to prison."

He led her over to the back porch and then nudged her to sit on the steps. "We're okay. We're at a safe house, remember? And there's nothing about this that we can be sure connects to you."

She glanced up at the cloudless blue sky. "I . . ."

"Tell me what happened to you, Aubrey."

Dare she trust him? Had God put Ethan in her life for this reason?

Aubrey drew in a breath and forced herself to start talking before she lost the nerve. Once she began, the words came too fast, skimming the surface of the truth instead of diving beneath it. "Judge Mullinax had a case in his federal courtroom."

She swallowed against the lump in her throat. "One where I had to testify against a hardened criminal." She kept her eyes on the floor, on the safe, solid ground. Porch steps. A home. A safe house.

Still, the words still felt unreal, even after all these years.

"We found out later he was wanted by Interpol." She spoke quickly, as if speed could keep the memories at bay. "More murders. Multiple countries. Europe." She swallowed. "After the trial, my family was threatened. They didn't stop until the feds put my family in witness protection—my parents, my younger sister Kristen, and me."

She wiped at her cheek when a tear escaped, annoyed by the betrayal of it. "The judge checked in, wrote me letters through the secure mail witnesses use. I got to tell him how hard it was going, how strained things were with my family being in danger because of me. About six years ago, he suggested I move. He didn't order it—he gave me the choice to leave my family in witness protection so they could get on with their lives, and I came here. Renegade seemed far enough away. Quiet enough." Her voice softened. "I thought I was safe."

What she didn't say pressed hard against her ribs.

She didn't say fear like that never really went away. Because if Donovan ever got out of prison and decided to come after her, then she would have to relive every moment she'd tried to forget. And she wasn't ready to open that door. Not yet. Not out loud.

"You *are* safe," Ethan said gently.

Oh, how she wanted to believe him. Even if her instincts were screaming at her that this peace she'd enjoyed for so long wouldn't last forever. No matter how safe she'd felt, Donovan wouldn't ever stop wanting to kill her for testifying.

Ethan's whisper entranced her, pulled her in, made her want . . . more. She leaned into him, absorbing some of his strength. His warmth. He draped his wrists over his knees, and they sat there for a moment, him allowing her to decompress after that wild ride.

"You mentioned being scared." His gaze was focused on the backyard. "We've all been scared at one time in our lives."

"You? Scared?"

He let out a soft chuckle and glanced at her. "Yeah. Me."

"I find that hard to believe, Mr. Two-Time White Water Kayaking Champion."

"Yeah, well, just a few years ago, I didn't think I was going to make it out alive after my team and I were ambushed." Ethan's body radiated tension, his muscles stiff against her side.

"That had to be scary."

"I should've known better. We walked right into a trap."

"How could you have known it was a trap?" She searched his face. A muscle in his jaw twitched.

"There were signs." He turned to face her. "I ignored the red flags."

She shook her head. "I find that hard to believe. You're a good marshal, Ethan."

A bitter laugh escaped his lips. "If I'd been focused, I wouldn't have lost most of my team. I couldn't protect them."

Aubrey shifted, angling her body toward him. "You are not

responsible for their deaths. Isn't that what you told me about the judge and his housekeeper?" She nudged his shoulder with hers.

"How about we agree to disagree?" He looked at her, his pull magnetic. Even if she wanted to look away, she couldn't. He tugged a folded piece of white cloth out of his pocket. "Handkerchief? I promise it's clean."

She smiled and accepted the offered hanky, then wiped the moisture off her cheeks. "Thank you." Her voice was a hoarse whisper.

"You missed a spot." He pointed to her cheek and wiped the remains of the dirt and tears with the handkerchief. "All better."

Ethan studied her a moment, then leaned close.

She licked her lips, and his gaze dropped to her mouth.

Suddenly, he stood and wiped the dust off his jeans. "I, uh, I think we need to get inside. Let me call Roberts and check in." He entered a code into the keypad by the door. "This house happens to be vacant right now, but I'm still going to clear it first. Stay on the porch. Don't move until I come back."

Her fingers tightened on the railing. "Don't go."

"I'll be quick," he said, already drawing his weapon.

He disappeared inside.

Aubrey counted his steps without meaning to, listening to the faint thud of doors opening, closing. Silence stretched. She forced herself to breathe, to stay still. Waiting in the dark wasn't new. She'd learned long ago how to sit with uncertainty without letting it break her.

The lights snapped on. She jumped anyway.

"All clear." Ethan stepped back onto the porch and gestured her in.

The safe house was exactly what it needed to be, with its dated appliances, clean linoleum, lack of personal touches. A place to disappear into, not settle in. Aubrey took it in quickly, cataloging exits and sightlines the way she'd been taught years ago. Old habits didn't fade.

Ethan guided her toward a vinyl chair. She sat while he pulled out his phone and put it to his ear. "Roberts. What's the status back at the festival? Any sign of the shooter?"

He paced as he listened, the tension in his body radiating off him in waves.

"Okay. Thanks." He glanced at her but said to Liam, "We're secure. Pine Ridge Trail. For now. Keep me posted."

When the call ended, he leaned closer to her, his voice dropping.

"I'm going to tend to the horse and let her graze out back. You okay?"

"Yes." The answer came easily, even if it wasn't entirely true.

Ethan hesitated, then gently turned her toward him, forcing her to meet his gaze. "I won't be long."

She nodded. She needed something to do.

She found enough coffee in the pantry to start a pot. Measure, pour, wait. Anything to keep herself busy. The familiar motions grounded her, but the weight of the day pressed in anyway. The judge. The shooting. The realization that danger hadn't stayed where she'd left it.

The screen door slammed and she startled *again.* "Ethan?"

"What's wrong?" Ethan washed his hands in the sink.

She shook her head, keeping her voice steady. "I don't want to spiral."

"Talking helps." He waited.

"I can't . . ." She stopped herself from spilling all her secrets. "I need to sit." Her head spun.

He pulled out a chair and handed her a bottle of water. "Drink."

She did, spilling some as her hands shook. "Perfect." She stood, grabbed a dishtowel, and began to wipe up the mess she'd made.

"Let me . . ."

"I'm fine." But the tears came anyway.

Ethan set the towel aside and cupped her face gently. "You don't have to hold it together right now."

She stepped into him, surprising herself. It wasn't desperation. It was trust. His arms came around her, steady and sure. She pressed into him as if he was her lifeline.

When her breathing finally evened out, she pulled back and wiped her cheeks. "Sorry."

"Don't be." His voice was quiet. He moved closer until only a fraction of an inch separated them and she could smell the peppermint he'd eaten earlier. Was he going to kiss her? Instead, he brushed a strand of hair behind her ear. "You've had a couple of brutal days."

The closeness lingered and the kitchen shrank. She was too aware of him, his presence. The air was charged with an underlying current—until his phone rang, breaking the mood.

She stepped back first. "You should get that."

"Yeah." He glanced at the screen. "Liam?"

Aubrey got two mugs down from the cupboard.

"What about the plane? And the sniper?" Ethan asked.

She glanced back to see all the color had drained from his face.

Ethan shook his head. "Okay. Got it. Drive my truck over to the safe house, please. I'll have someone drop off your car later. Thanks."

Ethan ended the call and stood there for a moment, his phone still in his hand. Aubrey watched the shift happen, how his posture changed, how the easy reassurance drained away and resolve took its place.

"What is it?" She held a mug between her hands.

"Liam's on his way," Ethan said. "I need to go back to the office."

Her disappointment flickered, but she pushed it aside. "Okay. What aren't you saying?"

He hesitated, then leaned back against the counter. "We don't have confirmation yet. No ID on the shooter. No arrest."

"But?" she pressed.

"The plane crash wasn't random," he said. "Someone transported a prisoner to Renegade under false credentials, marking it with a code we use for high-risk transports—they don't land on the usual records. They used a decommissioned Marshals plane and pulled off a prison break in South Carolina. Whoever planned this went to a lot of trouble."

Her pulse picked up. "A prisoner brought here?"

"Yes."

"And you think that's connected to today?"

"I do." He met her gaze fully now. "Which means we have to consider motive. Not just opportunity but intent."

The words settled heavy in her chest.

"You think this was aimed at someone specific," she said slowly.

"I think it's possible," he replied. "And if that's the case, then we have to be honest about who might be in the crosshairs."

Her instincts sharpened. "Me," she whispered.

If Donovan was out of prison . . . She closed her eyes for a moment, forcing back the memories. The last glimpse she'd had of her older sister's face before they ran and she never saw Kayla again.

Ethan didn't say it right away. That alone told her enough.

"Finn Donovan is loose," he said finally. "Someone transferred him out of the federal facility in South Carolina and brought him to Renegade."

The name hit like a sudden drop in altitude—not shock, not panic, but a cold, familiar gravity.

"He hasn't made contact," Ethan continued. "We don't know that he was involved today, but we don't know he wasn't. We don't know who's behind this attack or why they would go to so much trouble to bring him here. But if he is in Renegade and has been for several days, we have to assume his plan involves revenge."

Her throat tightened, but she kept her voice steady. "Against me."

"Yes." His tone softened, just slightly. "Which is why I need you to be careful. Watch your routines. Don't go anywhere alone. And don't assume today was an accident, but we can't assume it *was* him either. Not until we're sure."

She nodded, absorbing the distinction. This wasn't certainty. It was preparation.

"So Renegade Days . . ." she began.

"May have been an attempted murder," Ethan said. "Or a diversion. Or it may have had nothing to do with him at all." He held her gaze. "We won't know for sure until we have more information."

A knock sounded at the door.

"That should be Liam, but stay here while I check," Ethan said. "He's going to stay with you while I get eyes on this."

She straightened. "I'll be fine."

"I know." His voice was firm, but his eyes lingered. "But that doesn't mean I'm not worried."

She gave a small nod, accepting that much.

As Ethan moved toward the door, Aubrey stayed where she was, steadying herself, not with denial but with resolve.

Because if Finn Donovan was back in play, then she couldn't afford to cower in fear.

She needed to stay ahead of him.

The men shook hands, and then Ethan looked at her over Liam's shoulder, his eyes conveying the depth of his feelings that he couldn't voice.

She waved, and he simply nodded his head, spun on his heel, and walked out of the house.

She prayed for his safety and that he would come back to her.

Ethan gripped the steering wheel as he navigated the streets of

Renegade. Gone were the enthusiastic crowds from earlier in the day, replaced by debris and empty venues.

He knew better than to allow his emotions to override common sense. His ex, Melissa, used to say he was emotionally stunted. That didn't seem to be the problem with Aubrey at all.

Aubrey wasn't Melissa, and what he was feeling for Aubrey was definitely stronger than anything he'd felt in the past. Still, it was hard to quit allowing the wounds of the past to color what was developing between them.

He removed his Stetson and tossed it on the passenger seat. A stray balloon floated across the street. He rolled down the window and rested his arm on the edge. This cowboy getup was hot and sweaty, and he couldn't wait to return the costume to Jenna.

The caller ID lit up with Mrs. Hanover's smiling face. "Hey, Mrs. Hanover. What can I do for you?"

"I'm so glad I caught you, dear. I heard about the shooting today during Renegade Days. Simply awful. How are you? Are you safe?"

"Yes, ma'am."

"Oh good. I hope you don't mind, but I'm checking on my babies."

Ethan turned down Main, on the west side of downtown. "They're fine. I fed them this morning."

But was *he* fine? He glanced down at his shaking hands. Flashbacks from a couple of years ago steamrolled through his mind. He had to temper his emotions and focus on the task at hand.

"I know you're busy, but I wanted to assure you that I'm praying for you."

"I appreciate that." His phone buzzed with another incoming call. "Mrs. Hanover? I'm sorry to cut you off, but I have to take this call."

"Certainly, dear. I'm going to send you a picture of my great-granddaughter. I was planning to be home tomorrow, but with what happened there today, I'm not sure."

"That's probably not a bad idea. Stay as long as you like, and don't worry about the cats." He checked his rearview mirror and changed lanes. "You take care now."

"I will." He heard the uncertainty in her voice, but it was best if she delayed her return. He ended the call and clicked over to the next call. "Butler."

"It's Adam. Everything good with you and Aubrey?"

"She's safe, and Liam is looking out for her. I'm on my way to the office." He turned on his blinker to make a right in front of the courthouse. Almost there.

"The rest of the team is coming in as well."

"Good." Ethan waited while several pedestrians ran across the street, fearful looks of distrust on their faces. "Tell Stanton to find everything he can on Finn Donovan. Convicted criminal, the case was years ago. Find out how long he was given in prison, what the charges were, any known associates. We need the whole case file." In the past, his gut instincts had failed him. This time, he was going in prayed up, seeking God's wisdom.

"Copy that. He involved?"

"Unconfirmed. Could be unrelated. See you in a few." Ethan disconnected the call and parked behind the imposing structure, which rose like an impregnable rock face. Right now, he couldn't seem to get a foothold on exactly what'd happened.

A cool blast of air greeted him as he entered the courthouse. He waved at the court security guard as he worked through the metal detector security checkpoint.

Deputy Marshal Nick Stanton met him at the elevator. A tattoo of an American eagle was visible on his right forearm. Normally, Nick didn't wear short sleeves, so the plain black T-shirt he was wearing was out of character, even if the cool weather from this morning had morphed into a blazing hot afternoon.

"Butler."

"Stanton." Ethan pressed the up button and stared at the arrows above the car. "What did you find out?"

The elevator door opened, and Stanton waved Ethan in first. Even though they were evenly matched in height, Stanton had at least twenty pounds of muscle over Ethan. Nick made him nervous—and glad they were on the same team.

Nick pressed the button for their floor and crossed his massive arms over his equally massive chest. "I'll tell you when we get to the offices."

"I need to change first, then I want everyone gathered." Ethan scanned his badge at the door.

Emma Kennedy sat at the reception desk, covering Aubrey's job while she was off.

"Butler, Deputy Marshal Roberts left you this." She handed Ethan a file with Rousseau's name written across the top.

"Thanks. I'll be back in a second." Ethan shut the door to his office, quickly changed out of the costume, and headed back to Aubrey's desk, where he picked up the file.

Stanton poured himself coffee at the credenza. "Where's Sunshine?"

"Who?" Ethan paused from reading the file.

Stanton came back over with two mugs, handing one to Ethan. "You know, Sunshine. Aubrey."

Emma chuckled. "Aubrey is in a safe house. Liam is with her."

Ethan glanced between the two grinning deputies. "What's 'Sunshine' supposed to mean?"

"Nothing." Nick raised his hands. "I was just asking about her. You're testy today."

"Let's go." Ethan pointed his chin at the conference room. "Everyone else should be waiting for us in conference room A." He glanced back. "That means you too, Emma."

"Right." She cleared her throat.

Ethan ignored the byplay he didn't understand and entered the larger conference room, which held a long table and twenty chairs. A small cabinet sat off to the side, where refreshments were usually available, and the high windows allowed the afternoon sunshine to warm the room.

It reassured him more than he'd realized to see the rest of the deputies were there.

Hank Green, whose main job was courtroom security, and Albright, who'd been shot a few weeks ago, were missing. Liam was watching Aubrey. But there were still plenty of deputies to work this.

Supervisor Howard stood at the front of the room. "As you are aware, we had an attack during Renegade Days this morning. Thankfully, no one was killed, but the stagecoach team driver, Frank Petersen, was seriously injured and is in critical condition. Kennedy, can you pass out the information, please?"

Emma gave each deputy a stack of stapled papers, which included the flight manifest from the downed plane. Whoever had stolen it knew they'd never take off without a manifest, so they'd filled one out. How much they could trust the information remained to be seen.

Howard continued. "As you can see, there was only one inmate on the plane that crashed: Finn Donovan. He has been locked up in federal prison on the East Coast for the past twenty years. Now someone's taken it upon themselves to bring him here. He should be considered armed and dangerous."

A low murmur moved through the room.

Stanton said, "That why you asked me to find his file, Butler?"

Ethan shook his head. "I didn't know it was him at the time." More murmurs rippled across the room, but Ethan didn't wait for it to settle. "Sir, something like this doesn't happen without multiple people being involved. This was a conspiracy, and they pulled it off. Until the plane crashed."

Howard narrowed his eyes. "Right. It's up to us to apprehend him and bring in those who stole the plane and concocted this elaborate plan to bring him here."

The deputies began talking at once.

Howard held up his hand. "Hold on now. We will be working around the clock until we find this plane and apprehend Donovan and his coconspirators." Howard looked at Ethan. "Given the black box in the judge's car, are there any leads as to who killed the judge and his housekeeper? It's likely the same perpetrator."

Ethan leaned forward. "The judge's outside cameras had been disabled. And there was no clear picture of anyone other than Aubrey showing up as seen from the neighbors' cameras either. So no leads there until forensics gives us something."

"I did find something interesting." Adam Montgomery spoke up. "I called the Denver office, and there were rumors that the judge was fixing trials. Maybe he finally decided he didn't want to do that anymore and they killed him."

Emma glanced around. "The Denver office got us a warrant for Mullinax's financials. We were able to get access to the judge's bank accounts and found he had a lot of extremely large deposits over the past ten years. But the past sixteen months, he's had a lot of large withdrawals as well."

Howard leaned back in his chair. "Keep pulling that thread. Find out if he was taking bribes. Butler, in light of the circumstances, I'm putting you in charge of the manhunt. Montgomery and Roberts can take the hunt for the plane. I need to make some phone calls to get the support we need. Dismissed."

They stood and filed out of the conference room, but Stanton held out his hand and motioned for Ethan to follow him back to his office.

Once inside, Stanton closed the door. He pulled a file out of his drawer and pushed it across the desk. "Seems our friend Roger Rousseau has a few skeletons in his closet."

"Was there a reason why you didn't share this in the meeting?" Ethan opened the file folder and read the contents.

"I figured you'd want to hear this in private before deciding what to do with the information." Stanton sat in front of him like a stone sentinel. Unmoving. Stanton had good instincts, and Ethan trusted him.

"Okay." Ethan looked up from the file. "These bank transfers look like the same numbers that the judge was receiving."

Stanton crossed his arms. "Looks to me like whoever was paying off Mullinax is also paying off Roger Rousseau. Which, as far as we know, connects both of them to the syndicate."

"But that doesn't mean Roger has anything to do with this plane crash, or with the deaths of Judge Mullinax and his housekeeper."

"No, but if you look further, we were given some copies of emails from an interested third party. They wanted to remain a confidential informant. Rousseau mentions the 'syndicate'"—Stanton made quote marks—"asking for a personal favor."

"Could be anything."

"Maybe." Stanton leaned forward. "But when you look at the date of the email and the date of the judge's death and the plane wreckage, they match up."

Holy crime scene.

Ethan closed the file and pinched the bridge of his nose. "Finn Donovan was brought here by the syndicate."

"Yeah."

Stanton sat back in his chair, a smirk tilting his mouth up. "Turns out Sunshine has a few secrets."

Ethan said, "Doesn't mean she's part of it."

"Of course not." Stanton picked up a pen and twirled it between his fingers. The man didn't say a whole lot, but he studied human behavior. Probably could've been a shrink. "After you got Aubrey out of there, how was she?"

"Scared, and rightfully so. Given we now know that Donovan is on the loose."

"You're gonna help her, right?" Stanton asked.

"Isn't that part of my job?"

"I mean beyond your duties as a marshal." The old office chair squeaked as Stanton adjusted his weight. "I think you're the man God sent to help her." Stanton pointed the pen at Ethan, his deep-brown eyes burning with an intensity that caused Ethan to shift in his seat.

"My purpose is to chase down felons, put them behind bars, and make sure they never hurt another living soul."

Stanton said, "Exactly."

Ethan exhaled slowly. Maybe he and Stanton weren't talking about two different missions after all.

EIGHT

THE SAFE HOUSE WAS QUIET IN A WAY THAT made her skin prickle.

Not peaceful. Not comforting. Just . . . hours and hours of emptiness. Enough hours that Liam had gone back to work when Ethan showed up again with his laptop and piles of files.

Aubrey sat at the small kitchen table, her fingers wrapped around a mug she hadn't taken a sip from yet. The coffee had gone cold sometime after Ethan left the room to check in with the deputy on duty. The hum of the refrigerator was too loud. The ticking clock on the wall felt like it was counting down something she couldn't see.

She stared at the worn linoleum floor and tried to breathe through the tightness in her chest.

Safe.

That was the word everyone kept using.

She knew the procedures. She knew the logic. But logic had never stopped a bullet. Or a blade. Or Finn Donovan.

Her sister's face rose up without warning, wide eyes, mouth open as if she'd tried to scream her name. Not a memory but a nightmare she'd had over and over. Aubrey's grip tightened on the mug until her knuckles ached.

She hadn't told Ethan everything.

Footsteps approached down the hall. Controlled. Familiar. Ethan stopped just short of the doorway, giving her space instead of crowding her. She appreciated that more than he probably knew.

"The deputy from Denver is outside. He's all set," he said quietly. "We'll rotate shifts outside and inside every few hours."

Aubrey nodded, though she hadn't been listening closely. Except to the part earlier where he'd told her deputies from Denver had come down to help out. Her pulse was still too loud in her ears.

Ethan hesitated, then moved to the other side of the room and sat facing her. Not too close. Not too far. Like he was aware that one wrong move might shatter something fragile between them.

"How are you holding up?" His question was gentle.

She gave a humorless huff. "You want the polite answer, or the honest one?"

His mouth twitched, but his eyes stayed serious. "Honest. Of course."

Aubrey looked down at her hands. They were shaking again. She pressed them flat against the tabletop, grounding herself.

"I keep replaying it," she said softly. "Renegade Days. The noise. The crowd. The way everything went from normal to chaos in a second." Her throat tightened. "I thought I'd moved past that kind of fear. Turns out I just learned how to hide it better."

Ethan didn't interrupt. He just listened.

She swallowed. "When you said Finn Donovan's name earlier . . . something snapped. Like a door I've kept locked for years just flew open."

His posture shifted, alert but careful. "Aubrey—"

"I didn't just know him." She cut in before she could lose her nerve. "I didn't just recognize the name because I testified against him."

The room seemed to hold its breath.

"He killed my sister."

The words landed heavy and final between them.

Ethan stilled. "I'm so sorry, Aubrey."

Aubrey's vision blurred. She blinked hard, refusing to cry. She'd done enough of that years ago.

"They told me that my testimony meant he'd never see the outside of a cell again. And I built my life around that promise." She laughed softly, bitterly. "Turns out promises don't mean much to men like him."

Ethan's hands clenched on his knees. She could see the tension running through him now. Controlled, contained, but fierce.

"That's why you froze today." It wasn't a question.

"Yes." She nodded. "Saying his name out loud makes it real again. Makes him real again."

Silence stretched between them, thick with unspoken things.

"You should have told someone," he said gently.

Her shoulders sagged. "But I was tired of being the girl with the dead sister. The witness who identified Finn Donovan as a killer. I just wanted to be . . . Aubrey. And for years, it worked. I was living my life, and Donovan wasn't part of it."

Ethan leaned forward, resting his forearms on the table. "You didn't do anything wrong, you know."

She finally met his eyes. "But he's coming for me, isn't he?"

Ethan didn't lie. "We have to assume you're a target even if it turns out there's another reason the syndicate brought him here."

Fear flared hot and sharp—but beneath it was something else. Resolve. "Then I'm done staying silent. If he's loose, I want to help stop him."

Ethan shook his head immediately. "Your safety comes first."

"And my sister?" Her voice wavered, but she held his gaze. "Doesn't she count too?"

Pain flashed across his face—fast, raw. "Of course she does, but her safety isn't the issue here. Yours is."

He reached across the table, stopping just short of touching her hand, giving her the choice. After a beat, she slid her fingers into his. He said, "I won't let him hurt you again."

Aubrey squeezed his hand, grounding herself in the warmth, the promise.

For the first time since Renegade Days, the fear didn't feel quite so suffocating.

Finn Donovan had come back from the shadows.

But unlike when she'd been on the witness stand, she wasn't facing him alone.

Minutes ticked by, time he should be working. Sitting with Aubrey was what he wanted to do, but it was also time he could be using to chase down Finn Donovan.

But a marshal's job wasn't just hunting fugitives. It was protecting the people in the crosshairs. He could work the case from the safe house just as well and keep Aubrey within reach.

She didn't look at him. Instead, she stared at their joined hands. Hesitating about whether to share more of her story?

Could he share his?

"I'm here all day." His thumb brushed over her knuckles. He didn't want to rush her, but he'd seen the fear in her eyes earlier this morning. It was imperative that she tell him everything. "Aubrey."

She opened her eyes, which shimmered with tears.

"I'm not going anywhere." He pointed at the door. "The team is here for you too, and we're not going to let anyone hurt you.

You have to tell me, if for no other reason than to keep others from dying."

"I know." She gave him a wobbly smile, and she slowly slid her hands out from under his. "I don't know where to start."

"The beginning is good."

She barked out a mirthless laugh. "Yeah."

Her gaze drifted to look outside the big picture window and then back to him. So much hurt in her expression.

Perhaps if he shared a little bit of himself, she'd open up to him. If he didn't, she might never confide in him. But if he did tell her, she'd probably run. Being vulnerable was risky, but right now, their lives might depend on it.

"You know I lost my team two years ago." Ethan cleared his throat. "Part of the reason it happened was that I didn't want to seem weak and I didn't want to put my new team in danger. But by withholding information, I did just that."

She raised soulful eyes to his. "What happened?"

He shifted in his chair. "It's an ugly story, one I'm not proud of."

"I've got nowhere else to be."

Ethan exhaled. "My team and I were protecting a high-profile witness." He pulled back and stuffed his shaking hands in his pockets. "He was a horrible human being, but he helped us bring down a Mafia leader. Anyway, I was feeling pretty smug after the court case and conviction. I was on top of the world. But I'd become lax, sloppy in my work. I was distracted."

"Don't be so hard on yourself."

"It was my fault they died." He shook his head. "I'm to blame. I was so focused on my success and the accolades I'd received. I thought . . . I was invincible." His breath caught. "I'd pushed God out of my relationship with my fiancée, stopped praying and asking for His direction."

She raised her hand. "Been there, done that."

"Yeah, well, big mistake." Emotion clogged his throat. "A good friend of mine, Rob, was also on that team. We were getting ready to move the witness into the protection program. We had everything set up. New name, new identity. All of it."

"Standard operating procedure."

"Yeah." He stood, pacing the small room, each pass burning off restless energy. He'd never spoken this out loud to anyone. Until Aubrey. And now that he'd started, the truth clawed to get free.

Aubrey stayed seated, watching him carefully, like she was tracking a storm only she could see forming. "You don't have to carry it alone just because you survived it."

He stopped and looked at her. "You want the short version?" His voice grated like tired metal.

"No." She shook her head. "I simply want the truth."

He exhaled once, dropped into the nearest chair, forearms braced on his knees. "My fiancée wanted me out. Not because she knew too much about the dangers I face, but because she didn't want to be tied to a marshal. This life is stressful. She hated the badge, the risks, the distance it put between us." His jaw worked. "I thought I could fix it by loving harder. But you can't rebuild something when only one person is still fighting for it."

Aubrey's brows drew together. "And then the ambush."

"Yeah." His gaze hit the floor. "Autopilot that morning. Same route. Same schedule. I missed the signs. Someone else didn't." He swallowed. "They hit us from the alley. Blocked us front and back. Came from all sides. Bullets everywhere." His hands curled into fists. "I survived. Most of them didn't."

Silence crackled between them. All it would take was one match, one comment, and this would all blow up in his face.

"And Rob?" she asked, voice low.

He closed his eyes. "Bullet to the spine. Eighteen months of surgeries. Rehab. Paperwork. He'll never walk again. He resigned last spring." His throat tightened. "My error opened the door for the wrong moment to happen on the wrong road."

Aubrey rose and crossed the room, kneeling in front of him, steady, present, fearless in the face of grief. She placed both hands lightly on his forearm. "Evil ambushed your team, Ethan. That wasn't a decision you made."

He blinked down at her, throat working, and then ducked his head.

Aubrey let silence hold a beat. She didn't let him hide. Instead, she let him breathe.

Then quietly, but with iron-core sincerity: "You didn't pull the trigger. The bad guys did. And guilt doesn't get to rewrite God's truth. Something I should probably remember."

His head snapped up.

She stood, brushing dust from her jeans. Met his eyes. "And the God who kept you alive that day didn't do it just to watch you drown in blame."

He surged to his feet again, but this time it wasn't an explosion. It was protest wrapped around panic. "It's best if you stay far away from me. You'll eventually be hurt."

"You're assuming all the guilt." She stepped into his path, forcing him to halt. "Remorse isn't proof you're dangerous. It's proof your conscience still works." A breath. "What you lost was devastating. But you aren't the one who cost people their lives or ruined the plan."

He stared at her, his chest caving as though trying to bear an impossible weight.

She touched his arm. "I have to remember that grace doesn't erase the worst day; it meets you in it. And God's mercy is big enough to hold both of us."

This moment belonged to two humans standing at the edge of a spiritual fault line.

Her hand slid down his arm until her fingers laced with his. She gave a soft squeeze, the small gesture settling between them like a prayer. "You don't get to sentence yourself to isolation for the crimes of evil men, Ethan Butler. God didn't save you just to watch you disappear from the world."

His pulse hammered, but the metal taste was gone.

Because maybe—just maybe—love hadn't been the distraction that killed his team.

Maybe love was the appeal that could finally save him.

"Aren't you doing the same thing?" He held her gaze, the frustration from earlier ebbing into something closer to concern than accusation. "I know you're scared of Finn Donovan. That maybe you blame yourself for what happened to your sister."

She looked away. "I don't want to talk about it."

He nodded once, absorbing the deflection without striking back. "Okay." A beat. Then, with a sigh that carried more disappointment than irritation: "I open the vault, you shut yours. Just feels . . . uneven."

Aubrey blinked. "Ethan . . ."

"And I don't mean the case," he clarified, his voice gentling another degree. "I mean us. You asked for truth, so I gave it." His tone dipped low, steady now. "I don't expect you to pull the wall down all at once. I just hoped you'd trust me enough to hand me a brick."

She swallowed. "It's not the same."

Ethan shifted back half a step, putting a sliver of space between them while keeping hold of her hand. "Maybe not, but fear is fear. And running is running." His thumb brushed once over the back of her hand. "So tell me this much. What are you fighting that you don't want to name?"

She swallowed, her throat raw from the emotion, and tugged her hand from his. A faint tremor moved through her, and she crossed her arms over her middle. "The devil." Her voice was barely audible in the quiet room.

Ethan stilled. No rebuttal. No pressure. Just a slow exhale.

"Then you're braver than you think," he murmured. "Because most people don't admit the shape of their enemy."

Aubrey pulled her hand from his and he let her.

But his voice followed her retreat, soft, stripped of battle. "And if the devil is what you're up against, then maybe you and I are on the same side after all."

He watched as she struggled with the emotion of it all. He could almost see the fear as old memories resurfaced. With tentative steps, he went over and sat on the loveseat. He had to keep his distance, for both their sakes. "Tell me what happened, Aubrey."

She nodded once and inhaled, as if fortifying herself for the story she was about to tell. "As a kid growing up, you have no idea of the evil that exists in this world."

He nodded his encouragement. "And that's why, as adults, it's easy to become jaded."

"When your childhood is ripped from you, it's an entirely different story." Her eyes took on a faraway look. "When I was twelve, I saw a man commit murder in broad daylight."

"Where were you?"

"In a small Southern town in North Carolina."

"Quite different than Colorado. I thought I detected a slight Southern twang." He smiled to soften his words.

"Yeah, I've worked hard to get rid of my Southern accent. It's difficult but makes me harder to trace." She took another deep breath. "It was a hot summer day that morphed into a hot summer night. My older sister, Kayla, was my best friend. We were invited to go swimming in the neighbor's pool after dinner. Since it was still daylight, our mom let us ride our bikes. It was less than three blocks away, but we decided to take a shortcut through one of the neighbors' yards." She bit her lower lip, looked away.

Ethan gently squeezed her clenched hands. "You're doing great."

Aubrey nodded. "We knew the path well since we always traveled back and forth between the neighbor's house and ours. It was humid, and our T-shirts clung to our backs. I remember the scent of honeysuckle."

She closed her eyes and exhaled. "At the back of the fence line, there were only trees and some small shrubs. The streetlights hadn't come on yet. We were laughing but stopped when we saw some shadows move. There was a huge man with lots of muscles. It looked like he was hugging and kissing this woman. Or rather, we thought he was."

Aubrey opened her eyes. "But she was trying to remove his hands from around her neck. He was strangling her. Kayla yelled, and I told her to ride away, but she sat there on her bike and screamed and screamed. He saw her."

She bit her lip. "The neighbors had a motion detector light in the backyard, and I saw him, saw his face and the tattoo he had on his neck."

He had to tread carefully. "What happened next?"

"He strangled the woman, and she slumped to the ground. We hightailed it out of there, and I thought Kayla was right behind me. She wasn't. He'd caught her, and I kept going because I didn't know."

Dear Lord. "I'm sorry, Aubrey."

"My parents called the police, and everyone searched the neighborhood for the woman and my sister, but they didn't find anything. My parents were frantic. A couple of days later, the police found the woman's body, along with Kayla's, in the wooded area, in a shallow grave."

"And your family went into the WITSEC program?"

She nodded. "But as long as Donovan is alive, the threat will always be there. That's why I'm here. I left my family in Idaho—my parents and my other sister. And I left WITSEC when I moved here, so I could keep them safe, because if they're near me, then they'll always be in danger."

He placed a finger under her chin and tilted her face toward him. "How long is it since you've seen them?"

"Six years, since I moved to Renegade." She pulled away from his touch, then stood, arms crossed over her waist, and moved to the window overlooking the front yard.

He watched as her shoulders moved up and down, as if the struggle to tell him everything was overwhelming. "You did the right thing testifying."

"Testifying changed my family forever."

He shook his head. "Finn Donovan did that."

She inhaled and turned back to look at him, her eyes wide with fear. "If he was on the plane that crashed, then he's here. In Renegade." Goosebumps rose on her arms, and she tried to rub away the cold seeping into her bones. "He's coming after me."

Ethan cupped her shoulders. "We're going to keep you safe while we find him."

Aubrey's lower lip trembled. "The anniversary of Kayla's death is coming up."

He pulled her in for a hug, and she wrapped her arms around him. Ethan held her. "You're going to be safe. I'll make sure of it."

His phone buzzed in his pocket.

Minutes later, when he checked it, he found a message from Adam.

Adam

We know where to look for the plane.

NINE

ETHAN CHECKED OFF THE VOLUNTEER GROUPS as they trickled back into the command-center lot. One by one, they filed by, tired faces, dusty boots, radios returned with sheepish half smiles and apologies for coming up empty. The clipboard in his hand grew heavier with each slash of his pen.

Still nothing.

Ethan had been sure the teams were searching the right grid. Which meant the mountain was either hiding the wreckage . . . or the plane wasn't where it should be.

He dropped into a camp chair beneath the awning and rolled his shoulders, trying to loosen the tension that had built between his shoulder blades all day. The command center smelled like dust, pine, coffee gone stale, and the faint chemical bite of hand sanitizer. Clipboards. Flagging tape. Mud on boots. A thousand small signs of movement without progress.

He pulled up Aubrey's phone number and stared at it for a beat. He hit Call and it went straight to voicemail.

Ethan frowned and tried again, thumb pressing hard against the glass.

Voicemail.

That was odd. If she'd stepped out from an area where there was signal, the phone should still ring first. Even if she'd silenced it, it should bounce once or twice before the carrier gave up. Straight to voicemail meant her battery was dead. Or her phone was off.

Or she was somewhere she shouldn't be.

He forced his mind away from the obvious spiral. He didn't do spirals. Not anymore. Not after losing too much. This was the first major task force he'd headed up since the fiasco two years ago. Since he'd walked away with a file full of dead names and one living man in a hospital bed who would never walk again.

He needed this search to bring results.

To prove to his superiors, and to himself, that he was still capable of leading a team.

With all these volunteers, they should've been able to find at least a trace of the downed plane: a shred of metal, a gouge in the tree line, the scent of fuel, anything. But the mountain had swallowed it whole.

A few gray clouds scuttled across the horizon, low and fast, dragging a cool breeze over the parking lot. The air shifted the way it always did in Colorado right before the weather turned—sharp and restless, as though the sky couldn't decide whether to forgive or punish.

If it rained like the forecast predicted, it would wash away evidence and turn the trails into slick mud and gravel. It would create havoc for the volunteers, who were already tired. Mudslides weren't uncommon after a heavy rain, especially in ravine country, where loose shale and debris waited for an excuse to move.

Daylight was bleeding out. The sun slid behind the mountain range, leaving the peaks silhouetted in bruised purples and deepening blue.

Supervisor Howard stepped beneath the awning and handed back a roll of flagging tape with the same absentminded ease a man might return a borrowed pen. He and Aubrey had shown up this morning with a bunch of supplies, but Ethan had assumed they'd returned to the office after that. Maybe Howard had come back out to check on the progress of the search at the end of the day.

"Did you ever hear back from the FAA about the black box?" he asked Ethan now.

Ethan forced his gaze away from the line of volunteers and down to the map spread across the folding table. "Yeah. It's not good."

He tried calling Aubrey again. Voicemail.

Ethan kept his voice even. "Apparently, instead of writing over the recording from the previous flight, there was no information. It was blank. Probably a malfunction of some kind, or so they think."

Howard's brows went up. "Is that normal?"

"From what I understand, if the boxes aren't maintained, yes. It can be."

Howard stared at the mountain like he could intimidate it into producing the wreckage. "So we're back to square one on who broke out Donovan and brought him here."

Ethan exhaled through his nose. "It appears so." He lifted the walkie and thumbed the channel. "All remaining volunteer groups, return to the command center. We'll resume the search tomorrow."

Static. Then a chorus of tired voices.

"Ten-four."

"Copy."

"Returning."

Ethan lowered the radio and looked at Howard. "And given the weather conditions and the terrain, we were hamstrung today. We'll regroup in the morning with SAR, when the light's better."

Howard's expression softened, an unfamiliar sight. He clapped Ethan on the back. "You'll find the wreckage. It's just a matter of time. I'm heading back to civilization to grab something to eat."

Praise from Howard felt like rain in a drought: rare, and somehow still not refreshing. Because they didn't have time. Time was always the thing they ran out of. Ethan didn't deserve the praise. Not when he couldn't even get a straight ring on Aubrey's phone. The longer Finn Donovan was out there, the higher the chance someone innocent got hurt.

Ethan pulled his phone out again and tried Aubrey another time.

Still no answer.

The volunteer groups were trickling in now, handing over walkies, returning maps, nodding farewell as they headed off to homes and loved ones.

He glanced up. Heavy clouds concealed what remained of the late-afternoon sun. Wind picked up, leaves and grit swirling across the gravel parking lot. Montgomery and Roberts were still out there—staying late to chase a last promising lead.

Ethan checked his watch.

Almost six.

Which meant the Renegade Marshals office staff should be gone for the day, unless someone had stayed behind.

He turned away from the commotion and walked to the edge of the lot, where the reception improved by a bar or two. He dialed the office.

"US Marshals Service, Renegade Office, this is Deputy Marshal Kennedy speaking."

"Kennedy." Ethan kept his voice level, even as his pulse started to tick faster. "Hey. Is Aubrey there?"

Silence hummed on the line. A pause long enough to mean something.

"I thought she was with you," Emma said finally.

Ethan's stomach dropped, cold and heavy. The wind suddenly felt sharper. The world tilted in a way that had nothing to do with the mountain. "She was here earlier, but when I didn't see her, I figured she'd gone back to the office."

A beat of static. Then Kennedy's tone sharpened. "Do you want me to—"

"I need you to call in the SAR groups for tomorrow." Ethan forced the immediate task out first. "Make sure they know we may be extending the grid."

"You got it."

"And Kennedy?" Ethan's jaw clenched hard enough to ache. "If Aubrey contacts you, let me know. I don't care if it's the middle of the night. I want to know where she is."

"No problem."

The line went dead before Ethan could add anything else. He stared at his screen for a second, then shoved the phone into his pocket like it had betrayed him.

He checked the last volunteer group off his list. Everyone was accounted for. He rolled up the laminated map, shoved it into the plastic bin with the walkies, and closed the lid harder than necessary.

Howard was halfway to his sedan. The last person to have seen Aubrey.

Ethan caught up to him before he reached the driver's door. "Howard. Wait up."

Howard turned, impatience already forming, but it shifted when he read Ethan's face. Before Ethan could speak, the walkie crackled to life.

"Butler, do you copy? This is Roberts." Liam sounded out of breath, and that alone tightened Ethan's shoulders.

Ethan lifted the radio. "Copy. Go ahead."

"We have a situation," Roberts said.

"What is it?" Ethan and Howard spoke in tandem.

"We found the plane." Roberts's voice cut through the static. "The thick foliage was obstructing our view into the ravine.

Montgomery and I climbed above the ravine on the east side of Renegade Mountain and spotted it. It's sitting at an odd angle, and tree branches are hiding most of the fuselage."

"I'm sending you some photos and the coordinates," Montgomery added, his voice coming in a second later, steadier but tight.

Howard straightened, all command now. "Good work. Send the exact location to Kennedy. She's back at the office. Make sure she forwards it to all the marshals, then we'll send coordinates to search and rescue. This information is not to be released to the public yet. Got it?"

"Copy," Roberts said over the radio.

As if Ethan or any of the other deputies would leak it. The moment the press got wind of a downed plane, this mountain would be crawling with camera crews and civilians desperate to insert themselves into the tragedy.

Ethan thumbed the radio again. "Have you guys seen Aubrey?"

A brief pause, then Roberts replied, "I saw her join up with one of the last groups to go out this morning."

Ethan's gaze snapped to the lot. Only a handful of vehicles remained—his truck, Howard's sedan, Roberts's SUV, and Montgomery's truck. "She wouldn't have put herself in greater danger by going out. Surely not."

Howard rubbed the back of his neck. "Perhaps she caught a ride home with another volunteer when they came back."

Ethan stared at him. "Her phone's off. She's not answering."

Howard's mouth tightened. "Well, where could she be?"

Ethan paced under the awning, boots grinding grit. "Of all the dangerous things to participate in . . ." He stopped, forced himself to breathe. Howard was the one who'd brought her out here in the first place. Complaining would undermine his boss and risk creating even more problems with his supervisor. Still . . . "Didn't Aubrey go back to the office with you this morning, sir? You brought her here, didn't you?"

"I didn't see her when I left, so I figured she'd either gotten a ride already or decided to help with the search. She knows how to take care of herself." Howard nodded as if that answered it.

Ethan gripped the handset. He couldn't believe Howard was being so blasé about this. "Liam, which trail did you see her on?"

"She attached herself to a small group hiking the Avalanche Trail."

Avalanche Trail. Ethan pictured it instantly. Long, winding, dirt and gravel, steeper than it had any right to be for volunteer groups, and threaded too close to ravines for comfort.

"Have you seen her since then?" Ethan's hand shook.

"That's a negative," Roberts said. "We saw the group later, but she wasn't with them."

Ethan's chest tightened. "What time was it when you last saw her?"

"Around eleven," Roberts said. "Right after we handed out the maps and the walkies."

Eleven. That was a long time to be missing, especially with the weather turning. It was nearly six thirty now. Why on earth had she gone out there?

Ethan made a decision. "Here's the plan. I'll take the four-wheeler and meet you and Montgomery at your coordinates. We can search for her from there."

"Copy," Roberts and Montgomery said together.

Ethan refused to let his mind wander into what-ifs. What-ifs were poison. He needed action. He needed Aubrey alive.

"I'll contact Deputy Marshal Kennedy." Howard shifted into command mode. "Have her get a couple more people out here. I'll man the command center."

"That works." Ethan shoved his phone into his pocket again and looked toward the mountain. Clouds rolled over the ridgeline, thick and black, swallowing what little light remained. "I don't like the look of those clouds. Hopefully Aubrey didn't go far."

Howard nodded once. "I'll contact EMS dispatch and have an ambulance waiting."

Ethan checked his service weapon out of habit—mag seated, holster secure—then shoved the thought away. A firearm wouldn't fix an exposed woman lost in a storm.

"I'm headed your way, Roberts."

"Copy," Roberts said.

The low rumble of thunder rolled through the valley like a predator coming to life. Ethan felt it down in the bones of his feet. He climbed onto the ATV, started the engine, and aimed the headlights toward the trailhead.

The deepening twilight cast long shadows across the well-worn dirt-and-gravel path. But it was the silence of the woods that unnerved him, the way the trees absorbed sound, the way the world narrowed to his beam of light and the growl of the engine.

He pushed the ATV as fast as he dared. The trailhead barely allowed the width of the vehicle. Pines crowded close, trunks thick and dark, branches whipping at his shoulders. Very little light pierced the canopy now.

God, I need Your help.

The prayer slipped free. Not polished. Not pretty. Just honest.

"Aubrey!" he called once, stopping briefly in the middle of the path to listen. He waited for the echo to die.

Nothing answered but the wind.

He started again, lights cutting forward. Lightning cracked somewhere to the north, sharp enough to make the fine hairs on his arms rise. Thunder followed almost immediately.

The storm was moving in fast.

At the edge of a small clearing, Roberts stood waving, his flashlight a jittering white slash.

Ethan braked and killed the engine. Silence rushed back in, heavy and watchful.

"That doesn't look or sound good." Roberts nodded toward the sky, where lightning threaded through deep-purple clouds.

"I know," Ethan replied. "That's why we've got to find Aubrey."

Roberts jerked his chin toward the trees. "You're going to have to leave the ATV here. It's too dense."

"That's what I was afraid of." Ethan pulled the key, pocketed it, and swung his pack onto his shoulders. "Which way?"

Roberts pointed left, into thicker timber and a steeper incline. "Rough climb."

"Let's go."

They moved fast, breathing hard almost immediately as the trail pitched upward. Dirt and gravel gave way to loose stone and damp leaf litter. Ethan's boots slid and he adjusted, leaning forward. "Aubrey!"

No answer.

At a fork in the trail, Roberts stopped and lifted his light to reveal a ravine ahead, choked with shrubs and young pines. Farther down, Montgomery stood about twenty yards from something darker than shadow. The wreckage, tucked into foliage like a secret.

"Maybe she didn't even reach the plane," Roberts said. "We tried to get down there, but yesterday's storm loosened a lot of rocks. It's a bad slide."

Montgomery climbed up toward them, face grim under the beam. At the top, he let out a breath. "We marked it as best we could. Photos and pins are already sent."

Ethan swept the ravine with his light, seeing only broken angles and a hint of metal when lightning flickered. "I can see why you didn't find it at first." He pulled out a strip of flagging tape from his kit and marked a nearby pine, pressing the adhesive hard so wind wouldn't steal it. "Good work, both of you."

But the plane could wait. The mountain had it contained, at least for the next hour.

Aubrey couldn't.

Which direction would she have taken if she'd left the trail in a hurry?

Ethan shoved the question down and replaced it with action. "Spread out," he said, already moving. "West sweep from here. Stay within visual range. Call anything that looks like her."

The three marshals split west from the crash perimeter, backtracking with their boots grinding dirt, loose gravel shifting as the storm dimmed the last wash of light. Their flashlights carved shallow, bouncing arcs through pines and wind-whipped dust. Branches hissed overhead, and thunder rolled like a countdown.

"I found a sneaker!" Adam's voice carried through the trees from upslope, where he'd cut a wider angle. He lifted a white-and-pink shoe into his beam.

Ethan angled toward him long enough to glance. Too small. Too bright. "Not hers. Keep going."

The team advanced another fifty yards, spacing themselves to cover as much ground as possible without losing each other. Ethan kept his light low, sweeping the packed dirt and gravel, searching for any type of disturbance. A scraped stone, snapped twigs, scuffed prints.

He stopped at a fork. The main trail angled north, but the other path continued west, narrower and looser, edged with gravel and sliding shale that cascaded toward ravine country.

Something snagged his beam beneath a low, broken branch.

Teal.

He crouched, fingers brushing fabric half buried under pine needles and stone. He lifted it carefully.

A hoodie. Mud-dusted and torn.

His throat tightened. "Aubrey." Certainty settled heavy in his gut. "She went this way."

He waved Montgomery and Roberts over, holding the hoodie up in the light.

Roberts's face tightened. "Yeah. I remember her wearing that this morning."

Montgomery whistled under his breath. "Oh man." His gaze tracked into dark timber. "She's headed the wrong way."

The statement landed like a weight. *Wrong way* meant rough terrain. *Wrong way* meant ravines and loose shale. *Wrong way* meant a person could get disoriented fast, especially if they weren't an experienced hiker.

The ground was torn up—a warning sign Ethan would heed in any other circumstances. Shoe prints skidded along the dirt in a frantic, uneven pattern, deep in the heel, shallow in the toe, like someone fighting for balance. Pebbles were scattered downhill in a fan. Freshly broken twigs dotted the slope, snapped mid-stride, not intentionally cleared aside. The disturbance was short but violent, ending at a drop no more than six feet down the ridge.

A fall, not a detour.

Ethan knelt, studying the scuffed trench. No hesitation prints. No doubled-back drag. Just momentum and collapse.

His stomach tightened. "Of course you'd push yourself." He muttered the statement into the wind. He pulled evidence tape and marked the pine beside the fork, pressing it firmly as gusts tried to peel it away. "Trail. Down there."

He angled down the ridge, boots slipping in loose gravel, each step tested before he trusted it. The descent wasn't long, but it was steep enough to punish speed. Rocks shifted under his weight. Dry soil skittered toward the trees below. He kept his light low, scanning the ground like he'd been taught—read first, run second.

Halfway down, the scuff marks resumed.

The slope leveled into a narrow basin choked with pine shadows. Wind hissed through branches overhead. Thunder growled again, louder now. Raindrops began to fall, fat and cold, peppering his bare arms and turning the dust into paste.

Then Roberts's voice cut through the wind.

"Butler! Over here!"

Ethan pivoted and hurried toward the beam of Roberts's light. Roberts was crouched near what looked like a shallow pile of leaves mounded unnaturally against a log. It looked like someone had tried to disappear by dragging the forest over themselves.

Ethan knelt, studying it.

The dirt beneath was disturbed in an oval shape.

"She hid," Ethan said quietly. "Right here."

Montgomery stepped closer, scanning the perimeter. "Smart."

"Desperate," Ethan corrected, eyes tracking the trail ahead.

Roberts whistled low.

Ethan's jaw clenched. The wrong way wasn't just geography now. It was time. It was weather. It was risk.

A ball of dread settled in his gut, but he shoved it down and forced his mind to stay calm. "She's still walking, so that's good."

Roberts didn't look convinced.

"But we don't know how far she's traveled," Ethan continued, voice tightening. "And now the storm's coming in hard. Visibility's dropping. Sound carries weird. If she's disoriented, if she's scared, she'll keep moving."

Montgomery lifted his light, scanning the dark timber ahead. "This way." He took off into the underbrush.

Ethan and Roberts followed immediately, boots sliding on damp, leaf-covered ground. The rain picked up, cold needles against Ethan's skin. Wind whipped through the trees, smaller branches bending low, swiping at their shoulders and catching their lights.

Ethan shivered. Not from cold, but from the sick certainty settling deeper with every step.

If he didn't find Aubrey soon, this excursion of hers would end badly.

For her.

For him.

For everyone involved.

And somewhere beyond the trees, thunder cracked like the mountain's warning . . . or its promise.

TEN

AUBREY PUSHED A STRAND OF HAIR OUT OF her eyes as she leaned against a pine tree, the bark biting into her skin. She'd been walking for hours, and she was tired and uncomfortable. She hadn't seen the team she was supposed to be with for at least an hour. And daylight was rapidly fading, the trees becoming restless in anticipation of the approaching storm.

She shouldn't even be out here!

But Howard hadn't given her a choice.

Howard leaned close. "You think one of my marshals should ignore their duties to babysit you in the middle of a crisis? We have a plane to find and a fugitive out there! If you were in real danger, you should never have left witness protection. That's on you."

She glanced over his shoulder at the command center. Looking for a familiar face, a friend to come to her rescue. Ethan.

But Howard was right. She would be hindering them from doing their jobs. Expecting them to help her fight her battle.

"Sir—"

"Deputy Marshal Kennedy is at the office doing your job." He leaned close, his hot breath fanning her face. "So I suggest you get out there. Join one of these teams and make yourself useful, Aubrey."

"But I—"

"That's an order, Richardson. Join a team or you're fired."

The wind dragged voices toward her. Two men arguing near a clearing. Aubrey wiped tears from her face with her sleeve.

Her foot caught, pitching her forward and slamming her palms against the rocks. A sharp sting ripped through her ankle as she rolled sideways down a short embankment. *Ouch.*

Breathless, she pushed upright. Pain lanced up her leg. As she stood, her hoodie snagged on a branch behind her, then tore free from her shoulders. Nightmares of Finn Donovan grabbing her—grabbing her sister—filled her mind.

She kept going, limping to the edge, pulse hammering. A lone shoe sat half buried in the dirt. Her stomach dropped. Someone else had come through here.

They could help her!

She crouched behind a massive pine, every breath tight and burning, and was able to make out two men in the dim light.

She recognized Roger Rousseau instantly from the files Ethan had been looking over at the safe house. The other man was taller, and when he shifted, her blood iced over.

Dragon tattoo. Flames exploding around the scaled head. Blood dripping from the claw.

Donovan. Finn Donovan. The man who had stalked her nightmares since the summer he killed her sister. The man she had testified against to lock away forever.

She swallowed the scream that wanted out and surged to run, gravel skidding underfoot. She stagger-ran another thirty yards before the forest forced her to stop. Her ankle throbbed in violent, synchronized beats with her pulse. She dropped behind a curtain of deadfall, splintered logs, loose stone, and brittle brush. Dust puffed around her as she landed on one knee.

The trees here were thick, trunks wide, branches low. Good for cover. Terrible for mobility. *Lord.*

She killed her breathing, one hand clamped over her mouth. Gravel bit through the thin fabric of her leggings. Pain screamed to be acknowledged. Fear screamed louder.

Boots crunched toward her. Heavy. Confident. Closing.

Donovan didn't call out. He wouldn't waste breath and risk being overheard. He hunted silently, the way predators conserved energy before a strike.

She slid sideways, dragging herself into the shadowed pocket between two ponderosa roots. The soil was dry, coarse, slippery like loose sand. She swept the forest debris of needles, dust, and chipped bark over the front of her legs with shaking fingers. Camouflage by desperation.

A twig snapped behind her. She flinched. No. Just her. Just gravity. Just panic. She shivered as a gust of wind brushed over her skin. She'd lost her hoodie and her phone when she slipped and fell.

She had to get out of here. Fear clawed up her throat. She stepped on another twig, the noise halting her escape.

"You hear that?" Finn Donovan said.

Aubrey ducked into a shadow. Where was he? She couldn't tell where the voices were coming from.

"It's nothing," Rousseau said. "Probably some small animal in the underbrush."

A sob worked its way up her throat. Aubrey placed a hand over her mouth and bit her lip to keep from gasping too loudly.

She pressed back into the tree trunk, trying to make herself as small as possible. Her heart pounded against her rib cage. Good sense, or maybe it was fear, held her in place, muscles frozen, unable to take a deep breath.

"Naw, this sounded like footsteps."

Roger laughed. "You're just not used to all the sounds of nature."

"I'm telling you . . ." They paused their conversation for a moment, then Donovan laughed. "Yeah, you're probably right. I'm just jumpy. Haven't been out of the big house in twenty years."

Aubrey waited as the sound of their voices faded.

She lifted her eyes to heaven. *Thank You.*

Now she had to find the others—find safety.

She took a step, and her foot started to slide. The leaves on the forest floor were damp, and she lost her footing, tripping over a hidden root.

Aubrey went down on all fours, debris and rocks digging into the sensitive skin on her palms. Her knees took the brunt of the fall, burning as they made contact with the forest floor. All the air ripped from her lungs, and she forced herself to breathe in and out.

Heavy footfalls thundered near her, along with the distant rumble of the storm.

Were they coming back?

She held her breath for a moment, then found a sturdy branch and, using it as a walking cane, managed to stand without crying out.

The trail should be around here, somewhere close. Slowly, she pivoted in a circle, uncertain which way to turn. Unable to find the trail. Between the trees, she spotted a structure.

A cabin.

She had to make her way back to the command center. The marker she'd put up earlier should've been easily visible, but it wasn't there. She couldn't have strayed that far from the path.

How on earth was she going to find her way back? Aubrey stayed flattened behind the brush, body wedged into the shadow of a fallen log.

The two men in front of the cabin argued like thunder had taken human shape.

She crawled until she could see them.

Rousseau paced the porch, his boots grinding the warped boards. Donovan stood closer to the door, tall and still, like he owned the space and the air around it. Even from here, Aubrey could see the dragon tattoo curl along his neck above a US Marshals jacket.

The sight punched a hole clean through her lungs all over again.

Wind yanked at the pines overhead. The storm was moving in fast. She pressed herself lower, praying the men wouldn't hear the uneven hitch in her breathing.

A third man stepped out of the cabin and joined them, broad-shouldered, unfamiliar. What made Aubrey's stomach drop wasn't his face; it was the jacket.

US Marshals. Same as Donovan's.

Her chest tightened, panic trying to boil over.

How many of them are wearing those jackets? How many people have they fooled?

She squeezed her eyes shut for half a second, trying to keep her mind from fracturing. The sounds and smells of twenty years ago crashed into her: heat, fear, the metallic taste of adrenaline, the way the world narrowed when danger decided your life for you.

Thunder boomed, close enough to rattle her ribs. It drowned everything—voices, wind, even the frantic heartbeat pounding in her ears.

It's fine. I'm fine.

The lie repeated in her head like a broken record.

Pine needles and small rocks dug into her stomach as she curled tighter, trying to blend into the forest floor. Tears burned hot behind her eyes. An iron band cinched around her chest, squeezing until she couldn't draw a full breath.

Please, God.

The prayer tasted unfamiliar on her tongue. She hadn't prayed with this kind of desperation in years—not since life had veered from her plans and she'd tried to shut the door on faith because it felt easier than hoping. Lately she'd started to reconsider faith being part of her life. She'd even counseled Ethan about spiritual things. But still . . .

Would God even listen to her now?

She swallowed hard, forcing air in quietly, forcing her body not to shake. Trying to get her thoughts straight.

Rousseau's voice rose over the storm. "Look, Frost, I'm doing my best, okay? I've got a couple of US marshals who aren't the type who can be persuaded."

"And that's my problem?" Frost shot back.

"We need to get rid of the evidence," Rousseau snapped. "But I haven't had time with all these people crawling through the woods today. Eventually they're going to find the wreckage, if they haven't already. And they'll figure out one of the officials in town is helping us."

Aubrey's blood went cold.

Evidence. Wreckage. Officials.

This wasn't just about a plane. This was definitely a cover-up. A conspiracy. Something big enough to pull Donovan back into town. Involving Rousseau and this Frost person. A syndicate plot.

Donovan's voice cut in, amused. "What about the pilot?"

Frost grunted. "Dead."

Aubrey clamped a hand over her mouth to keep from making any sound.

"You're just gonna leave him outside?" Donovan asked, like he was asking about trash.

"Probably."

Donovan laughed. "You're a cold, heartless piece of work, you know that?" Admiration coated the insult.

"That's priceless, coming from you," Frost said.

Rousseau shook his head. "Maybe we ought to at least drag him inside. An animal will try to drag him off."

"Do whatever you want," Donovan replied. "I'm just here to finish a job that I should've taken care of a long time ago."

The words slammed through Aubrey, stealing her breath.

Fear rippled through her body in frissons that had nothing to do with cold. She wrapped her arms tighter around her middle, trying to stop shaking. She needed to get away from here. She *had* to. But her knees were banged up from earlier falls, and her ankle still throbbed from the twist she'd tried to ignore. Darkness had closed in, and rain was beginning to fall—slow, fat drops at first, quickly picking up to a steady downfall. She had no phone and no sweater.

If she moved now, they'd hear her.

So she stayed.

Minutes stretched, too long, too tight, too loud. Their voices rose and fell, arguing details Aubrey couldn't piece together through the wind. Then the argument stopped abruptly, as if someone had made a decision.

Rain increased, coming down in sheets. Water poured off the tin roof in rivulets. Donovan and Rousseau stepped inside first. At the open doorway, Frost paused and looked out into the trees, scanning as though he could feel her watching. For one terrible second, Aubrey was sure his gaze would lock on hers.

Instead, he shook his head like he'd dismissed a thought, then slammed the door shut.

A dim light from a small window spilled over the dilapidated porch, turning rain into silver needles.

This was her chance.

Aubrey crawled backward on hands and knees, slow and careful, dragging herself through wet leaves until she was beyond the reach of that thin window glow. Only then did she push up, every muscle trembling, and limp away, praying she was heading back the way she'd come.

She hadn't gone twenty yards before her boot snagged on dense brush.

She lurched, nearly falling. Her hand shot out to catch a trunk, the bark scraping her palm. Lightning flashed and glinted off something pale in the bushes.

White fabric.

Her gaze dropped to a shirt, shoulders marked by dark epaulets.

The dead pilot.

Leaves clung to his uniform. The blood on his right shoulder had dried into a dark, brutal stain across his chest. His skin was gray. His eyes were open to nothing. One boot was unlaced, the leather tongue twisted where the ground had tugged it loose.

Aubrey's breath stopped.

Her pulse didn't.

A sound clawed up her throat—half gasp, half sob—but she swallowed it down, choking on panic. She scrambled backward, hands skidding over stone and bark, heart screaming at her to run.

Death is here.

And so was Donovan.

She didn't scream. She didn't waste breath.

She ran.

The undergrowth rustled behind her.

Aubrey veered off the faint footpath into a denser patch of trees. Footsteps pounded after her. Fast and heavy.

No. How?

Faster. She had to go faster.

She fought back tears and shoved through nettles that slapped her arms and tore at her leggings, stinging and drawing blood. The forest floor was a slick blanket of dead leaves. She slipped, regained balance, slipped again.

She glanced back once and saw two silhouettes cutting through rain, closing the distance.

Momentum carried her downhill, but the slope turned

treacherous. Her boot caught on an exposed root. She went to her knees hard, and her ankle twisted at an ugly angle.

Pain detonated white behind her eyes.

She bit back a scream, teeth sinking into her lip. Tears burst free anyway as she shoved herself upright, but her injured ankle buckled. She fell onto her backside and slid, leaves and gravel carrying her down until she rolled to a stop.

She crawled, desperate, toward the faint outline of boulders, an outcropping that could hide her if she could wedge herself beneath it. She flattened her back against the uneven rock, pulling her knees in as tight as the pain allowed.

Now that she'd started praying, she couldn't seem to stop.

Please. Please, God.

Aubrey finally inhaled, shallow at first, then deeper, shaking. The storm clouds had swallowed the light. Even if the day had been warm, the temperature would drop hard overnight.

She shivered, not sure if it was cold or shock.

Her ankle throbbed viciously. She probed it and winced. Swelling was already visible, tight and ugly.

She rested her head against the cool rock and closed her eyes.

Good grief. How am I going to get out of this?

Wind whipped her hair across her face. She brushed it back, arms crossing over her middle to conserve heat. Rain softened into scattered drops, a steady plop-plop on leaves. The forest held its breath.

Voices echoed from the opposite side of the clearing. Aubrey shrank tighter against the rock.

Think.

She couldn't sit out here all night. But she couldn't risk moving while Donovan was nearby either. Tears tracked down her cheeks. She swiped them away hard.

She prayed the information she'd overheard didn't die with her.

Her stomach grumbled. She pressed a hand against it, then

blinked, realizing she'd lost time—dozed off, maybe. The leaves shuffled above her head.

"I don't know where she could've disappeared to," a man muttered.

Aubrey's heart seized.

Then another voice. Familiar. Rough. Close. She knew that voice.

Ethan.

Thank You, Lord.

"I'm here," she rasped, voice barely more than breath. "Help me . . . please."

"Did you hear that?" Ethan's voice sharpened.

"Here," Aubrey tried again, louder, raw. "Below you."

Pebbles and leaves slid down. A flashlight beam swept the rock face. Ethan lay flat on his stomach above the outcropping, rainwater beading on his forehead, his expression taut with relief and fury braided together.

"Aubrey." The word came out like a prayer and a reprimand at once. "Thank the Lord." He vanished from view, and panic flared until his voice snapped over the radio. "Howard, we found her. She's hurt."

"Roger that," Howard replied through static, barely audible from her spot. "Ambulance is staged and waiting."

A moment later, Liam and Adam appeared behind Ethan, breathless and soaked. Aubrey's lungs finally pulled in a full breath.

Ethan's gaze assessed her from disheveled ponytail to muddy hands to torn leggings. She braced for the tongue-lashing.

Instead, he reached down and took her arm, helping her stand.

The moment her injured ankle took weight, she stumbled and fell into him. Ethan caught her automatically, arms going around her in an awkward, instinctive embrace. For one brief second, she was pressed against warmth and solid muscle and the faint, woodsy edge of his aftershave.

For one brief second, she forgot Donovan. Rousseau. That other scary guy, Frost.

The dead pilot.

The hug ended too soon. Ethan stepped back, hands still on her arms like he was making sure she stayed upright.

"Don't ever scare us like that again," he said, voice low but rough with leashed emotion.

A curl of warmth unfurled in Aubrey's chest. He really did care, even if his delivery was always . . . Ethan.

Heat rushed to her face. Stiff and aching, she stared at her knees, at the gaping holes in the leggings, dried blood at the edges.

Liam broke the moment. "We need to move. Aubrey needs medical attention."

Liam and Adam started up the hill. Aubrey remained rooted, her heart pounding.

"Coming?" Ethan held out his hand.

She swallowed hard. "Hang on. This is important."

Ethan's posture shifted instantly.

"I saw Finn Donovan," she said, forcing the words past her throat. "He was with Rousseau. And there was another guy—they called him Frost. They were wearing Marshals jackets."

Ethan's lips thinned. "Are you sure?"

"I'm telling you, it was him." Her voice shook. "And there was a pilot. Dead. They were arguing about what to do with him."

"Where?" Ethan demanded.

"Back the way I came," she said, pointing upslope. "I got turned around, but there's an abandoned cabin up there. The pilot is under a bush nearby."

Ethan's gaze flicked toward the storm-darkened trees. "Okay. We need to get out of here. We can't search for the cabin tonight. It's too dangerous."

She took one step and grimaced, pain knifing up her leg.

Ethan bent, fingers probing her ankle gently but firmly. She hissed, unable to hide it. "Yeah, that's swollen bad." He straightened. "Arm around my shoulder. Other arm around Liam's. We're getting you out."

"Thank you," Aubrey whispered, voice breaking. "If you hadn't found me—"

Ethan didn't let her finish. "We did," he said, more promise than comfort. "And we're not leaving you again."

ELEVEN

AUBREY STARED AT THE OFF-WHITE CURTAIN that separated her from the other patients in the ER. She shivered under the thin hospital blanket and huffed out an exasperated sigh.

Seeing Donovan had brought back a boatload of memories—none of which she wanted to revisit. Being stuck on that mountain in the cold and rain, not knowing if she would make it home, had turned out to be one of the scariest moments of her life.

And when Ethan showed up? Relief. She'd known in her heart that he'd do everything in his power to get her back to safety. Ethan exuded a peace and a calmness that soothed. Eased all the tension she'd experienced.

She glanced out the window, watching the rain pelt the glass, and pulled the blanket up under her chin. When were they going to release her?

Aubrey glanced at the clock. She'd been here over three hours, the time inching closer to midnight. She stifled a yawn, and a deep, throbbing pain in her ankle made her wince.

"Oh, thank the Lord you're all right!" Jenna burst through the curtain, her long hair trailing behind her, a cup carrier in one hand, a plastic bag in the other. "I was so worried when I got that call from the hospital." Jenna paused, taking in the surroundings. "Where's Ethan? He told me you might be in danger when he returned his costume, but refused to give me details. I thought he'd be here protecting you."

"He stepped out for a second to make a phone call." Aubrey swallowed. "He was right not to tell you much. I don't want you to be in danger."

"I was worried you were here by yourself." Jenna's expression darkened.

"I'm fine, just a badly sprained ankle." Aubrey shifted her position on the uncomfortable hospital bed.

"You don't look fine to me."

"There's a dangerous man out there," Aubrey said. "But Ethan is keeping me safe."

"He better. Who is this guy?"

Aubrey told her about Finn Donovan and her sister's murder. In the end, Jenna swiped a tear from her face and said, "I'm so sorry, Aub. That's horrible."

"It was a long time ago. Right now, I'm safe, and Ethan is going to find Donovan."

"Sure you're okay?"

"I don't like my boss at the moment, but I'm fine." Auburey told her about the conversation with Howard that got her out on that mountain. His anger.

Jenna shook her head, about to say something when Aubrey cut her off.

She didn't want to talk about this anymore. "Honestly, I'm just hungry and thirsty. What did you bring me?"

Jenna's eyes twinkled with mischief, but her expression still held grief from hearing Aubrey's story. "Your favorite: a Sprite and a double bacon cheeseburger from the Gourmet Junction." She pulled the food from a take-out bag, the savory aroma of bacon and onions filling the small area.

Aubrey's mouth watered, and she held out both hands. "Hand it over. How did you manage to get me a meal at this late hour? I thought they closed at nine." She bit into the burger, and her eyes rolled into the back of her head.

"I called in a favor with one of the line cooks."

Aubrey paused mid-bite. "Thank you. This tastes so good."

"Best burgers within a four-state radius, or so I'm told." Jenna flipped open the lid on another to-go box and grabbed an onion ring. "And you're welcome."

"Mm. So good," Aubrey said around a mouthful of food.

Jenna laughed and grabbed a napkin from the bag. "You have a big streak of mayo on your face."

Aubrey shrugged. "Who's gonna see me?"

"Me." She handed Aubrey the napkin.

Their laughter stopped as Ethan stepped through the makeshift cubicle.

Aubrey coughed. "I thought you had to take a phone call."

Jenna passed her the Styrofoam cup, and Aubrey slurped up most of the contents. Anything to keep her mind focused and her gaze off the intimidating man.

"I did. And now I'm waiting on you to finish your dinner."

Huh. "Funny guy. Want some of my fries?"

He reached into the bag and snagged a couple.

"Well, since you're in good hands, I'm gonna head out." Jenna grabbed her purse and leaned over to hug Aubrey. She whispered in Aubrey's ear, "Call me when you get out of here, no matter the time, and tell me all about *you know who*." She nodded in Ethan's direction.

"It's not like that," Aubrey hissed. "This is serious."

Jenna waved and then winked at Ethan. "Deputy Marshal Butler, nice to see you again."

"You too, Jenna. Be safe."

"Always." She paused at the opening and whirled around. "Don't do anything I wouldn't do!"

"Jenna!" Warmth crept up Aubrey's neck and face.

She could feel her cheeks flame. Ah, the curse of being a redhead. She wanted to hide her face under the sheet and wait until Ethan left. If she weren't still in protective custody, she'd find her own way home. Call a rideshare. But that wouldn't be smart, and she'd already caused enough trouble today.

Instead, she raised her chin only to see Ethan fighting laughter. "I'm sorry about that," she told him. "I don't know what came over her. If she thought you were going to be here, she would have brought you a burger as well."

Ethan shook his head. "I'm fine, Aubrey. Thanks."

He didn't say anything else. Instead, he rummaged around in the small bedside table and found an individually packaged wet wipe. His woodsy cologne teased her senses, and she leaned closer to get a whiff. He gave her the side-eye, and she moved away and cleared her throat.

He opened the packet and handed a wipe to her, then pointed to her cheek.

Great. She still had a glob of mayonnaise on her face. She quickly wiped her face and tossed the used cloth on the table, waiting for him.

He studied her for a moment, and she almost shrank back under his intense gaze. Her hand automatically drifted to her hair, making a crunchy noise. Slowly, she pulled out a dried leaf and a small twig. She must look like she survived hurricane wind gusts, while Ethan smelled shower-fresh and, of course, looked as if he was ready for a magazine shoot.

He moved the only chair in the room closer to her bed and sat.

He hadn't offered her forgiveness.

Yet.

"Aubrey, what were you doing on that mountain today? You could've died." A flash of pain washed over his stoic face, then was gone an instant later. Perhaps she only imagined the emotion.

This Ethan was so unlike the man she was used to dealing with the past two years at the Marshals office. He seemed softer, more compassionate. Did he want to hear a horrible story about his boss threatening to fire her because the marshals had important jobs to do? Because Howard thought she should've stayed in witness protection?

"I, uh, wanted to help. I've hiked a few of the trails."

"Aubrey . . ." He exhaled her name on a sigh and hung his head.

"I—" They spoke at the same time.

The doctor pushed aside the curtain and glanced between them, her brow furrowed. She had thick, dark hair pulled back in a ponytail and olive-skinned, Middle Eastern features. "Everything okay in here? I'm Dr. Yassan, head of emergency medicine."

Aubrey pulled the blanket higher and forced herself to smile. "Fine. It's fine. I'm ready to get out of here, is all."

"The nurse will be back with your discharge papers. I've written a couple of prescriptions. One for pain and the other is a muscle relaxant, which you're going to need after your adventure today." The doctor gave the prescriptions to her.

"Thanks, Doctor. I'll be sure to get these filled." Aubrey set the prescriptions on the bedside table.

"Make sure you ice that ankle once you get home, and take it easy. Keep the foot elevated. No standing for long periods of time." The doctor continued to talk and make notes.

"What about work?" She didn't want to stay in her house, or any house, longer than she needed to. There were far more marshals at the office to protect her—not to mention it being a federal building with security at every door. She was way safer there than at home or even in a safe house.

Aubrey winced inwardly. She just needed to go there—and stay there.

"What do you do?" Dr. Yassan asked.

"I'm an administrative assistant for the US Marshals Service."

The doctor looked up. "Oh, that's good. Seated work is fine. Just make sure to keep your foot elevated." She left, and an awkward tension settled between Aubrey and Ethan.

Just when she was ready talk again, a blonde nurse breezed through the curtains. "Here we are!" She handed Aubrey a stack of papers and had her sign away her life. "You're free to go. No more hiking."

Yeah, thanks for that advice.

Ethan's mouth twitched. He was having too much fun at her expense. He held out his arm, apparently over his irritation with her. "Ready?"

She held on to him. "I can't wait to shower and wash my hair."

He plucked another twig out of the back of her hair. "Yeah, probably a good idea."

"Haha. So funny."

He escorted her to the lobby. "Think you can walk?"

"Lead the way."

The parking lot lights cast an eerie yellow glow over the cars. Ethan's older-model truck sat near the hospital entrance. She stared at the passenger door. Just great. She'd never be able to get in the cab of his truck.

Before she could protest, he scooped her up, and her arms automatically went around his neck.

"Didn't we just do this?" Ethan looked down at her and smiled. And oh my word, when he smiled, it transformed his entire face.

She couldn't look away and simply nodded.

"You'll have to open the door for me," he said.

"I need you to forgive me first."

He stared at her. "Aubrey, I forgive you. I just want you to be safe."

She nodded.

"The door?"

"Oh yeah, sorry." She fumbled with the handle, but she finally got the door to open. Ethan bumped it wider with his hip and slid her into the back seat of his king cab. His truck was clean, orderly, and smelled like him.

"Is this okay?"

His words pulled her out of her dreamy state. "Hmm? Oh, yeah. It's great."

They stopped by the twenty-four-hour pharmacy first, filled her prescriptions, and then headed to her place so she could grab a bag of clothes and other things she needed. It seemed like forever since she'd been at home, and she needed her Bible.

"Hang on a second." Ethan got out of the truck.

She watched as he reached for his service weapon.

She shifted, but it was difficult to see around the seat. A few moments later, he returned, slid into the seat, and slammed the door shut.

Aubrey frowned. "What's wrong?"

"We aren't going inside." He turned on the engine.

Aubrey leaned over between the seats. "What? Why?"

A muscle ticked in his jaw. "The front door was open. I walked inside and the entire place was tossed." Ethan's knuckles were turning white as he gripped the steering wheel.

She sank back against the seat. "I don't understand." Her fingers tightened around the seat belt strap.

Ethan started his truck, then backed out of the driveway at an unsafe speed. He tossed her his phone. "Call 911, please."

She fumbled to dial, then put the phone to her ear.

"911, what's your emergency?" The dispatcher's voice filled the cab.

"My house has been broken into. Everything is a mess." Aubrey struggled to keep her voice calm.

"What's your address?"

"526 Sycamore." Aubrey stared out the windshield, her gaze drifting to Ethan. He gripped the wheel as he drove, tension in his body language.

"Are you in danger?" the dispatcher asked. "Are you still at your residence?"

She cleared her throat. "No. I'm with Deputy US Marshal Ethan Butler. We're headed somewhere safe."

Safe. It seemed that she wasn't safe anywhere, even when she was with Ethan.

"Police have been dispatched. Can we call you back on this number?"

"Yes."

The operator recited Ethan's number and disconnected the call.

Aubrey placed his phone in the cupholder. "The police are on their way."

Ethan's gaze met hers in the rearview mirror, his jaw tense but eyes warm with concern. "Good," he said, voice low and sincere.

His gaze shifted back to the road. "I'm sorry, Aubrey. You've already survived enough. Coming home to this is just . . . wrong."

Shock and exhaustion clogged her throat, trapping every word she tried to form. She swallowed hard and turned toward the window, fingers twisting in the edge of her seatbelt as the dark ribbon of road slid past. Ethan softened further. "Listen to me. Bravery doesn't mean you deserve more pain. It means you deserved protection long before now." He reached over the seat, grasped her hand and squeezed. "We get you safe. Then we take the next step together."

"Right. Thank you."

He nodded, his attention pulled back to rain-slick city streets.

Aubrey gazed out the window, the streetlights passing by in a blur. They drove in silence until they entered an older housing development.

Ethan pulled into the gravel driveway of an older brick ranch home. Low-lying shrubs hedged the perimeter of the house. He unlocked the front door this time and ushered her inside, turning on the hall lights. He led her gently to the overstuffed couch in the living room. "Stay put for a second, okay?"

She watched as he disappeared down the hallway, his footsteps echoing against the bare walls. He spoke to someone in the kitchen, his voice low. A few beats later, he returned with a glass of water, a dish towel, and a baggie filled with ice cubes.

"Here you go." He set the glass on the coffee table, then opened her prescription bottles and handed her a muscle relaxant and the higher dosage ibuprofen. "You're going to need those tonight."

She nodded and tossed back the pills with a sip of water. "Thank you."

Ethan nodded once and sat on the coffee table, their faces at eye level. "Stretch out your leg." He placed a crocheted blanket across her legs, then wrapped the bag of ice in the dish towel, lifted the corner of the blanket, and placed the ice around her swollen ankle.

She hissed. "Cold."

"I know." He patted her calf. "Leave it on for fifteen minutes max. I'm calling one of the female marshals to sit with you tonight."

Panic clawed up her throat. Donovan was out there. "Why now, after all these years?"

She had to get out of here, away from Renegade. If she stayed, the people closest to her would be hurt. She tossed aside the blanket and stood, wanting to be anywhere but here.

Ethan held out his arm. "Where are you going?"

"I don't know. Just—not here." Anywhere that didn't smell like mud and fear. Anywhere that wasn't Renegade.

Ethan caught her hand and gently guided her back to the sofa. Pain flared through her ankle and she winced, the fight draining out of her.

She scrubbed her hands over her face. She needed a shower. Clean clothes. Her purse, her phone—some piece of her life that hadn't been left on that mountain.

She had none of it.

Except Ethan.

He touched her elbow, careful, grounding. "Hey. You're safe. I've got you."

"I know." Her voice wavered. "My brain just hasn't caught up yet." She managed a tired, apologetic smile. "I know you'll keep me safe."

Arguing would take energy she didn't have. She sank back into the cushions, exhaustion pulling her under.

The doorbell rang, and Ethan rose immediately, posture shifting, alert. "I'll be right back. Stay put."

She lifted her bandaged ankle an inch. "Pretty sure I'm not going anywhere."

Voices in the foyer cut through the spiral of her thoughts, pulling her back from the brink of panic.

"Hey, Aubrey." Emma Kennedy stepped into the room, a bulletproof vest strapped over her shirt, her service weapon holstered at her waist. "Am I glad to see you."

"Same." Aubrey adjusted the icepack on her ankle.

Ethan rocked back on his heels, hands in his pocket. "So, do you two need anything else?"

"I'm gonna check the windows and doors." Emma wandered out of the room.

Looking up at his handsome face, Aubrey had to swallow back all the emotion from the day. He was right. She could've died out there today. But God had been looking out for her. Maybe it was time to stop being so angry.

His expression softened. "What is it?"

"It's nothing. I just . . . Thank you, Ethan." She smiled and stifled a yawn.

"You're welcome." He held her gaze. Steady. Like him. "And don't forget to lock the doors."

"Already on it." Emma walked back through the room. "I re-checked all the windows and the patio door."

Ethan stood there as if he wanted to say something else. An awkward silence filled the small space. Finally, he simply said, "Good night."

Emma followed him to the front, and after a moment, Aubrey heard the lock click into place.

"Night, Ethan." She whispered the words as his footsteps echoed against the concrete walkway outside.

Emma came back in. "I have clothes if you want to clean up."

"Sounds amazing."

Later, Aubrey drifted off to sleep in an unfamiliar bed, a smile on her lips. Despite everything going on, it seemed like things were changing between her and Ethan.

And she kind of liked it.

The next morning Ethan sat at his desk, no further along with the case. He glanced up from his laptop every few minutes, checked his phone.

Why hadn't Deputy Marshal Kennedy called in yet? He needed an update. Or at least an ETA for when she'd show up with Aubrey. With that right foot of hers, Aubrey couldn't drive.

Ethan leaned back in his chair. This was getting ridiculous. He wasn't interested in Aubrey. He was just worried after hauling her off that mountain in the dark.

Yeah. Keep telling yourself that, buddy.

Ethan abandoned the illusion of productivity and shoved out of his too-warm office. He needed air. Coffee. A mental off switch. Anything to stop reliving the moment her arms locked around his neck, her breath unsteady against his shoulder.

"Get any sleep last night?" Liam Roberts appeared as Ethan reached for the coffeepot.

Ethan poured a cup, more for something to do than for the caffeine. "A little."

Liam's brow arched knowingly. "Was it the late-night ER visit with Aubrey, or something else bothering you?"

Ethan's shoulders tightened, a different kind of exhaustion pulling at him. "I thought I was prepared for what she carries. Turns out, I wasn't even close."

Liam nodded, no judgment, just understanding. "She trusts you, Ethan. That says something."

Ethan exhaled, his gaze dropping to the steam curling from his mug. "Maybe. I just hate that she needed a reason to."

Liam clapped his shoulder once. "Give her a reason to keep trusting you. Starting now." He angled his cup toward Ethan's.

The ghost of a smile tugged Ethan's mouth for a second. "Copy that."

Liam added more cream to his coffee. "You gonna admit how you feel, or keep pretending it's just concern?"

"Concern for a dangerous fugitive on the loose and no leads on where to find him? The Denver agents found nothing in the woods. Just an empty cabin."

Liam nodded. "Come on, man. You like her—and we both know it runs deeper than protecting her from Donovan."

Ethan's gaze drifted to her empty desk. The sunlight hit her chair, soft and golden, like she'd just stepped away for a second.

"She's a ray of sunshine on a cloudy day. Got under my skin before I even realized it." He met Liam's eyes. "She's already in my heart, and I'm not sure I could let her go, even if I wanted to."

Liam grinned and slapped his back. "Then don't."

Ethan shook his head. Liam was right. But first, he needed to head out and check on the Marshals team he'd sent out to the crash site to collect evidence. The FAA had arrived in Renegade late last night, before he'd even found Aubrey. With the storm settling over the mountain community, he hoped the plane hadn't shifted. Collecting evidence was going to be impossible in the rain as it was.

He still needed to ask Aubrey some questions. And check with the police about what had happened at her house.

Speaking of . . . Aubrey stood at the door, Emma Kennedy behind her. Had she overheard him talking to Liam? That was not how he wanted to declare his feelings.

A red tint crept up Aubrey's neck. "Good morning, Ethan."

"Morning." His greeting was gruff. Great.

An awkward silence settled between them. A smile spread across Emma's face as her gaze bounced between him and Aubrey. "See," Emma said. "Everyone's fine."

He cleared his throat. "Did you two have any problems last night?"

Emma stifled a yawn. "Apart from a lack of sleep? Nope. I'm going to fill out a report and then head home and grab some shut-eye myself." She saluted with her cup of coffee as she headed into her office.

Ethan glanced down at Aubrey's foot. "I thought Dr. Yassan told you to take it easy."

"Pffft." She waved him away, but he saw fear in her gaze. "You were there when she said desk work is fine. I feel pretty good today. A little sore, but other than that?" She shrugged and placed her bag in her desk drawer and locked it. "Better to be here than twiddling my thumbs on a couch and stopping a deputy marshal from working an important manhunt."

She did look good today. The green of her shirt emphasized the green of her eyes, but her black skirt looked a little out of place with the bandaged ankle.

"What? What's wrong?" She glanced down at her outfit and contorted her torso trying to see behind her. "Do I have dirt or something on my skirt?" Her low whisper held a tinge of panic.

"No." Ethan shook his head and laughed. "You're fine. You look, um, great." *Ouch. For pity's sake, Butler. You messed up that compliment.*

"You sure?"

He held up his hands in surrender. "Yep." He turned toward the coffee bar and opened a pastry box, the savory aroma of cinnamon rolls hitting him in the face. And was that cream cheese icing?

"Oh man . . ." He was just gonna have to make an exception today. He was running on caffeine and carbs. What was one cinnamon roll? He'd get back in the gym soon enough. He groaned as he bit into the buttery, melt-in-your-mouth pastry.

"Good?" She watched him chew.

"Better than good." He stopped mid-chew and swallowed. "Do you really feel okay?"

She stood over her desk, rearranging some files, never looking at him. "After the pain meds wore off early this morning, I was wide awake. Don't blame Emma. I called Howard, and he told me it might be best if I show up."

"At least you're safe at the office."

She looked over. "Oh, for crying out loud . . ." She trudged over and slapped a napkin against his chest. "You have cream cheese icing on your nose."

Heat flooded his face, and he caught the napkin as she released it. No woman had made him blush since his neighbor Laura in the sixth grade. He'd tried to kiss her on the playground. For his romantic gesture, she'd gifted him with a bloody nose. "Uh, thanks."

Aubrey studied him for a moment, head tilted to the side, a small smile forming. She shook her head, and he watched as she clomped back to her desk, her uneven gait a reminder that her little adventure yesterday could've ended much differently. He grabbed his coffee and the pastry and headed back to his desk.

In his office, he crumpled the napkin and tossed it into the trash. How had she gotten under his skin in such a short period of time?

Glancing out the window, he studied the mountain in the distance, covered by a thin layer of clouds. The plane wreck, the dead body at the judge's house, the judge's body, and Aubrey's ransacked house—they had to be connected. But how?

He sent an IM to his friend in the Denver Marshals office, Sebastian Carlsson.

Ethan

You available to talk?

Sebastian

Yes.

Ethan's phone rang immediately.

"What's up? I sent the information about the prisoner transfers to your admin. You typically don't call me unless there's a problem."

"Yeah, I've got a problem all right." Ethan raked his fingers through his hair.

"Tell me."

"You know that some local kids found the wreckage of a plane on Renegade Mountain."

Sebastian chuckled. "We were apprised of the discovery." He must've put his hand over the speaker, because Ethan heard muted voices in the background. "Sorry about that. I had to answer a question."

"No worries."

"About this plane wreckage . . ." Sebastian left the thought hanging, but that one sentence felt like a two-ton anvil hanging over Ethan's head, with the rope about to snap.

Ethan said, "It's odd."

"How so?"

"Well." Ethan pulled the file closer. "The plane appears to be an older-model plane used by the Marshals' transportation services. The emblem on the tail is outdated, and we found a bogus flight manifest."

Ethan heard the squeak of Sebastian's chair and then a sigh. "Tell me more."

"There's not really much more to tell. The call letters are missing, like someone scraped them off the tail. Where the wreckage is, there's only one way in, and I've got a team out there now collecting evidence. Some kids found the plane while hiking and recorded their discovery live. I'm sending you the link now. This plane was stolen, and we think it was used in an escape to break Finn Donovan out of jail."

Ethan sent the link and watched the beginning of the recorded feed.

After a minute, Sebastian responded. "Okay, but why go through all this trouble for one guy?"

Ethan pinched the bridge of his nose, nerves stretched thin from the night before. "Sebastian, I'm pulling pieces together, and I need a federal angle."

"I'm listening."

"Aubrey saw Roger Rousseau yesterday," Ethan said, the words weighted now. "Not in court, not in a file, *on the mountain*. He was with Donovan. Talking to him. Casual. Like old friends. And Draven Frost."

"The guy Rousseau met with in Denver?"

"Now he's here. And they're working together. Which makes me wonder if they're *both* syndicate."

The line crackled. "That's big. You sure?"

"She wouldn't make that up," Ethan said quietly. "She testified against Donovan twenty years ago for her sister's murder. Summer case. Jury conviction. And now he's back in her orbit. But she identified the other two. I think they brought Donovan here to kill the judge, and in return, he gets to have his revenge on Aubrey."

Sebastian whistled. "Okay. That's motive, proximity, and witness confirmation. But a warrant still needs federal sign-off."

"That's why I'm calling," Ethan said. "Stanton pulled intel on Donovan's prison transport history. If you can get a judge in Denver to accept Aubrey's sighting, then we can tie Roger and Frost to an active fugitive. That's enough to request a warrant."

Ethan heard the rapid-fire clack of Sebastian's fingers on the keyboard. "It's a long shot, but not impossible. I can reach out to chambers and ask off record if a Denver judge sees warrant weight in it just with Aubrey's testimony. I'll push for an ETA too."

"I know it's a reach without the pilot's body," Ethan said. "But if there's even a chance to shield her from what's circling back . . . I have to take it."

Sebastian paused, then: "I'll try. Give me a day. If it fails, I'll shoot you a text—'no dice.'"

"Thanks," Ethan said quietly. "And Sebastian? Don't sugarcoat it if it's no dice. I'd rather know fast."

"Copy. And Ethan? Get some sleep before you start chasing ghosts yourself."

A tired laugh escaped him. "I'll try."

Ethan disconnected the call and leaned back, hope flickering, fragile and imperfect but finally pointed in the right direction.

His gaze drifted out the window. Clear blue skies, but underneath the peace, something darker was hiding.

No matter what, Ethan was going to keep Aubrey safe.

TWELVE

BETWEEN THE ANKLE INJURY, A BUSIER-THAN-NORmal office, doing her best to avoid Supervisor Howard all day, and dealing with Ethan's overprotectiveness, Aubrey was ready for a hot bath, her pj's, and a good book.

Renegade was supposed to have been safe.

This week, her safety net had disintegrated.

Yesterday on those trails, lost on the mountain, she'd realized that ignoring her past had been a luxury.

She wanted this nightmare to end.

"Ready to go?"

She jumped and almost fell out of her seat. "Ethan! You scared me."

"Sorry." Ethan stuffed his hands in his pockets and rocked back on his heels. "Let me help you with your bags."

She clomped over to the coffee station and threw away the boxes and pastries that'd sat out all day. She needed to get her emotions under control. Glancing down at her shaky hands, she squeezed them into fists.

She huffed out a lungful of air. "Ethan, I'm fine carrying my things."

Besides, he needed two hands free to fight off all the bad guys.

She restacked the coffee cups and turned to face him. Anything to delay returning to the safe house. She needed to calm down and maybe accept his help. But he was so different than how he normally acted around her.

"Sure?" he asked.

"I appreciate the offer, but I'm fine. I'll be fine." Maybe if she repeated that mantra enough times, she'd actually believe it herself. But she wasn't fine.

She could almost see the wheels turning in that analytical brain of his. If there was one thing she knew about Ethan, it was that he thought through everything he said before saying it.

Finally, he spoke. "Aubrey, I just got the initial report from the coroner's office concerning the judge."

The words startled her, immobilized every coherent thought. She gave herself a little shake. "What did the report say?" Words and feelings scraped against her throat as she tried to rein in her emotions.

"He was killed prior to the fire. No soot in his lungs."

She closed her eyes, trying to process what he was telling her. Slowly, she met his steady, compassionate gaze. "So the car didn't just spontaneously combust in front of the church with the judge in it?"

"No, considering accelerant was used."

"I see." She resumed cleaning up around the office—anything to keep her hands busy and her mind from rushing to conclusions. Then she stopped and whirled around to face him. He was standing in the same spot as before, studying her.

"How . . . ?" She shook her head. "Maybe I don't want to know."

He moved into her personal space, his blue eyes holding a storm of their own, edged with worry instead of case-hardened detachment.

"Blunt force trauma to the back of his head," he said quietly. "The report confirms it most likely killed him instantly."

Aubrey's breath thinned. The hallway suddenly felt too narrow.

Ethan softened his stance, though not the truth. "And the lab rushed the DNA. The housekeeper had Finn Donovan's DNA under her fingernails. Defensive wounds." His jaw tightened, but his tone gentled—anger for the dead, ache for the living. "They're working on the assumption he killed them both before he took the shot at you in the crowd."

Aubrey's pulse kicked, sick and sharp. "Shot at me in the *confusion*," she whispered, pieces clicking coldly into place.

"Not randomness," Ethan said, softer still. "Confusion he was counting on." He let the words land before adding, "You were the target. The chaos was the camouflage."

Aubrey's shoulders folded as regret crawled through her body, cold and suffocating. She'd brought danger here.

"As for leads, they're thin. But that DNA isn't. It gives us direction and enough weight for a warrant to dig more." He eased back just enough to let her breathe. "And you're not facing any of this alone. Not on my watch."

She nodded once, reining in all the emotion that wanted to rise to the surface. "Thank you for letting me know."

If she'd thought seeing the judge's car engulfed in flames had been bad, this was even worse. She'd held on to the hope that it had been someone else in the car. Anyone else but Judge Mullinax, although that was a cruel thought. It would mean an innocent victim had been killed.

The judge was the one person who had listened to her fears, helped her work through her trauma, and paid for her therapy.

He'd even set up the job interview for her here at the Marshals office.

Now there was a killer on the loose. The judge and his housekeeper had been murdered, and she was probably his next target.

She tried to sound strong when she asked, "What happens now?"

Ethan held her gaze, tone firm and measured. "We're going to tighten security around you. I'm taking you back to the safe house for the night. Work and safe house. You only go those two places, okay? And you're never alone."

Oh, he was good. She didn't want anyone's sympathy. That's why she'd hidden out here all these years. "I really need to grab some clothes from my house. Can we swing by there first? Or maybe Jenna can bring me some of my things." She tossed the remaining used napkins into the trash.

"We don't need to involve Jenna." He picked up her tote bag and opened the office door. "Coming?"

He propped the door open with his hip, watching her, assessing her reaction. Always assessing.

She stood in the hallway and exhaled. As they waited on the elevator, she glanced over her shoulder. Ethan stood behind her, his back ramrod straight, staring at the steel doors. What was up with him? Had Howard told him about their conversation? Maybe he agreed that she was hindering the search for Donovan by needing protection. That was why she'd jumped at the chance to be at the office today. But it wasn't her fault that she couldn't go home alone.

"Aubrey! Ethan! Wait up!" Liam called after them.

The elevator doors opened, but she stepped back into the hall, Ethan glued to her side. Her foot ached, she was tired, and she really didn't feel like talking.

"I'm glad I caught you before you left the building."

"Can this wait?" Ethan said. "I'm taking Aubrey to the safe house."

"Not really. You see . . ." He massaged the back of his neck, never looking at her, just the bright red numbers above the elevator. "My niece, Sophia, is having a party next week at my house, and I was wondering if Aubrey could make some of those fancy cupcakes. I want to surprise her and her friends."

Was that all? A slow smile spread across her face. "Yeah, sure. I'd love to do that. Email me and let me know what kind, colors, how many."

Liam grinned. "Thanks so much. She's gonna love them. At least, I hope she does. Let me know how much I owe you for this."

"No charge."

"I can't. At least let me pay for some of the ingredients." He pulled out his wallet and handed her a twenty-dollar bill.

"Really, Liam. I don't want your money. Besides, you helped rescue me. Consider it a reward for saving my stupid behind." She needed something interesting to do at the safe house, and this was perfect.

He stuffed the twenty in the side pocket of her bag. "Too bad." He glanced over his shoulder and addressed Ethan. "I'll be in the conference room when you return. Have to get back to work. Adam and I are going over the notes from the team. Discussing our next plan of action."

She gave Liam an encouraging smile. "Maybe you'll find a clue from the plane."

"That's what I'm praying for."

She pushed the down button again. What was taking this thing so long? The ding of the elevator doors opening cut off their conversation. "See you tomorrow."

Liam waved as the doors shut, and she leaned against the wall, but not before pressing the "G" for the courthouse's first floor. Soon enough, she could relax.

Well, relax as much as possible in a house that wasn't hers, with a fugitive on the loose.

They paused at her bungalow only long enough to grab a bag, the realization that her diffuser—cinnamon, apple, home—sat forgotten on the counter not hitting her until they stood on the porch of the safe house. The safe house smelled like nothing. Like survival. Safety, she realized, was a scent she'd left behind.

Her pulse hammered as Ethan unlocked the door.

"Let me check it out first before you go in," he said, already reaching for his weapon.

She barely nodded, one hand tightening around her duffel strap. Was this her life now? Forever scanning shadows, waiting for footsteps only she could hear?

Ethan stopped short as the door swung open, and stood in the entryway, unmoving.

"What's wrong?" she asked, bag thudding to the ground. He hadn't drawn his gun, so it wasn't that he faced a threat.

The answer hit her as she peered over his shoulder.

Couch cushions were slashed open like gutted fish, stuffing scattered across the room like tufts of snow. Lamps lay sideways, tables had been overturned, and every drawer yawned, its contents spilled out like confessions beaten loose. The calm of the bungalow had been destroyed.

This couldn't be happening *again*.

Panic surged up her throat, denying the oxygen her lungs needed. She stumbled forward and into a solid wall of muscle.

Ethan.

His hands locked around her upper arms. "Aubrey. Look at me."

"He found it." She gasped. "A Marshals safe house. How did he even—"

"No time." Ethan's voice snapped—firm, urgent, cutting through the spiral. He turned her toward the steps, guiding her out with controlled force, boots hitting the boards fast. "We're leaving. *Now.*"

She stumbled onto the gravel as he steered her toward the truck, his service weapon drawn, eyes burning with protective fury.

"Lock the doors," he ordered, opening the passenger side. "I'll handle the rest."

He slid behind the steering wheel, his phone pressed to his ear. "Yeah, this is Butler. We had a break-in at the safe house. Send a unit to 1107 Pine Valley Road." He cranked the engine.

"Ethan . . ." Her voice broke off in a sob. "How did they know?"

He shook his head. "I don't know." His mouth formed a tight line. "But I'm gonna find out." He glanced over and held out his hand.

She grabbed it, a lifeline in this nightmare.

She shivered, and it felt as if her entire body was encased in ice. Ethan placed his arm around her shoulders, and she leaned into his warmth, enjoying his nearness for a brief moment. Because eventually, she'd have to leave.

Over the years, she'd been so brave. Carried on. Moved to a new town and made new friends. Kept her secrets.

Now her past had caught up with her and was pursuing her with a relentlessness she hadn't expected.

What if Finn Donovan or one of his buddies actually found her?

"Come on. Come on!" Ethan pounded the steering wheel with his fist as he tried to maneuver around a slow-moving sedan. The vehicle swerved in front of him, and he honked his horn. "Get out of the way."

This had to be an inside job. But who would betray the location of a safe house? Anger surged through his veins as he threaded through heavy rush-hour traffic.

He used his hands-free device and called the office.

"Roberts here."

"Someone broke into the safe house. I'm taking Aubrey to the secondary location. Is it usable?"

"Yeah. The building inspector said it was good to go."

"Good." He glanced over at Aubrey, but she was focused on the passing scenery. "I need you and Montgomery to meet me at Rousseau's place. We're gonna make a house call. See if mommy dearest knows where he is."

"On our way."

He glanced at Aubrey, her fingers white from gripping the door handle. "I'm gonna find out who did this. What could they be looking for?"

She turned toward him, her eyes wide with fear. "I don't know. But if they want to scare me, they're doing a really good job."

He ran a hand through his hair. "Hey now. You're safe."

"No one is really safe, are they?" Her voice was a strangled whisper, breaking through the last of his defenses.

Yanking the steering wheel to the left, he swung his truck around the older-model sedan, focused only on one thing—keeping Aubrey safe.

He wanted to push his truck, floor the accelerator, but didn't dare draw attention to their flight. After fifteen tense minutes of backtracking through side streets, they halted in front of another small safe house. He threw the gear shift into Park and cut the engine.

Adrenaline pounded through his body.

Someone was grilling in the neighborhood, the savory aroma of barbecue drifting on the warm breeze. The scent was comforting and an unlikely accompaniment to the past frantic minutes.

Aubrey sat in the passenger seat, unmoving.

"Aubrey. Hey. We're at the safe house."

Her laughter was tinged with panic. "Another safe house." She shook her head. "I don't know if I can do this. Maybe I'll just leave . . ."

Ethan reached over and grabbed her arm. "It's going to be okay."

She shook her head, and he placed a finger under her chin. "Aubrey. Please. Look at me."

Her tortured gaze met his, and the look in her eyes made him want to wrap her in his arms.

"Come on, let's get you inside." He opened his door, then skirted the front of his truck and opened hers. He held out a hand. "It'll be okay."

She hesitated a moment, then placed her chilled fingers in his. He led her into the house and then closed and locked the door.

This home was older than the previous one, but clean. "Aubrey, stay here where it's safe while we clear the house." He left her in the foyer, unholstered his weapon, and began clearing each room.

He needed to be quick. Leaving Aubrey by herself wasn't optimal, but he had to make sure everything was safe.

"All clear." He holstered his weapon and then looked through the blinds and checked the road. Went back to her.

Before he knew what was happening, Aubrey wrapped her arms around his neck. He awkwardly patted her back and gently tugged on her arms. "Shh now." He lowered his voice. "You're safe."

Focus. He needed to stay focused on the task and not the woman with him.

Swiping her hair from her face, Aubrey nodded. He slipped his arm around her shoulders, then led her over to the small family room and guided her to the couch, where she dropped onto the cushions, an aura of defeat surrounding her.

He headed toward the door to call for backup, unable to look at Aubrey for fear that he'd convince himself to stay nearby.

She stood. "Where are you going?" Her panicked tone tore at his heart.

"I have to go back out and find Donovan and Rousseau. You're staying here, where at least I know you're safe." Just as soon as backup came.

"Ethan." Her tone had an underlying bite that hadn't been there before. Her low whisper pierced the armor around his heart. "I don't know if I can trust anyone in the Marshals office."

He nodded. He already knew the cost of misplaced trust.

As he stood at the door, indecision warred within. He needed to protect her, but he also needed to protect the citizens of Renegade. He pulled out his phone and sent Stanton a text.

Ethan

Need you at the new safe house on Eagle Drive.

Three green dots appeared. *C'mon. Answer.*

Stanton

I should be there in twenty. Why?

Ethan

Need you to patrol the outside of the house and keep Aubrey safe.

Stanton

Got it.

Ethan stuffed his phone into his pocket. "I have to leave, but Stanton will be outside. Don't go anywhere without him."

"'Kay." She plopped down on an older upholstered chair.

He stared at her for another second, then headed outside. If he stayed in there, he would never leave.

As soon as Stanton showed, Ethan took off.

His truck rumbled into the shadow of Renegade's outskirts. *Donovan had help.* That was no longer a theory. It was a working direction for the manhunt. But Ethan focused on the unseen operator, the one who didn't need to be present to pull the strings. Questions were giving way to patterns. Hesitation to action. He was finally at the part of the case where things were starting to make sense. The ransacked safe house proved someone was steering the aftermath of the plane wreckage on the mountain into something personal and precise.

His phone buzzed again.

Carlsson

No dice.

No warrant yet. Still, Ethan didn't need one to knock on a door the law might soon be forced to kick in anyway.

But he *wouldn't* be doing it alone.

He pulled into the driveway of what could only be described as a mansion. Four stories, with balconies on the upper floors. The massive stone structure overshadowed the driveway, the manicured shrubs and lawn like something out of a landscaping magazine cover.

He cut the engine as Liam's truck rolled up behind him, gravel spitting beneath law-enforcement tires. Adam pulled up behind Liam.

Montgomery stepped out first, hand already near his belt, eyes scanning timber shadows. Roberts followed, pulling the SUV door closed with a thud that sounded a lot like containment.

Roberts nodded once. "You sure about this?"

Ethan met his gaze. "Safe house got hit. I'm not asking questions anymore, Deputy Marshal. I'm closing windows."

Montgomery exhaled low. "Copy that."

Ethan cracked his jaw once, trying to dispel the tension. His eyes lifted toward the tree line beyond town, where Aubrey had unknowingly seen a meeting she was never meant to witness.

A medieval-style wooden door with brass hinges graced the front. Ethan rang the doorbell, which sounded like ancient bells.

"Do you believe this place?" Adam glanced around and whistled.

The door opened, and a man in a black tuxedo answered. "How may I be of service, gentlemen?" His gaze roved over the trio.

"We'd like to speak with Roger Rousseau." Ethan tried to peek around the butler, determined to find out if anyone who lived here knew where the guy was.

"I'm afraid he's not here at the moment."

Just great. And he didn't have a warrant either. "Well, then . . ."

"Jasper, who's at the door?" The woman had to be Destiny Rousseau, Roger's mother. Petite build, overly botoxed forehead and cheeks. She held a martini glass in her left hand. Her tight black dress clung to her curves. Ethan felt heat crawl up his neck, and he looked at the tips of his shoes.

"Ma'am, these men are looking for Mr. Roger."

Ethan opened his wallet and flashed his ID. "Mrs. Rousseau?" He cleared his throat. "I'm Ethan Butler, Deputy US Marshal." He held out his hand.

She sipped from her glass. "Call me Destiny." She stared at his hand as if it were covered in manure.

"Your son was recently spotted in the company of an escaped federal fugitive and another man wanted for questioning. We need to know where he is and if you've heard from him."

"As our butler has stated, Roger isn't here."

"When do you expect him back?"

Destiny shrugged. "I don't know. He's a big boy and can take care of himself. Now, if you'll excuse me, I have guests arriving in about twenty minutes." The door closed with a bang.

He shook his head. "Well, that was interesting."

Liam smirked. "What now?"

"We head back to the office. Discuss what was found at the plane site." And pray. "Did the Denver team find anything in the cabin Aubrey mentioned?"

"Cabin was cleared at 0600," Roberts said. "No occupants. No prints. They bagged a few items—energy-bar wrappers, an empty sports-drink bottle, and a pair of disposable gloves. Lab's running touch DNA, but nothing came back in the field. If someone used it, they didn't stay long."

The evidence was substantial enough to log, but thin enough to frustrate his investigation. Submitted. Tested. *Inconclusive.* The kind of clues that whispered without saying much.

Adam popped a piece of gum in his mouth. "The FAA has shut down access to the mountain trails. They've expanded the grid search to look for debris."

Ethan leaned against the truck's hood. "Adam, head back to the office. Liam, head over to the safe house. And don't tell anyone else where Aubrey is."

The fewer people who knew where she was staying, the better.

Ethan pulled out his phone and made a quick call to Emma.

"Kennedy. Everything all right?"

Ethan waved as the other two drove off in their cars. "I want you to drive Aubrey's car around Renegade. Gas station, grocery store, the usual routes—anything to make Finn Donovan think Aubrey is still moving freely."

"Got it. But I'll need her keys."

"Her keys and the car are at the office," Ethan said.

"Copy that."

"Aubrey's at a safe house. Stanton is there. Liam's heading over to relieve him." Ethan opened the truck door and sat staring at the Rousseaus' house through the windshield. "And Kennedy? Be safe."

"Always."

He disconnected the call and sent Aubrey a text.

Ethan

Liam should be at the safe house within thirty minutes.

Aubrey

Thank you.

Ethan

He'll be there for the first shift, and then I'll come back later tonight, closer to midnight, for my shift. Don't tell anyone where you're at.

Aubrey

Not even Jenna?

Ethan

Sorry. Not even Jenna. If there is a mole at the Marshals office, you're not safe. No matter where I send you.

Aubrey

You're scaring me.

Ethan

I don't mean to scare you, but . . .

Could he finish what he needed to say to her? He'd looped in most of his team because the truth was that he trusted them. So who was the leak?

Aubrey

But what?

Ethan

I care about you. I don't want to lose you.

Aubrey

I care about you too. I'll see you later tonight. Stay safe.

A fierce protectiveness rose within him, a feeling he hadn't experienced in an awfully long time.

He promised himself and the Lord that he would protect Aubrey, no matter what.

Even if he had to sacrifice his own life.

Because no one should have to live in fear.

THIRTEEN

SHE HATED SITTING HERE, ALL ALONE, IN A strange house. Aubrey stared at the walking boot on her left foot, which Emma had brought from home, from an injury she'd had years ago. This thing was a pain in the neck and made her feel like she was dragging a ten-pound weight behind her with every step.

She picked up the remote and turned on the television. Scrolling through the stations, nothing appealed to her, and she tossed the remote on the couch. She flopped back against the cushions. At least the couch was comfortable.

She picked up her phone—the replacement Emma had arranged for her. Five missed calls from Jenna and a handful of text messages. Good grief. With everything going on last night, she'd forgotten to turn the notifications off. She fumbled to unlock the phone and sent off a text to Jenna.

Aubrey

Hey. Sorry I didn't answer your texts last night.

Jenna

You scared me! Where are you?

Aubrey

Yeah, about that. I can't tell you.

Aubrey watched as three small dots appeared, then disappeared, until finally her best friend responded.

Jenna

I'm calling you. Now.

Oh boy. Jenna was persistent and would eventually ferret out the information.

Aubrey's phone rang, and she answered it before the first ring finished. "Jenna. I'm so sorry."

"Girl, I'm worried about you. What're you doing?" She heard Jenna exhale. "A better question is, *where* are you? First, anyway."

Aubrey paced the small room. Front window to the back wall was less than twelve steps.

"Aubrey?" The hurt in Jenna's voice threatened to break Aubrey's resolve.

Aubrey glanced around the corner into the kitchen. Liam and Stanton had traded off security detail a couple of hours ago. She heard the water running in the bathroom, so Liam wasn't far.

She placed her hand close to the microphone. "Look, my house was broken into. Everything is trashed."

"Oh, Aubrey, I'm so sorry. You worked so hard to make that place livable."

"I'm fine," Aubrey said—too quickly, too lightly. So she reached for the safer truth instead. "Okay, not *fine* fine. But safe. That's the part I'm clinging to today."

"Copy that," Jenna said softly. "Technically alive. Emotionally . . . debatable?"

Aubrey barked a humorless laugh that turned genuine at the

edges. "Yeah. Something like that. Anyway, what are you up to?" she asked, steering them away from the storm's center.

"Not much," Jenna said. "Props are boxed. Costumes inventoried. And don't worry, I'm not accusing you of abandoning me to solo costume purgatory." A quiet sigh threaded through. "I just keep thinking how much easier it was when we did this stuff together. You plus me plus too much caffeine plus terrible wigs. Simpler times."

Aubrey's throat tightened. "Simpler times," she echoed. "I miss those."

"If you were here," Jenna continued, "I'd make you carry the heaviest bin. But I'll survive without you today. I always do." She paused a beat, her tone warm. "I just want you to survive too."

Aubrey swallowed, breath thin, heart heavy. Jenna was her person. The woman who'd show up with duct tape and cupcakes if the Marshals allowed it.

That was exactly why Aubrey *couldn't* tell her where she was.

She couldn't let Jenna start searching Aubrey's house, sniffing for clues, or inserting herself into a federal radius she didn't belong in. Not when the threat was still breathing free air.

Aubrey pressed a palm to her forehead. "I'm not at the house. I'm somewhere secure." The mask returned—not defensive, simply protective. "And I need to stay here until they find Donovan."

Jenna didn't push. She simply absorbed. "Okay."

Aubrey continued before Jenna could step into danger with her loyalty. "If you see *anything* that feels off—strangers asking questions, someone showing up who knows too much, someone watching a little too long—you walk away. You call me. No hero moves. Just distance and instinct. Promise me that much."

"Distance and instinct," she repeated softly. "I can do that. I know what Finn Donovan looks like. I looked him up online. That guy is creepy."

Aubrey gave a wry half smile. "Welcome to my world."

"I'll respect the perimeter," Jenna said, "even if I hate the distance it puts between us. Because I want you alive to twist my arm into being in charge of costumes again next year."

Aubrey exhaled, small, shaky. "Deal."

Jenna's voice softened further, steady as Renegade Mountain that had stood the test of time. "And hey . . . just stay reachable, okay?"

"Reachable, I can do." Aubrey's throat tightened with emotion. "I need to go. I promised to make a batch of cupcakes for Liam's niece, Sophia. It's her birthday. And don't worry, I've got the US Marshals watching over me."

"Don't forget God," Jenna reminded her. "He is with you, even in this."

God. If He was protecting her, why hadn't He done the same for Finn's victims?

"I've got cupcakes to bake." Aubrey tried to infuse her words with a lightness she didn't really feel at this moment. "But I'll check in later."

Jenna disconnected the call. Aubrey held the phone against her chest and sighed.

Whenever Jenna talked about God, Aubrey felt a heart tug. She'd pushed Him to the side off and on. Hadn't come to Him until in desperation, when she was stranded on that mountain. And He had answered her prayer. *Thank You for keeping me safe yesterday.*

Why had she waited so long to renew her relationship with the Lord?

In the kitchen, she made a list of the ingredients she needed for baking. The cupboards were bare of even the basic essentials. She knocked on Liam's door. "Liam, we need stuff from the store."

"Hang on a sec."

She heard a low rumble of voices.

Finally, he came out.

"I need baking supplies for the cupcakes."

"Right. Special delivery coming up." He pulled his phone out of his pocket and made a call. "Hey, Emma. Can you do me a favor?" Pause. "Aubrey needs some groceries. I'll have her text you the list. Thanks."

Today was a beautiful day. Calm. No hint of what had happened just the other day during the festival. Or last night. A lawn mower rumbled in the distance, and a tentative peace settled around her. And her heart.

She finished her list and sent it to Emma.

Aubrey picked up the remote and surfed through the channels. Nothing interested her, so she shut off the television. She flopped against the cushions and sighed.

Liam was still on the phone. "He is?"

Aubrey straightened. "What's wrong?"

A small V formed between his brows. He shifted the phone away. "Emma's being followed."

Her heart stopped for a brief moment, then resumed beating at a frantic pace. She knew it. That's why she needed to leave.

Liam said, "Ethan sent Emma out, driving around in your car. Now Donovan is following her. Or at least, she thinks it's him." He refocused on the call. "Phone Ethan. Now."

Liam hung up.

Aubrey rose halfway from the couch, then stopped herself, heart giving one uneven thud. She wasn't bait. She knew that. But fear had a long memory.

"She trained for this," Liam said, unwavering. "Emma knows exactly what she's doing. If Donovan does recognize your vehicle, he takes the bait and we control where it leads."

Aubrey sank back into the chair, the tight coil in her chest loosening. "Okay," she said softly. "Then we wait." *Please let her be okay.*

The blinds were already drawn tight against the windows, lights kept low—standard procedure since the shooting at Renegade

Days. Liam straightened as his phone buzzed. "Roberts." A brief pause as he listened. He glanced at Aubrey, his movements steady, unhurried. "Copy. Still clean. No sign of Donovan near the house."

Aubrey released a slow breath, her pulse finally leveling out.

Liam ended the call and offered her a small, confident smile. "See?" he said. "Still good."

Aubrey nodded, trust returning in quiet measure. "Then we're good."

Liam tipped his head once. "Yeah. We are."

She sat with her knees pulled to her chest, the safe house quiet but the silence pressing close.

How much longer will this go on? The question circled, unanswerable.

She closed her eyes and prayed—not the clipped, whispered prayers of habit, but the deep, wordless kind dragged up from the soul. Protection for Emma, Liam, Ethan. Protection for herself. Wisdom for all of them. And mercy, fierce and urgent, that Donovan would be found before anyone else paid the price.

The scrape of tires in her memory roared into the silence around her. Liam's hand found her shoulder, light but deliberate. Aubrey's eyes flew open. She had no idea how much time had passed.

"Hey," he said quietly. "Ethan's on his way with your groceries."

Her pulse stumbled. "What happened?"

Liam crouched so she didn't have to crane to meet his eyes. "Donovan pursued her, and Emma turned onto Route 8. He rode her bumper through the bends, and she forced him to speed up to follow." He paused a beat, allowing her to absorb the information. "He thought he was following *you.* He never realized Emma was driving."

Aubrey exhaled, the breath shaky but smaller now. "Oh no."

Liam paused before he continued. "Emma knows how to run a chase. I trust her with that." His tone was calm assurance. "Ethan was able to catch up and force the issue. To get Donovan stopped."

The relief lasted only a second. Then fear slammed back into her throat, cold and jagged. "No." The word scraped out hoarse. Small. Frail. She couldn't finish the sentence.

Liam knelt in front of her, hands open, voice low, cutting through spiraling guilt before it could take root. "Sorry, but he got away."

Aubrey swallowed. "That means he's still out there."

Liam nodded. "There was a crash at the Route 8 junction," he said. "Donovan's SUV blew the red, clipped the turn too fast, and hit your car broadside. It wasn't stealth. It was rage and recklessness."

There was no blame in his words. Just facts. And truth.

"Emma's at the hospital now. Ethan stopped by the store on the way here."

Aubrey's breath went thin. "Will she . . . make it?"

"Yeah." He set a hand over hers, grounding, warm, present. "Broken arm. Cuts. Concussion. But she'll survive. And she'll be madder at that crash than you are, trust me."

Aubrey swallowed once—painful, but possible now.

Liam squeezed her hand and, voice a quiet promise, added, "You didn't put her on that road. Ethan did. She stepped into the chase for the right reason. She'd do it again."

Aubrey nodded, worry still there but quieter, steadier now.

Liam patted her shoulder, reassurance returning even in the gravity. "She's tough," he said. "Just like you."

Aubrey managed a small breath. "Then she's going to try to replace my car, isn't she?"

Liam smiled, but faintly. "Oh, she definitely will offer."

All the tension in her back released.

"But your insurance will cover it, I presume." The doorbell chimed. "Hopefully, that's Ethan." Liam stood to answer the door.

Aubrey rose to meet Ethan in the kitchen, where he dumped the shopping on the table.

Ethan took off his sunglasses and peeked inside the bags. "Vanilla, flour, sugar, baking chocolate, heavy cream."

"Thanks, Ethan." Right now she could barely remember why they were so important before.

The house was quiet, too quiet, and she shivered. The blinds were drawn tight, light filtered down to thin slats along the walls. Still, a warning tension gathered at the base of her neck.

Not sight. Not sound.

Instinct.

The unmistakable sense of being watched.

Her chest tightened. It didn't make sense. She knew that. Donovan had followed her car out of town. Emma had taken the hit. The collision had happened miles away. There was no reason for him to know where she was now.

And yet . . .

She stepped away from the window, pressing her back to the wall, breathing through the sudden rush of adrenaline. Her hands trembled. Too little sleep. Too much pain medication. That had to be it.

"What is it?" Ethan asked.

Aubrey shook her head, forcing herself to focus. "I didn't see him," she said quickly, needing to be precise. "I just . . . felt it." She shrugged. "It's difficult to explain. Donovan followed my car earlier. If he realized Emma wasn't me . . ."

He would have no idea where to find her.

Unless someone told him where she was staying—again.

Ethan's gaze sharpened. "Then he'll understand he took the decoy," he said. Calm. Controlled. "Which means he'll start reassessing."

Liam was already moving, phone in hand. "And when Donovan reassesses, he circles."

Aubrey's pulse kicked harder. "Back toward town."

"Toward what he knows," Liam confirmed. "And his friends, right?"

Aubrey stared at the closed blinds. "I hate that he recognized my car."

Ethan checked the front door, then rested a steadying hand on her shoulder. "You're not alone," he said. "Not tonight. Not until he's contained."

Aubrey swallowed, fear settling into something sharper. More focused. "Okay."

"Good," Ethan said, already turning away. "Let's get to work."

Not flirtation. A reset. Purpose.

A sudden slam cracked through the afternoon—a car door closing. Aubrey startled anyway, her chair scraping as she lost balance.

Liam caught her elbow instantly. "Easy. That's probably one of ours."

She steadied, breath coming fast but controlled. She lifted her chin. "Then let's finish this."

Frustrated energy rolled off Ethan as he stopped in front of her. He dragged a chair back and sat, elbows braced on his knees, gaze fixed on the floor like he was choosing his words carefully. For a moment, neither of them spoke.

Her breath caught. "Ethan . . ."

"I've lost enough people. I don't want to lose you too. I like you too much for that."

The admission hung there in the space between them, raw, unfinished.

Aubrey stared at him, heart pounding. This wasn't the time. Not with Donovan still loose. Not with adrenaline still burning through her veins.

He stood abruptly, decision made. "Come on."

She took his hand as he helped her up. "Where to, Deputy Marshal Butler?"

"The kitchen," he said. "You've got cupcakes to make. I've got a criminal to catch." Ethan's hand tightened briefly on hers, grounding. Then he slid his aviators back into place. "I'm heading out. Call if anything changes."

He was gone before she could argue.

Aubrey watched his truck disappear down the street, emotions whipping faster than she could sort them out. Fear, relief, something warmer she wasn't ready to name.

Flinty one moment. Protective the next.

And somehow, that version of Ethan unsettled her far more than the one she used to know.

What was he thinking? He was an idiot, letting his emotions control him.

This was supposed to be a professional relationship. That's it. End of story.

Seeing Aubrey in the emergency room the other night, pale, shaken, and hurting, had defeated the last remaining stronghold. He couldn't contain how he felt about her any longer. He gave himself a mental slap. He *liked* her?

Lame. Lame. Lame. What was he, in seventh grade again?

He admired her strength to survive despite being chased by a ruthless killer. He admired her starting over at a young age. Man, he more than liked her.

He sat behind the steering wheel and used his Bluetooth to make some calls.

"Montgomery here."

"Adam, I need to meet with everyone on the team. I'll be in the office in a few."

"Oh, good. Because there's an FBI special agent here by the name of Rudy Patterson."

Ethan stopped at the intersection and yawned. All the emotions of the past twenty-four hours hit him in the solar plexus. He needed sleep. But he needed answers more than anything else.

"Good. Who's in the office?"

"Glover, Albright . . ."

A car horn honked, and Ethan waved. He accelerated slowly. Only a couple more blocks to drive. "What aren't you saying, Adam?"

"Howard is here too. But he's on a rampage, if you know what I mean."

Yeah, he knew what the kid meant. But that was Howard's MO. "I'm pulling into the parking lot now. Get everyone assembled."

He breezed through security, and instead of waiting for the elevator, took the stairs. He scanned his ID and strode down the hall to the conference room. The door opened and all conversation stopped.

A suited, dark-haired FBI agent stood, his hand extended. "I'm Rudy Patterson. FBI special agent."

"Ethan Butler." They shook hands.

Patterson nodded. "I've heard a lot about you. You're quite the legend with this group."

"That's what I was trying to tell you on the phone." Adam squeezed Ethan's shoulder and sat. He grabbed a doughnut from the box in the center of the table and began eating.

Ethan opened the file in front of him. "Let's begin. Special Agent Patterson, would you like to start?"

"Thank you. As you are probably aware, I've been sent in to help with the apprehension of Finn Donovan. I'm passing around a recent photo of Donovan. And you can see it on the screen as well. Make a note of the dragon tattoo that climbs up his back and across his neck, finishing under his left ear."

Ethan stared at the mugshot projected on the screen. The chatter in the briefing room faded to a low hum.

Finn Donovan.

Agent Patterson's voice broke through his haze. "We've been tracking his visitors since he was convicted. No one visited him. Until about six months ago."

"Let me guess. Roger Rousseau," Stanton said.

"Well, we think it was him. We can't be certain because he was wearing a disguise and gave us an alias. But it tracks. He visited one time. Donovan didn't receive any packages. No mail. Nothing."

Ethan leaned forward. "So what you're telling us is it had to be someone on the inside passing information."

Patterson turned toward Ethan, his dark eyes assessing. "Correct. Since Rousseau lives in Renegade, we looked into this Frost character you spoke with."

No accusation over the fact Ethan had chatted with him and never realized he was involved.

"We have him traveling to South Carolina twice over the past six months. And with him being a known associate of Roger's . . ."

Ethan nodded. All this information made sense. There was no way Donovan could find his way around town without someone assisting him. "What other information do you have?"

Patterson leaned against the table. "There's a house we've been watching in Southwold. Roger Rousseau has been meeting with some sketchy individuals. We don't have enough proof, and we haven't figured out who the top dog is. Yet. I'm working on a plan to get us that information. But for now, two officers from that precinct will meet us in about an hour. Let's raid the place and see what we kick up."

Adam exhaled. "About time."

Ethan smiled. "Everyone, suit up. We'll carpool. Take the unmarked cars." Ethan glanced around the conference room table, emphasizing the importance of this operation. "Special Agent Patterson, you're with me."

Agent Patterson nodded, and everyone headed to their respective offices to gear up.

The time between the decision to go to the house and arriving felt like the longest hour of Ethan's life.

"Stop here." Agent Patterson pointed to a small strip mall. A tattoo parlor anchored the far end, with a pawn shop and a Vape shop rounding out the businesses.

Ethan hit the brakes. "Team. Once you're parked, move into position. Adam, take the west side of the house. Glover, cover the back. Patterson and I will enter the front."

"Roger." The team responded in unison and then went silent.

Ethan parked the SUV on the far end of the parking lot, across the street from a row of run-down bungalows. These small houses had seen better days. Now, with lopsided porches, peeling paint, and overgrown yards, an air of neglect hung over the neighborhood. A dog barked in the distance, and the rumble of a jacked-up car with no muffler disturbed the relative peace.

The sun began to set, dark-purple clouds hovering on the horizon. Ethan pulled out his binoculars. All quiet. For now.

"You have the search warrant?"

Agent Patterson pulled the warrant out of an inside pocket and held it up, his leather jacket creaking with the movement. "My informant told me that Rousseau makes a weekly visit to this house, usually between seven and eight today."

Ethan glanced at the clock on his dash. Almost seven. His inner earpiece crackled.

"Butler, this is Stanton, do you copy?"

"Loud and clear," Ethan said.

"A new model luxury sedan just rolled up in front of the house. Right on time."

"I see it." Ethan didn't need the binoculars to see who was exiting the car. Roger Rousseau, handsome, entitled, and rich. He buttoned his suit coat and put on his sunglasses. His extravagant clothes and car were out of place, like neon beacons. He looked around once, then walked up the rickety steps and inside.

"Wait for our signal," Ethan added.

Ethan and Patterson exited the car and crossed the street, weapons drawn.

A loud bang sounded and then shouts, before they even breached.

"That was a gunshot! I'm going in," Stanton said.

"Let's go!" Ethan barked into his mic. Ethan covered Patterson while he sprinted up the four steps on the front porch, then stood with his back against the outside wall, weapon ready.

"Go, go, go!" There was no time to wait.

"FBI, open up!" Patterson pounded on the door frame.

"Cover me." Ethan kicked the door open, his service revolver drawn, clearing the room. Patterson followed him, checking behind the door.

The floor shifted under his weight. He barely had time to register the sharp crack of wood splitting before his boot slipped on something loose and he went down hard, his head striking the edge of a low table. Pain exploded behind his eyes, and he dropped to his knees, stunned.

A prearranged death trap for law enforcement that Roger would've known how to avoid.

The sound of retreating footsteps echoed down the hall. A door slammed and he heard Stanton shout.

Ethan forced himself upright and immediately stumbled, vision swimming. Dust motes floated on the stale air, and in the dim light across the room, a dead body was sprawled across the scarred hardwood.

Blood pooled beneath the victim's head. A male. Late twenties, maybe. Long, stringy hair. Sallow skin. He had all the earmarks of a drug addict.

Ethan braced both hands on the doorjamb, jaw locked. "Scene's not clear," he said evenly into the radio. "Secure it."

"Copy," Patterson said, already moving. "Backup and medical en route."

Every breath felt like driving a spike through his skull, but he stayed upright.

A beat later, Patterson was at his side. "You okay?"

Ethan grunted. "I am, but not this guy." He pressed the call button on his radio. "Montgomery, call the local PD and tell them we've got a body."

"On it," Montgomery said.

Ethan and Patterson swept the living room and the kitchen, their footsteps echoing through the empty house. A few dirty dishes were scattered across the counter, along with the remnants of takeout from a local restaurant.

Two chairs sat at lopsided angles in the kitchen. Ethan gritted his teeth. "Stanton, Glover, check in."

The rest of the team slowly entered the kitchen. Adam didn't look happy. "There were a couple of them. They were out before we breached. They ran."

Through the window, he saw a police cruiser stop at the curb, and an officer, along with his K-9, stepped out. When the duo reached the kitchen, the officer said, "Heard you needed backup." He gave his German shepherd a hand motion and the dog sat. "I'm Boothe and this is Ranger."

Boothe looked to be in his early thirties, tall and fit, dark hair streaked with gray. His brown eyes flicked over the scene with practiced calm and a dry look that said he'd already sized up the trouble.

"Butler. Deputy US Marshal." Ethan squinted in the waning light. "I need you to check the perimeter. Suspect fled through the back door."

"Sure." Boothe shortened his grip on the leash. "Ranger. Find."

The dog surged forward, nose lifting and sweeping the air as much as the ground, muscles coiled with purpose as he worked the perimeter in a tight arc around the house. Boothe moved with him, controlled, giving the dog just enough lead to work without breaking contact.

Patterson frowned. "You don't need a scent or something?"

"He's not tracking," Boothe said, already following Ranger's pull. "He's searching for anyone hiding in the area. If he finds a person, I'll know."

Ethan sat on the top step and massaged his throbbing temples. Someone squeezed his shoulder. "Hey, you might want to get that looked at." Patterson stood next to him, concern crinkling the corners of his eyes.

Ethan gently probed the area on the back of his head and grimaced. "It's a little sore, no blood, probably have a goose-egg-sized knot tomorrow." He gave the fed a tight smile. "I've had worse."

Crime scene rolled up and began collecting evidence, what little there was. Boothe brought the dog back, the dog's tongue lolling out the side of his mouth. "Good boy." He patted the dog's side.

"Well?" Ethan asked

Boothe shrugged. "Nothing. He might've caught a trail going through the backyard, but there was no one there. This place is a known flop house. Too many people have been through here."

"Too bad," Patterson murmured.

Stanton, Montgomery, and Glover grouped around, standing in front of Ethan.

"I'm going to meet with the judge and the prosecutor to get a warrant for Rousseau," Patterson said. "He already made one mistake. He'll make more now that he knows we're watching him for yet another death."

Ethan exhaled. "I can only hope. Let's get out of here. We'll figure out what to do in the morning."

"Let's go." Patterson held out a hand and pulled him to his feet. "I'll drive you back to the office."

Ethan tossed the fed his keys, and they headed back to the

parking lot. Quiet settled over the car, and they rode in silence back to the courthouse.

"Thanks for driving."

Patterson handed him the keys. "Thanks for the backup."

"Anytime."

Ethan waited until the other man pulled away and his vehicle disappeared before getting into the driver's seat of his truck. Habit. Protocol. One last scan of the street before he turned the key.

Aubrey's face surfaced unbidden. He admired her steadiness, the way she held herself together when everything around her threatened to come apart.

Something unfamiliar tugged low in his chest. He turned the key and put the truck in gear.

He needed to see her.

Not to say anything.

Just to be sure she was safe.

He rang the doorbell at the safe house, and Liam answered the door. Ethan filled him in on the operation and how Roger got away as they went into the living room.

Aubrey rushed past Liam and touched Ethan's forehead. "Are you okay? You look awful." She tugged him inside and into the kitchen.

"Thanks for noticing."

Liam chuckled.

"Let's get some ice and ibuprofen."

She handed him the pills and he swallowed. She smelled sweet, like chocolate and sugar. The entire house smelled good. He leaned for another whiff. *Mmm.* She'd baked.

Whoa. What was going on? Must be the hit to his head. He needed to put some space between them. Ice pack pressed against his head, he leaned against the counter, careful not to disturb the fancy iced cupcakes sitting on the cooling racks. "Can I have a cupcake? They smell amazing."

She pivoted and started arranging cookies in a huge plastic container. "Since you're injured, I suppose you can have one. After all, you did bring me to this lavish accommodation."

"Stingy." He bit into the chocolate cupcake and groaned. "You've got to stop baking."

"Why?" Her green gaze bored into his. "These are for a birthday party, remember?"

"Too much of a temptation." He ate the remaining section in one bite, his gaze never leaving hers. Aubrey's eyes widened, and a light-pink blush covered her cheeks.

The atmosphere in the small kitchen turned thick and sweet. Like honey. And he didn't want to leave.

Aubrey stepped back. "I thought you were immune to my baking." She held the plastic container in front of her like a shield.

He stepped closer. "Oh no. Not immune at all." She was captivating.

He watched as she swallowed.

"I, uh, need to let Liam know these are ready if he's leaving now." She matched him step for step until she backed into the kitchen counter.

He removed the container and set it on the small breakfast bar. They stood staring at each other. Him wanting to tell her, and Aubrey? Well, he didn't know what she wanted. After a long interval, she ducked around him and scooted to the family room.

Well, that little rejection just threw a bucket of cold water on his hopes. Which was a good thing. He did not want his feelings to override his good sense.

She stood in front of the television, eyes unfocused. Arms crossed at her waist.

"Aubrey . . ." He grasped her hand and slowly turned her toward him. *Ouch.* Any movement made his head pound, but he needed to see her reaction. "I'm sorry. I didn't mean to scare you off."

His gaze landed on her lips, and she inhaled. Time froze. They stood staring at each other until Aubrey looked away. Whatever had just passed between them disappeared like morning dew on a hot summer day.

She cleared her throat and stepped away, putting the brown sugar and chocolate chips in the pantry, then went to the freezer. "Why don't you sit on the couch, and I'll make another ice pack?"

"Since you asked nicely . . ."

"I did." She handed him an ice-filled freezer bag wrapped in a dish towel and pointed to the couch. "Sit."

"Yes, ma'am." He sank into the cushions, his head screaming for relief. She dimmed the lights, and they sat in companionable silence, shadows dancing across the gentle planes of her face. He sighed. "I need to leave."

But he didn't move. He wanted to sleep for at least a couple of days.

"By the way, if we apprehend Finn Donovan, why don't you come to Bible study with me tomorrow night?"

Panic flashed across her face. "I don't know."

He raised his hands. "Hey, no pressure. I need to recenter myself, that's all. Thought you might want to go."

He didn't want to push. This was a decision she'd have to make for herself.

He tossed the ice pack on the scarred coffee table. "See me out to the hallway?" He held out his hand, and she grasped it as he pulled her to stand.

"Sure." She smiled.

They stood in the foyer for a moment. He had so much he wanted to tell her—how he felt about her, what he really wanted in life—but now wasn't the time. Or the place. "Stanton will be by in the morning to pick you up for your appointment. The follow-up for your ankle. I'll see you after."

He stepped closer. Aubrey was so close he could see the gold ring around her irises. He leaned forward, then heard someone clear their throat. He glanced up and groaned.

Not someone. Liam.

"Hey, you two." Liam was eating a sandwich, his wet hair slicked back. "Leaving so soon, Butler?" He grinned, his gaze ping-ponging between Ethan and Aubrey.

Ethan glanced at his watch. "I need to get back to the office and write up a report. See you later, Aubrey."

"I'll be here," Aubrey said.

"Bye, honey." Liam closed the door, and the last thing Ethan heard was Liam's laughter.

Aubrey was searching, he knew it. He was pretty sure she was a believer, but it seemed as if she had lost her way. Like him.

He'd been trying to grow closer to the Lord for years, a little bit every day. God had never left him, and he wanted to show Aubrey that God was there for her too.

That no matter what happened, God was still good and He had a plan for her life.

And his.

FOURTEEN

THE RICH AROMAS OF THE BEANERY'S WHITE mocha lingered in the SUV long after Aubrey and Stanton left the drive-through, but her favorite drink sat like the proverbial rock in her stomach. Stanton glanced at her as he pulled the government SUV into a spot near the medical building.

Days later, and the fiasco of Renegade Days still echoed everywhere she went.

The failed reenactment. The injured bystanders. The dead judge, along with his housekeeper.

She shifted uncomfortably, adjusting the walking boot on her left foot. This wasn't her fault. She knew that. The fault belonged to evil men intent on destruction. Or worse.

Still, guilt had a way of finding cracks.

"You okay?" Stanton asked as he cut the engine.

"Just ready to get this over with." She forced a smile. "I promise I won't make a run for it."

Stanton gave a single nod, already scanning the lot. "We'll be quick. I've got you."

Inside, the waiting room buzzed with low conversation and daytime television. Aubrey lowered herself into a chair and pulled out her phone.

Jenna answered on the second ring. "Tell me you're still being guarded. That you're safe."

"I am," Aubrey said softly. "Stanton brought me to the doctor. Just for a checkup."

"Good. Because I don't trust you not to carry the weight of the world by yourself."

Aubrey smiled faintly. "You know me too well."

They talked quietly about the reenactment, the whispers still rippling through town, the things that had gone right even when so much hadn't. Jenna coaxed laughter out of her, the kind that eased pressure instead of dismissing it.

"I still feel guilty," Aubrey admitted. "I know I shouldn't, but . . ."

She didn't even want to talk about Ethan and how he'd been hurt last night. Trying to close the case so that she was protected. Rousseau was still out there. And that Frost guy, whoever he was. And Donovan.

God, don't let anyone else get hurt.

"You didn't plan the shooting," Jenna cut in gently. "You didn't unleash horses through town. You didn't pull a trigger. You survived."

"But why me?" Aubrey swallowed. "Why me and not others?"

"Only God can answer that," Jenna said. "The better question is, what are you going to do with that time He's given you? Even if your faith is only the size of a mustard seed, that's still enough. In fact, He said that's how much we should strive for. We only need a tiny amount."

Aubrey closed her eyes, letting the words settle. *Tiny faith.* "I really should go. They should call me back soon."

"Call me later," Jenna said. "And Aubrey? You're not alone anymore."

"Love you, girl." Aubrey hung up just as the nurse called her name. Stanton followed, flashing that silver star and convincing the staff it was imperative he wait in the hall.

When she came out, she showed Stanton her paper. "All clear, pending six to eight weeks of healing time."

Stanton rose from his chair beside the door. "Before we head back, restroom's down the hall if you need it."

"I do." Aubrey shifted her weight carefully. "You'll be right outside there as well?"

"Wouldn't be anywhere else." He nodded.

The hallway beyond the waiting room was dim and quiet, the sounds of the clinic muted behind her. Aubrey moved quickly, unease prickling her skin for no reason she could name.

Just instinct.

She reached for the door to the women's restroom, and movement exploded behind her. She spun to see Stanton react instantly, stepping between her and the blur rushing from the supply alcove. His hand went for his weapon, but he never got it free.

Something struck the side of his head, hard. Stanton crumpled to the floor, his body hitting the wall before sliding down, unmoving. Blood on his head. So much blood.

Aubrey screamed, instinct driving her to rush into the bathroom.

But there was nowhere to go. She was trapped.

The door slammed shut, the sound echoing off the tiles, and there he was. Facing her. Finn Donovan. "That's right, little girl. I haven't forgotten you."

Her heart hammered in her chest, and her lungs refused to expand. Someone in the doctor's office would realize she was in trouble and call 911 . . . right?

He stepped forward, and she rushed to run past him. She had to get out of here, and that was the only way out.

He seized her, a steel band locking around her. She screamed until a gloved hand smothered the sound, his forearm pinning her arms to her ribs. "The more you struggle, the worse it'll be for you. Much better to come quietly."

His voice. She remembered. His voice had the same evil timbre, and icy slivers of fear ran through her veins. He reeked of body odor and cigarettes.

Aubrey didn't care. She couldn't breathe! She wriggled, tried to position her body to break his hold. Blackness crept in around the edges of her vision, and she struggled for air.

"I've been thinking about this day for the last twenty years, sitting in that cell." The man's sour breath grazed her skin, and a cold ripple of fear moved through her before she could stop it.

No. Please, God, not him.

"We're going to have so much fun."

Pain exploded behind her eyes, and she felt herself falling, blackness closing in.

The steel tightened and everything went black.

Ethan sat at his desk in his office, a half-cold cup of coffee untouched beside his laptop. Stanton and Aubrey should be back from her doctor's appointment soon enough.

His phone buzzed, and he picked it up. "Butler."

"It's Roberts," Liam said. "We've got a witness. Civilian. Had a run-in with Donovan last night."

Ethan straightened. "Where is he?"

"Renegade Mercy General. Gas station clerk off Route 8. EMTs flagged it. Donovan was wearing a Marshals jacket."

Ethan was already on his feet. "We need to talk to them."

"Copy that," Liam said. "I'm two minutes out. I'll swing by and pick you up."

Liam pulled into the lot just as Ethan stepped outside. They didn't waste words. Ethan slid in and Liam pulled out. "You good?"

As the office disappeared in the rearview mirror, Ethan's jaw set. "I'm good."

Aubrey was still out there. And Donovan was wearing one of their jackets, pretending to be a fed.

Anxiety tugged at Ethan as Liam parked in front of Renegade Mercy General. He jumped out of the SUV and bolted for the automatic doors, every instinct screaming to move faster.

Liam grabbed his arm, halting his progress. "Slow down, man." Liam looked away and then back at Ethan, a muscle twitching in his jaw. "The witness asked to speak to us. He's awake. Banged up, but awake. And he's not going anywhere."

"We need to get in there and ask some questions." Ethan needed leads.

They stopped by the front desk, showed their badges, and rode the elevator up to the sixth floor.

The beep of machines, PA system pagers, and the squeaking of rubber soles on the tile floor gave off haunted vibes. A uniformed Renegade PD officer stood watch outside the witness's door. He held up a hand as they approached. "No one is allowed in there."

"US Marshals. I'm Deputy Marshal Ethan Butler, and this is Deputy Marshal Liam Roberts." The men pulled out their wallets for ID and showed him the badges on their belts. "We have some questions we'd like to ask the patient, if that's okay, Officer . . . ?"

"Ferguson. Andrew Ferguson."

Ferguson opened the door. "Go on in, but you can only stay about five minutes. Doctor's orders."

"Thanks, man." Liam shook Ferguson's hand.

The hospital room smelled faintly of antiseptic and old coffee. The patient lay propped against the pillows, a bandage wrapped around his forehead and one arm secured in a sling. He looked younger than Ethan expected, barely out of his teens, eyes still a little glassy, either from the meds or the pain.

Liam closed the door behind them.

"Mason Cole?" Ethan said. "I'm Deputy Marshal Butler. This is Deputy Marshal Roberts."

Mason nodded. "Yeah." He pushed the button to raise his head. Bruises covered his arms, and a purplish bruise ringed one eye.

"We understand you had an encounter last night," Liam said. "At the gas station."

Mason swallowed. "That's one way to put it."

"We'd like to know what happened. Take your time," Ethan said. "Start from the beginning."

"It was late. After midnight," Mason said. "I was closing up when this guy walked in. He was wearing a Marshals jacket."

Ethan's spine stiffened and Liam pulled a chair up to the bed.

"Did it look official?" Liam asked.

"Sort of. But it didn't fit right. Too big. Like it wasn't his." Mason frowned. "Smelled like cigarettes."

"What did he buy?" Ethan asked.

"Beer. Cigarettes. Chips. Candy bars." Mason gave a humorless huff. "Junk food. Like he was stocking up."

"Did you talk to him?" Liam asked.

"Yeah." Mason shifted, wincing. "I asked if he was here for Renegade Days when everything went down. Everyone's been talking about it."

"And?" Ethan prompted.

"He just . . . stopped. Not angry, just real focused." Mason's gaze drifted to the wall. "He said, 'This town's not done with me yet.'"

Liam's jaw tightened. "Then what?"

"He asked for directions. Said he was already staying in Renegade, just wanted to make sure he was headed the right way." Mason hesitated. "Then he pulled out his phone."

Ethan felt the room narrow.

"What did he show you?" Liam asked.

"A picture," Mason said quietly. "Of a woman."

"Describe her," Ethan said.

"Long, dark-red hair. Kind eyes and a pretty smile." Mason glanced up. "She looked nice."

Ethan's stomach dropped and his blood turned to ice. He pulled out his phone, his movements controlled, deliberate as he accessed the secured file. He didn't look at Liam when he turned the screen toward the bed.

"Is this her?" Ethan asked.

Mason's face drained of all color. "Yeah. That's her. Is she in trouble?"

Ethan locked the screen and slid the phone back into his pocket. "She's under our protection."

"Did he say her name?" Liam asked.

Mason shook his head. "But when I told him I didn't know her, he smiled. Just a little. And said . . ." His voice faltered. "'If you see her, tell her Donovan's looking for her.'"

The words settled like a weight. The air felt heavier in the room, and a steel band tightened around Ethan's chest.

"What happened next?" Ethan asked.

"I hesitated," Mason said, his voice unsteady. "Something about him felt . . . wrong. I was gonna call the police after he left. I pulled my phone out of my pocket, set it on the counter." His hand drifted to the bandage on his head. "I think he noticed."

Mason swallowed hard, his throat working. "He didn't say anything. Just stared at me, like he was trying to decide what I was." Mason shook his head. "Then he dragged me across the checkout counter and threw me into the shelves. Hard. Chips went everywhere." His jaw worked as he forced the words out. "He stood over me, hand on a gun, and then looked up like he heard something. Then he hit me and ran."

Liam kept his voice even. "Did you recognize him?"

Mason frowned. "Not right then. It didn't click until after."

Ethan leaned in slightly. "After what?"

"After he left," Mason said. "I saw the report on the news later about the prison escape in South Carolina, and it hit me." His voice dropped. "Same eyes. Same tattoo. Same look."

Silence pressed in.

"I didn't want it to be him."

Ethan and Liam exchanged a look.

"You did the right thing coming forward," Liam said. "We'll take it from here."

Mason nodded, relief flickering across his face.

Ethan handed him a business card. "My cell number is on the back. If you think of anything else, let us know."

"Take care of yourself," Liam said.

Outside the room, the door clicking shut behind them, the hallway felt too bright.

"That photo isn't public," Liam said quietly. "He got Aubrey's picture from somewhere. Or someone."

"We've got a leak," Ethan finished. "And Donovan's acting the part of a fed to get people off guard." Ethan pulled out his phone again, already moving down the corridor. "And now," he added, voice hardening, "we stop assuming he's reacting."

Because Finn Donovan wasn't chasing ghosts. He was hunting with information.

Ethan's phone buzzed as they left Mason's room. He checked the messages. "It's Montgomery. Renegade PD has a tip on the whereabouts of Finn Donovan."

"Where?"

"Southwold area. Near the old rail depot. There are a lot of places to hide. Abandoned warehouses, old row houses that are used by gangs. Someone spotted him hanging out."

Liam exhaled. "No way. There's no way he'd be that stupid and risk getting caught. More likely it's misdirection."

"That's what I'm thinking. Are we sure it's Donovan?"

"They used the prison description, photos on file. Montgomery texted Aubrey. RPD had an APB out on him."

"Good. Any word on Rousseau or Frost?"

"Nobody has seen or heard from Rousseau in a couple of days. He might be in Costa Rica for all we know."

"I hope not. Only problem is, lot of people in this town love the Rousseaus and would do anything for them." The elevator doors opened, and Ethan pressed the button for the first floor.

"Even hide a fugitive," Liam said.

"Let's not get ahead of ourselves. Rousseau has to be someplace close. There's too much at stake." Ethan tried to keep their conversation on a lower decibel level, although it was difficult to be heard with all the traffic around the hospital.

"Agreed. I'll go back and check with Destiny Rousseau once I drop you off at the office."

"Good. Take Montgomery or Albright with you. We don't need another ambush, and none of us needs to be alone with Destiny Rousseau." Ethan scanned the hospital parking lot.

Everything looked normal enough. Family members going inside to see a loved one. A florist delivery van. Transportation vans and wheelchairs lining the curb.

After Ethan dropped Liam off at the courthouse, he called dispatch and asked for backup from local PD at the house where Donovan had supposedly been seen.

The farther he drove from downtown Renegade, toward Southwold, the emptier the streets became. Abandoned cars had rusted where they'd been left, warehouse parking lots gaped open and unused, and the houses between them looked hollow—windows dark, doors sagging, no sign of life.

The hum of the tires filled the cab, but a thought nagged him. Stanton hadn't checked in yet.

Ethan's phone buzzed with an incoming call. "Butler."

"You going to tell me what's been going on with you?" Rudy Patterson asked over the line. "Because someone just handed me a missing piece to this case. Who, or what, is the Shadow Syndicate?"

Ethan slowed at an intersection where the traffic lights hung dark and lifeless. An abandoned sedan sat half on the curb, corrosion creeping along the doors. His hands tightened on the steering wheel.

"They're the reason I was suspended recently," he said. He let out a slow breath, unsure he'd meant to say that. But right now, there was zero point keeping anyone in the dark. Lives were at stake. "Except it wasn't a suspension. It was a covert assignment. I was tracking Roger Rousseau, and I ran into Draven Frost."

"And no one knew?" Patterson said. "You got no whiff of the operation they were working on."

"I couldn't risk anyone here knowing, so I leaned on a friend in Denver." His jaw flexed as he passed a dilapidated house. "I tailed Rousseau for days. I came back empty-handed, and now this? He and Frost must've gone to ground after they met, waiting for the right moment to hijack that decommissioned plane."

A rusted pickup sat on the side of the road, tires flat, windshield cracked. Ethan eased around it, eyes tracking the shadows between warehouses.

"The file I got didn't come through official channels," Patterson said. "Someone leaked it. Quietly. And whoever did that didn't want their name attached."

Ethan's jaw clenched. "Meaning?"

"Meaning someone inside law enforcement, or adjacent to it, knows what the syndicate is. And they're scared enough to stay invisible. Probably worried about backlash."

He turned onto a street with no streetlights. "Sounds right. After all, the syndicate has had several people killed recently."

"My boss, ASAC Kumar, and I think it intersects."

Ethan's grip tightened on the wheel.

"Two potential witnesses are dead, and anyone else who might've known something has gone quiet."

Ethan said, "From what Detective Martinelli and Luca Saxon have pieced together, the syndicate has been developing something dangerous. A designer drug, supposedly more addictive and profitable than anything on the market. We're starting to see it creep into the market around town."

"Watch your back, I guess," Patterson said, voice low. "Because if the leak is real, you're not just hunting ghosts. Someone's been watching who you talk to and where you go."

Ethan said, "Another potential witness, Dr. Torres, was killed before we could confirm who was pulling the strings. Our best guess? Someone higher up planned to sell the formula to the highest bidder. Might've had cartel involvement, they weren't sure. Everything went dark after Torres's death." He paused, glancing at street numbers. "Until now."

"I'll continue to work this on my end. Stay safe." Patterson disconnected the call.

For the first time, Ethan had said more than the official report ever had, and now the weight of it pressed heavily on both of them. But he wasn't facing this alone.

He wasn't sure what to make of it. There just wasn't enough evidence.

Ethan drummed out a beat on the console, ready to question Donovan. Their only hope right now was that the convicted felon would talk, implicating whoever was behind this scheme.

He drove up to a row of dilapidated houses in the Southwold area of Renegade. A couple of police cruisers pulled up behind his truck, lights off. Rusty chain-link fences in need of repair surrounded most houses. The tipster's house was no exception.

A couple of dogs barked from behind a fence, and the sound of a car backfiring split the air. Ethan cautiously exited the vehicle and stepped over a missing plank on the porch. An old aluminum storm door hung at an odd angle, the glass missing from the top portion and now covered with a piece of cardboard. He waved to one of the officers to take position off to the side of the house.

Ethan rapped on the door while the other uniformed officers crouched behind open cruiser doors, weapons ready. A single officer stood behind him at the door, backing him up.

A baby's thin wail drifted through the house. Then a hesitant squeak—the door cracked open an inch.

"Who are you? What do you want?" The woman who appeared couldn't have been more than twenty-five, but life had aged her, hard. Her skin hung loose against sharp cheekbones. Dark circles bruised the skin beneath eyes that had seen too much. A baby clung to her hip, and formula was smeared across the woman's faded rock-band tee.

Ethan kept his voice steady. "Ma'am, I'm with the US Marshals Service. I'm Deputy Marshal Butler. Did you send the tip about Finn Donovan?"

"Yeah." Her gaze darted past him, toward the street, scanning the shadows like she expected someone to be watching.

"I'd like to ask you a few questions," Ethan said gently.

"Make it quick. My old man'll skin me alive if he finds out I talked to you."

"Where is he now?"

"Not here." The rasp in her voice hinted at cigarettes and sleepless nights.

"How do you know Donovan?"

"He's friends with my old man." She hitched the baby higher on her hip, eyes restless.

"When did you last see him?"

A siren screamed somewhere down the block. The woman flinched, her eyes going wide with terror.

"'Bout an hour ago," she whispered. "Said he was meeting some guy named Roger. And another one. Down at the old warehouse on State Street."

Ethan knew that place. Before he could press further, she slammed the door hard enough to rattle the frame.

He exhaled slowly. "Finally, something I can work with."

As he walked back to the SUV, the officer who'd gone with him muttered, "That woman's scared out of her mind. Hope she makes it through the night."

Ethan glanced back at the house—paint peeling, curtains drawn, silence pressing in. "Me too," he said quietly. "Come on, I need backup over to the warehouse."

As soon as they were done, he needed to check in with Stanton.

Ethan cranked the SUV and sped through town, his mouth set in a grim line. He navigated the narrow streets, dodging potholes, until he finally pulled in beside the other cop cars.

The warehouse rose out of the dark, empty and watchful. Graffiti covered the brown brick, and windows were missing panes. Pieces of metal were scattered across the faded blacktop. He sat in the truck for a second, observing the area. No sounds or activity came from the old building. A flock of crows sat on the electrical wire strung across the lot.

"I don't like this," he muttered to no one in particular.

He hadn't heard from Stanton or Aubrey. No calls, not even a text.

Ethan

Stanton, check in.
Where are you?

His phone indicated the text was sent, but no answering bubbles. Unread.

An overwhelming need to pray tightened his chest, his pulse thudding hard enough to hurt. Lately, it felt like his words vanished the moment they left him.

Please, God. Keep Aubrey safe.

FIFTEEN

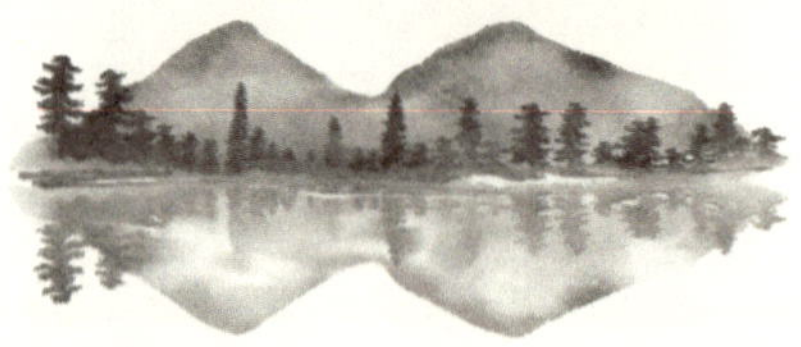

A DIM SHAFT OF SUNLIGHT PIERCED THROUGH her eyelids, and Aubrey grimaced.

She opened her eyes a sliver, only to be greeted by more pain with the light. Bile rose in her throat, and she licked her dry lips, the coppery taste of blood in her mouth. Her shoulder hurt from where she lay on the floor. She had to sit up, try to remove the ropes binding her wrists.

Think, Aubrey.

She inhaled slowly through her nose and exhaled through her mouth, trying to keep the nausea at bay. The old wooden floor was covered with dust, dead leaves, and other debris from the forest.

Using the wood beams of the wall and her good foot, she pushed herself up into a seated position, assessing her situation.

She heard voices through the door—one with Finn Donovan's dark tone, and the other man sounded familiar too.

"How long do you think she's gonna be asleep?" Finn asked.

The other man said, "I told you to be careful, not to hit her too hard. I told you to use the sedative."

Finn swore. "And I told you, I didn't have enough time. I caught the marshal in a blind spot and put him down. I shoved her through the window. Dead weight."

The sound of twigs breaking under their feet grew closer. Should she stay upright or pretend to be asleep? Their conversation paused, and Aubrey slowly lowered herself to the floor again.

Footsteps clomped across a porch or boards, wherever they were located. A few bird trills broke the silence. No traffic. No cars. Nothing.

They had to be back in the woods. But where? And if she was isolated with these two . . .

She closed her eyes as the door slammed open, and forced herself to slow her breathing. She hated to think what they'd do to her if they found out she was awake.

"Look, Rousseau, I helped you out, now help me out. The cops are lookin' for me all over. Do I need to remind you that I took out the judge for you after you screwed up and killed the housekeeper? You owe me. So after I make her suffer for what she did to me, you're gonna help me leave town."

Aubrey inhaled sharply, and Finn kicked her injured foot. Pain shot up her ankle and shin, and she winced, reluctantly opening her eyes.

"Well, well, well." Finn squatted in front of her, wrists resting on his knees. "Looks like the sleeping princess has awakened."

She watched as he took a stray strand of her hair and rubbed it between his dirty fingers.

"So soft."

Help me, Lord. She closed her eyes and swallowed back her fear. "What are you going to do with me?" She tried to sound brave, but her words were a weak whimper.

"Now, that depends." Finn stood.

"On what?" Aubrey watched him pace, wondering if Finn was in charge or if Rousseau was the boss here.

"On whether or not you tell us what you know about the judge," Rousseau said. "Why else do you think Donovan hasn't killed you yet?"

If she kept her head down, all she could see were the fancy Italian loafers that Rousseau wore and Donovan's scuffed biker boots.

She bit her lip. "I don't know what you're talking about."

"Sure you do." Now it was Rousseau's turn. She'd seen him in town. He even sponsored Renegade Days. His eyes were blocks of ice, his expression hard. "After all, you and the judge were, how shall I say it? Close?" His gaze traced to the top button of her blouse. "Pillow talk, right?"

"It wasn't like that."

"Oh, I'm sure it wasn't." Rousseau's laugh was condescending. "If you don't tell us where the judge kept the information on the syndicate, I'm gonna leave and let Finn do whatever he wants with you. Tell me and I'll kill you quickly."

"No, please." Her mouth was as dry as the Sahara Desert, the words raspy, scraping against her throat.

Ethan, where are you? Please, God, help him find me.

"*The Lord is my* rock and *my* fortress and *my* deliverer." Where had that Bible verse come from? Right. All those years ago, when Mom had made Aubrey and her sisters memorize a verse a week.

I trust You, Lord. She inhaled and began to pray.

Donovan grabbed her arm, his fingers digging into her flesh as he yanked her upright. "You better tell us the truth."

He squeezed harder, and she bit the inside of her cheek as he shoved her back against the wall, her head connecting. Stars swam in front of her, and her eyes watered from the impact.

She exhaled. "Just, let me catch my breath a moment. I need to think."

She only prayed she could stall them a little bit longer, until

Ethan found her. And if he didn't? Well, she'd be with Jesus, and that was an outcome she could live with.

Because she wouldn't be alone.

"Don't hurt me."

Ethan tossed his phone on his desk and leaned back in his chair. All that work for nothing.

The warehouse tip had gone nowhere. Hours burned, adrenaline wasted, the anticipated takedown collapsing into another dead end. False tips were part of the job—especially when there was a reward attached—but this one sat wrong.

Something was off.

A Post-it clung to his monitor in Aubrey's loopy scrawl.

Back by two. Have a doctor's appointment.

Ethan checked his watch.

Way after two. If she was running late, Stanton would've checked in. He was supposed to report every hour. It had been two hours since the last update.

Ethan pushed out of his chair and stepped into Liam's office. "Have you heard from Aubrey or Stanton?"

Liam shook his head. "No. Montgomery and Glover are over at Rousseau's place, asking mommy dearest a few questions."

Ethan nodded, but the unease didn't lift. He drifted back to Aubrey's desk, straightened a stack of files, busywork. He had to stay focused on Donovan. But where was she? Back at the safe house? He could call Jenna or the medical center. Find out when she'd left there.

Ethan dialed Jenna's number. "Hey, have you heard from Aubrey?"

"The woman you're supposed to be protecting?" Jenna asked. "That Aubrey?"

"One of the deputies took her to see her doctor. Have you heard from her?"

"Fine. She called me when she arrived at the doctor's office. Said Deputy Marshal Stanton was with her. I haven't heard from her since then."

"Call if you hear from her, okay?"

He went back to where Emma sat at Aubrey's desk. "Hey, where's Supervisor—"

She had the desk phone to her ear. "Yes, thank you."

Emma lowered the phone, her face pale.

"What is it?" Ethan's stomach churned.

"Police officers responded to a scene at the medical center. Aubrey's doctor's office. Stanton was found hit over the head, and EMTs have taken him to the hospital." She swallowed. "It doesn't look good." She took a deep breath, then added, "And no one can find Aubrey."

Ethan flinched. It had to be Donovan. Donovan had attacked Stanton.

And Aubrey was gone.

SIXTEEN

AUBREY LICKED HER DRY LIPS AND WINCED AS her tongue ran over the swollen part. She was so thirsty. How long had she been here? Shadows danced across the walls, and her shoulders felt as if they were stretched out of their sockets.

A third voice could be heard outside the flimsy cabin walls, and her cheeks hurt from being slapped. Donovan's hand had connected with her face multiple times before she'd passed out. Her throat was dry as sandpaper, and all she could taste was her own blood. Coppery and bitter.

She glanced down at her legs tied to the chair. Someone had removed the walking boot, and her left foot was now twice its normal size. Sharp pinpricks of pain skittered across her fingers, and she flexed them. With her injury, there was no way she could outrun her captors. She had to think. Outsmart them.

Please, God, help me.

Boots sounded on the porch planks, and she closed her eyes again. No way did she want them to think she'd awoken.

"How long do you think we have until those marshals figure out where she is?" Finn asked. She'd recognize his accent even with a blindfold on.

"How would I know? Could be on their way already."

One of the men grabbed her ponytail and yanked her head back. She yelped as needles of pain pulled at her scalp. "Told ya she was awake."

Aubrey opened her eyes and looked into the face of evil.

"Still refusing to talk?" Donovan lifted his hand to strike her, and she closed her eyes and braced for the contact. Only it didn't come.

Rousseau blocked his hand. "Donovan, just kill her. We can't let her go, and I don't want blood on my hands."

Donovan's evil grin made her squirm. "Oh, don't worry about that. You can save your own hide after I leave."

"This whole thing is a mess." Rousseau's phone buzzed. "Frost is on his way. He's ordered me to check with Howard."

From what Aubrey could tell, Rousseau didn't like being bossed around by Frost one bit.

Rousseau turned away. "Where are you? Hang on, I'm putting you on speaker."

"I couldn't get free." Howard's voice came through the phone speaker.

No. Aubrey's heart squeezed in her chest. Supervisor Howard?

Sending her up the mountain with those searchers made sense now. He'd wanted Donovan to find her.

Her boss said, "All my deputies are out looking for Donovan. You're on your own."

"And you're sure no one suspects you?" Donovan asked over his shoulder, his attention off Aubrey for a second.

"Positive," Howard said. "I've got the whole team out chasing phone signals, looking for our admin. You guys just need to make sure Mullinax didn't snitch to her." Car brakes squealed over the line. "I'm outside, coming in. Don't shoot me." The call ended.

Finn's voice was low and menacing. "You won't have to worry about her talking. I'll make sure she never says a word about me or you. Ever."

This was it. They meant to kill her. Fear surged through her body, hot and sharp. But she clung to one unshakable certainty—Ethan would come for her. She believed that with every breath she had left. And when he did, she would be able to give him important information again.

She needed these guys to tell her more.

Her lungs constricted as she listened to their conversation. Burned for lack of oxygen.

"Too mouthy for your own good, aren't you?" Rousseau grabbed a handful of her hair and yanked her head hard.

Flashes of pain pierced her scalp, her neck held at an odd angle, and she yelped, tried to move out of his grasp.

"It's too late." His hot breath almost choked the oxygen from her. But something told her he was just trying to act like he was in charge.

Was Frost the head of the syndicate?

Or someone else?

"Please . . . don't." The pain intensified the harder he twisted her hair. Her eyes clouded with tears.

The door flung open and her boss strode in. Rousseau let go of her.

"Supervisor Howard, I don't understand . . ."

Howard's reply carried a quiet edge of satisfaction. "Don't understand what, Aubrey? Why I'm helping the syndicate? Fixing federal cases for the syndicate? Manipulating investigations?"

He didn't wait for an answer before continuing. "Money. It makes the world go around." His bravado cracked, and she saw fury beneath his expression. "My wife cleaned me out when she left me. I have nothing. The syndicate pays well."

"Nothing but your oath." Aubrey croaked out the words. "Which you betrayed."

"Honor doesn't pay the bills."

Aubrey closed her eyes for a moment. "And the judge? Did you set him up?"

"Judge Mullinax was useful, for a time. Fixing trials. But then he developed a conscience. He was compromised, like the rest of us. But he wouldn't stay in line."

"I can't believe it." She closed her eyes at the thought of the judge's betrayal. Had she ever really known him?

"Believe it, Ms. Richardson. Your boyfriend sold out his oath and handed classified information to the cartel."

Donovan smirked, and she leaned away from his evil presence. He grabbed her chin between his fingers and pinched. "Turns out you were simply a means to an end, darlin'. Someone else he could manipulate."

No. The tears flowed freely now. She knew Stephen. He'd been her friend for years. She had to believe that the lies had come later—when he'd realized he was backed into a corner by these people.

"But why? Why not just scare him?" Aubrey's gaze bounced between the men.

"Where's the fun in that, darlin'?" Donovan leaned into her space. "I was brought in here to do a job." His smile thinned. "Turns out killing you is a perk." He dragged the knife along the scruff on his chin.

The word settled in her chest like a shard of ice.

Perk.

Aubrey swallowed. "Aren't you tired of all the killing? Being in jail or on the run?" Why live like this when redemption was possible?

For a moment, Donovan simply stared at her. Then his mouth curved, slow and humorless. "Listen to you." He leaned closer, his breath sour with tobacco. "Still trying to save souls."

Rousseau snorted somewhere behind her.

The faint *whomp-whomp* of a helicopter echoed across the mountain range. Conversation died. The men paused, listening, while Aubrey craned her neck toward the small window.

Her stomach dropped as the aircraft banked away from their position.

Almost dusk. No way Butler would find her tonight.

Even so, the men traded sharp, uneasy looks.

"I don't need any additional felonies added to my criminal record." Howard strode out of the cabin, the door slamming hard against its hinges.

Rousseau began pacing the length of the room, fists clenched at his sides. "You know the syndicate and Frost won't like it if we leave evidence behind."

"Calm down, Rousseau." Finn pushed off the wall and moved in closer. "What we do now depends on the little lady."

Donovan ran a dirty finger down her cheek, his cheap aftershave combined with body odor overpowering in the small space. He pulled a knife from his jacket and pressed the blade into the soft skin on her neck.

She whimpered. She didn't dare breathe for fear that he'd slice her open.

"You know, I could make you bleed out with a thousand tiny cuts."

He continued to push the knife tip into the soft skin of her cheek. Her neck. Her arm.

She cried out.

Fear seized her, paralyzing her mind. She couldn't push back, couldn't even form the words. Donovan's gaze raked over her, lewd and calculating. The cramped cabin pulsed with menace, and she shivered. She heard the chopper again, making another pass. Rescue was close. She shut her eyes in relief. *Jesus, help me! Keep me safe.*

"You know what? I'm leaving too." Rousseau stared at Aubrey a moment and then turned. "I don't need to be caught with you, Donovan."

He darted out of the cabin, leaving Aubrey alone with her nightmare.

She pushed down her fear and met Donovan's gaze. His eyes had a crazed look, dark and void as a night sky with no light.

Aubrey's heart pounded out a frantic rhythm. The events of the day she lost her sister repeated on an endless loop. *Please, God, send Ethan.*

"You really thought I wouldn't corner you at the doctor's office?" Donovan said, amused.

Aubrey forced a breath. His smirk didn't reach his eyes—those were flat and hungry.

"Howard stumbled across your connection to me completely by accident, you know," he continued conversationally, as though they were simply passing the time of day. "Got curious about your relationship with the judge, looked into your past. When they realized it was time for the judge to go, Rousseau contacted me. Made me an offer I couldn't refuse."

His words landed like stones in her stomach.

"Why kill the judge?"

Donovan's grin widened. "Frost and Rousseau wanted him gone." He shrugged as though that explained everything. "I helped them make that happen, and they helped me out of prison. Fair trade." He flicked his thumb along the knife's edge until a drop of his own blood dangled off the sharp tip. "Now I get to give you what you deserve. And ending the lives of some marshals in the process? That's dessert."

Her stomach dropped. Whoever came for her would be walking

into a trap. "Butler—" She shook her head. "You don't have to do this. You can let me go."

He moved into her space, his rancid breath ghosting across her face, and she recoiled. "The syndicate wants Ethan dead. He's been snooping around Roger's activities, talking to people he should never have talked to." His evil grin soured her stomach. "When Ethan comes for you, I'm gonna kill him too." Donovan looked like a caged animal, his body wound tight as a spring, ready to pounce.

Waiting for something—or someone.

Aubrey had to look away. She cleared her throat. A cold sweat covered her body. "I'm thirsty. Can I get a drink of water?"

Donovan grunted and held a bottle of water to her lips.

She drank greedily, but the water had a funny aftertaste. "Thank you." Her vision swam. "What was in that water?"

Donovan laughed. "Yeah, a little something to make you more compliant. That way, when Butler shows up, you won't be able to warn him he's in danger." He checked the window and then sat on the floor, his back propped against the closed door. "And afterward, we can finish our business. We'll have as long as I want to take."

No.

Her eyelids grew heavier, and she struggled to sit upright. A silent prayer was on her lips for protection for herself and Ethan.

But unable to stay awake, she couldn't form the words.

Ethan paced in front of Renegade Mountain State Park. The location-sharing app on Jenna's phone said that Aubrey was here.

A long shot, but he was willing to follow any lead if it meant he got her back.

The tops of the pine trees swayed in the early-evening breeze, and the deep purple of night descended over the area. No one was at the small picnic shelter other than a family of raccoons digging through the trash.

This couldn't be right.

He called the office, but it went straight to the main voicemail box. Emma had gone to the hospital to find out if Stanton would recover, but where was Howard?

Liam jogged up to him, out of breath. "Nothing, Butler. There's no sign of her around here, and the cabin is empty. They haven't returned to it."

"Either they messed with her phone or we're missing something." And they had no idea where to search for her.

The raccoons tipped over the trash can and scurried away. A flash of silver caught his eye. Ethan knelt and used a twig to move away some of the wrappers and uneaten food. There, among a pile of cold fries, sat a phone.

He stood and pulled his phone from his pocket and called Aubrey's number. The phone on the ground vibrated and rang.

Ethan swore under his breath. "They obviously left the phone here to send us on a wild-goose chase." He kicked the pile of trash and stomped away, trying to get his emotions under control. Lack of control had cost him his team two years ago, and he was determined not to make the same mistake.

Liam, Montgomery, and Glover stood around in a circle, staring at the pile of trash.

"So, what are we going to do now?" Glover asked.

"It's late." Montgomery gestured at the sky. "We're running out of daylight."

"You don't think I know this?" Ethan felt anger rising, his face flooding with heat. He paced away from the group and inhaled, looking up at the sky.

God, I need wisdom.

Guilt tripped him up, and he turned back to look at his team. Regret and shame for his outburst heated his skin. He kicked a rock, bouncing it into the trash. "I'm sorry, guys. That wasn't necessary. I'm simply frustrated."

"We all are." Liam placed a hand on his shoulder and squeezed.

Ethan pinched the bridge of his nose. "Aubrey needs us. She's alone out here with a killer."

If he lost her now, he didn't know what he'd do.

He swallowed back all the emotion from the past few days. "I'd like to pray over her, and all of us, if you're so inclined." He held out both hands, needing the connection to stay grounded.

Ethan prayed.

He ended with a hushed amen, and the moment felt anchored in something bigger than them all.

A ball of emotion clogged his throat, and he looked at his team with a new appreciation. "I know not everyone is a believer, but I want to thank you for being here. We *will* find Aubrey."

Liam nodded in agreement.

Ethan thought about Stanton, in critical condition, fighting for his life. "We need our Sunshine back in the office."

Every person assembled nodded in agreement. He needed Aubrey—and once they rescued her, he would make sure she knew it.

"We move forward, but nobody goes anywhere alone. Whoever has Aubrey is still out there." Ethan nodded to his team, standing here in the fading light, determination on their faces.

A cool breeze kicked up some debris, and it tumbled across the picnic area.

"Albright and Glover, head into town," Ethan said. "Check the doctor's office again and the surrounding area. See if any other witnesses might've seen a car or where they went. Adam, Liam, and I will head over to Destiny Rousseau's house. I'm fairly certain she knows where Roger is hanging out and is our best lead."

Liam nodded. "She knows something but will protect her son at any cost. We just need the right leverage."

Ethan checked his watch. "Everyone checks in every half hour, beginning in thirty minutes."

The teams split up and headed their separate ways.

"You really think you'll be able to get any information out of Destiny?" Adam asked. "Seems like we've already been over things with her."

Ethan cranked his truck. "Roger is up to his neck in this, just like his dad was. She knows more than she's saying."

"Yeah, and we're running out of daylight." Liam's mouth was set in a tight line.

Tall pines flanked the entrance, and the driveway wound about half a mile through lush landscaping.

Ethan rang the doorbell, and this time a maid in a black uniform with a crisp white apron answered the door.

She squinted up at them. "Can I help you?"

Ethan stepped forward. "Yes, ma'am. I'm Deputy US Marshal Ethan Butler, and these are my associates, Deputy Marshals Roberts and Montgomery." He showed her his badge.

Her eyes widened. "I'm sorry, sir, but Mrs. Rousseau is otherwise engaged."

Destiny Rousseau sauntered up to the door just then, her deep-red dress accentuating her curves. "Miranda. Who do we have here?"

The maid looked over her shoulder and then stepped back. "They say they're from the Marshals office."

"Ah, yes, Deputy Marshal Butler. We meet again. As you can see, I'm rather busy with a Renegade Ladies' Auxiliary meeting. We're discussing improvements for the more unfortunate areas of Renegade."

Poor. Why didn't she just say the word *poor*? What a load of fake concern.

Ethan cleared his throat, forced himself to bite his tongue and not say what was really on his mind. "I promise I won't take up much of your time."

Destiny paused a moment. "In that case, come in."

They stepped into the marble-tiled foyer. Adam and Liam looked as uncomfortable as he felt among this opulence.

"Miranda, please show our guests to the sitting room. I'll be right back."

Destiny strolled on those impossibly high heels, clicking against the marble floor. Feminine voices drifted down the hallway.

Ethan studied the pictures over the mantel. Most of them were of Roger when he was young. Roger riding his bicycle in the driveway. Roger, probably pre-teen, holding up a small fish, the catch still attached to his kid-sized fishing rod. A teenage Roger in his high school soccer team uniform.

"Ah, I see you found my little gallery of Roger's exploits." Destiny took one of the photos and gazed at it, her eyes unfocused, as if seeing Roger as a little boy.

"Yeah. Looks like he had a great childhood." Unlike Ethan's. His had been full of uncertainty, until his grandma rescued him and took him home to live with her.

"I thought I answered all your questions when you were here a few days ago." Destiny glided onto the small love seat, crossed her ankles. Always the lady. But there was a sinister element underneath that polished exterior.

Ethan sat across from her. "I'll get right down to it. Do you happen to know where Roger is tonight?"

She laughed and waved her hand. "He's a forty-year-old man. He does what he wants. You really think he checks in with his mother?"

Ethan was beginning to think the guy did. "Roger is involved with the kidnapping of a woman who works for the Marshals office."

He waited for that to sink in.

"When was the last time you saw him?"

Her face seemed pinched. "Two days ago."

"Did he seem upset?" Liam asked.

Ethan studied her, and he was impressed she didn't shift in her seat.

"No. Why would he be?" She arched one eyebrow.

Ethan raised his hands. "Hey, we have to cover all our bases." He forced himself to smile. "Where is he now?"

"I have no idea."

"Where would he go? Does he have a place he hides?"

Destiny sighed, rising in one graceful motion. "If that's all, Deputy Marshal?" She let the question hang, daring him to keep her any longer than necessary. "I have nothing more to say."

And he'd need a warrant to press her further—which meant enough probable cause for a judge's signature. Ethan's head pounded. "We're finished. Thank you again for your time."

Off to the side of the main foyer, a foam-core board was placed on an easel, a small light illuminating an artist's rendering.

Ethan leaned in and studied the poster. "Adam, Liam. Look at this."

The other two leaned in, and a look of understanding passed between them. Out of the way. Not much traffic. Perfect place for someone like Donovan to hide.

"Excuse me, Mrs. Rousseau," Adam said.

She paused, and he watched as she visibly stiffened her back. When she turned around, a saccharine sweet smile graced her face. "Yes. Is there something else?"

Adam pointed to the diagram. "This your property?"

Destiny crossed her arms. "Yes. What of it? My dear husband left that farmland to me when he passed. We're in the process of developing all one hundred acres of it. We're calling it Rousseau's Landing. Higher-end homes with a mountain view."

Liam chimed in. "Did Roger ever go out there?"

She shrugged. "Sometimes. We've had problems with trespassers lately. He keeps the riffraff away."

"I see," Liam said.

She stared at Liam a moment and then gave the maid instructions. "Miranda, will you see the gentlemen out, please." She smiled at Ethan. "Always a pleasure, Deputy Marshal Butler."

Leaving the house, they quickly returned to his truck.

Ethan said, "Liam, text the other team members. Tell them to gear up. Get Glover to send us some aerial views too. We're going to get Aubrey tonight."

SEVENTEEN

AUBREY'S NOSE TICKLED AND SHE SNEEZED. Disoriented, she slowly opened her eyes.

Her backside was numb from sleeping in one position. Her shoulders were stiff from being tied behind her back. And her muscles spasmed from being held in one position. An ache settled in her jaw from where Donovan had slapped her repeatedly. Her foot was throbbing, stabbing pain climbing up her calf and thighs. She tried to move her ankle, but it was still swollen, and she couldn't move it without causing more pain.

A dim shaft of moonlight illuminated the old cabin. A whippoorwill cried a plaintive night song. It must be perched on a nearby tree. They were alone out here, in the middle of nowhere. She couldn't do anything. Except pray.

Please, God, let Ethan find me.

Maybe that was the point. Even in her darkest times, she'd forgotten to pray. She was so paralyzed with fear and grief, she'd forgotten to reach out to the Lord.

Her gaze drifted to the man who held her captive. He not only held her captive this night, but mentally, she'd been a prisoner to her fear. She could no longer live in fear. What was that verse? *Perfect love casts out fear*. God's love for her was perfect, and regardless of how this night ended, He loved her and wanted the best for her. Whatever that outcome looked like.

Selfishly, she wanted more time with Ethan.

Donovan's snores filled the small cabin. He sat propped up in the corner, facing her, a knife still clutched in his hand.

What was he waiting for? Why didn't he simply kill her now?

Donovan shifted in his sleep. Even though he appeared to be relaxed, there was tension in his body language.

You are my strong tower, Lord.

Donovan's entire body jerked, and he scrambled to his feet. Disoriented for a moment, he scanned the small interior, a crazed look in his eyes. "What's that? Who's there?"

"I didn't hear anything."

"Shut up!"

Aubrey clamped her mouth shut. Donovan was unstable, and she didn't want to chance another smack across her face.

All she heard was the wind whispering through the trees and the swishing of the overgrown grass. A lone owl called to its mate.

Donovan paced the interior of the small cabin. His frenetic motions were scaring her. He checked one window, then the other. Back and forth, checking and rechecking.

"Why did Rousseau leave?" A muttered curse followed the question. "He should be here with me. This was all his idea." He spoke to no one in particular, and his arms flailed wildly, as if he were fighting off some invisible opponent. He rummaged in his backpack and pulled out a brown bottle of whiskey, uncapped it, and took a long swig.

Fear unlike any fear she'd ever known raced through her body, and she shivered. This wasn't normal behavior. He was like a man possessed.

He paused, his chest rising and falling rapidly as he yanked his phone out of his pocket. It looked like one of those cheap burner phones. The kind that was untraceable.

Donovan glanced over his shoulder at her, spearing her with a look, and she shrank back in her seat. He resumed looking out the window.

"Rousseau, where are you?" Donovan screamed into the phone. "I need transport out of this town."

"I told you I was leaving." Roger's voice filled the tiny space. Donovan must've put the phone on speaker.

"That wasn't the plan." Donovan kicked the empty bottle across the room, and it shattered when it hit the wall. Dark-brown splinters of glass littered the floor.

"Maybe not, but guess what? Plans change." Rousseau's answer sent Donovan into another fit of rage. "It's following orders. You never did learn who was in charge here."

"I was stuck in that crummy jail cell for almost twenty years. This was supposed to be my way out. A new life. I want my money."

"Cry me a river. Stick to the plan and it'll work. And the money? Well, that's not up to me. You need to contact Frost if you wanna get paid."

Icy tendrils of fear swirled around Aubrey's chest.

Rousseau paused before answering. "Turns out freedom's just another kind of cage. You do their dirty work, or you end up in the ground with the rest of the ghosts."

Donovan swung around. "So tell me, Roger, what do I do with her?"

"She was your priority," Rousseau said. "Handle it, and those marshals."

Donovan inhaled through his nose, jaw flexing. He shoved the knife back into its sheath and resumed pacing. "I thought you said there'd be food in this dump. I'm starving."

"Well, that's a you problem now." Rousseau's voice oozed irritation through the phone. "Mother told me the Marshals were snooping around her house again today. I couldn't even go home for my bags. I'm not risking getting caught with you."

A flicker of hope sparked in Aubrey's chest. The Marshals were close—close enough to make Rousseau refuse to return. She bit her lip to keep from crying, forced herself to stay still.

"You owe me!" Donovan barked, pacing. "We had a deal!"

"I owe you nothing," Rousseau snapped. "You were sloppy. You were almost arrested yesterday, which is why I've already left. They'll never find me."

Donovan's jaw clenched. He ran the knife blade up and down his thigh, the scrape of metal against denim a steady threat. "You left me to take the fall."

Roger tsk'd. "Face it, Donovan. The Marshals were going to catch you eventually. Don't ever call me again. What's a few more years to a life sentence?"

The call ended with a laugh that curdled into static.

Donovan stared at the phone for a long moment before hurling it against the wall. It shattered—Aubrey's last hope of contact splintering with it.

When he turned back, rage had hardened into something colder, quieter. He stalked toward her, his steps deliberate, a predator choosing how to corner its prey.

Aubrey forced herself to meet his gaze. If she was going to suffer, she would memorize every detail—his expression, his words—so that when Ethan found her, she could tell him exactly what had happened.

Donovan stopped, eyes glassy and distant. For a second, his head tilted, as if listening to a voice only he could hear. He nodded once, lips twitching in a private conversation.

He's gone. Completely gone.

Then he moved. In a blur, he crossed the room, fisting a handful of her hair. Pain tore through her scalp. His breath hit her cheek—stale, sharp, reeking of whiskey and rage.

"Since we're alone up here"—he dragged the knife along her jawline in a slow, deliberate swirl—"we might as well pass the time. What do you say, Red?"

A tear slipped free, hot and unwanted. "No." Her voice trembled, her chest tightening as panic clawed at her ribs. "They betrayed you. It's over. Just leave me and go."

The knife traced her throat like a lover's touch turned cruel. He smiled—a dead, joyless expression. "Except for one thing. You and me, we've got history."

He stepped back, pacing again, restless energy radiating off him. Aubrey's mind screamed at her to stay calm, to *wait.* A flash of light cut through the window—brief but unmistakable. Not moonlight. Not a passing car.

Her heart surged. *Ethan.*

Donovan froze. Every muscle in his body went taut. "You hear that?"

She nodded once, pulse thundering in her ears.

"That's what I thought." A grin split his face, wild and unhinged. "Knew Butler would head this way eventually. Too bad we won't get to catch up before he dies."

Laughter erupted from him, jagged and mad.

Aubrey's body trembled, but beneath the terror, there was relief—sharp, fierce, and alive. This wasn't over. If she didn't make it out, Ethan would, surely. But she prayed they'd both live, because her future was freedom.

And Ethan.

Ethan parked his truck on an empty stretch of Highway 19, near Middleton Mountain. This part of Renegade wasn't as heavily populated.

The nearest neighbors were at least a mile or two down the road—perfect for hiding out. Too perfect.

Ethan and Liam climbed out of the truck. A low rumble of thunder rolled through the valley, wind whipping leaves and grit around their boots. Ethan hit the lock on his key fob, the sharp beep echoing against the darkening sky. Together, they started unloading the ATVs.

"Thanks, man." Ethan tightened a strap that didn't need tightening. "This means a lot."

Liam gave him a look. "I get it. I know what it's like to believe you might lose the person you love."

Love. The word hit harder than the wind.

Did he love Aubrey? The answer rose before he could stop it—*yeah, he did.* Somewhere between her stubborn questions and that soft, fierce smile, she'd broken through the walls he'd thought were permanent.

He'd spent too long pretending he didn't need anyone. Too long confusing control with safety. It had cost him more than he cared to admit.

Not this time. Not with her.

He climbed onto the ATV, jaw tight with determination. Once he found Aubrey, he wouldn't let fear—or pride—keep him silent another second.

The rest of the marshals pulled up, headlights cutting through the dusk. Doors slammed. They moved with practiced precision—vests, weapons, spare magazines clicking into place. Albright hefted a sniper rifle and slung it over his shoulder.

Everyone's phones pinged with the incoming aerial shots of the Rousseau development.

“Good work, Glover.” Ethan scanned the map. “If anyone gets separated, rendezvous at Highway 19 West and Hilliard Road.”

“Renegade PD is on the way too,” Adam added.

Ethan looked around at his team—his family—and sent up a silent prayer of gratitude. “This marks the start of Rousseau property.” He pointed to the Coming Soon sign driven into the shoulder. “I want you to know I’m thankful for each one of you.”

In the fading light, determination—and a flicker of pride—crossed their faces.

“Liam and I will take the far end near the tree line with the ATVs. Albright, Glover—head east. Montgomery—go west. Check everything. Phones on silent, ten-minute text check-ins. Let’s move.”

Engines roared to life. The wind picked up, carrying the scent of rain and pine.

Ethan spotted a narrow footpath disappearing into the trees. “Let’s head that way,” he shouted over the roar.

Liam nodded. They throttled forward, headlights slashing through the gloom as the storm gathered strength. Leaves and debris lashed their faces.

“I don’t like this,” Liam called. “We’re losing light.”

“I know. A few more structures though. We have to check everywhere.”

Ethan raised a hand, bringing them to a stop. Engines off. Silence. The headlights illuminated an old cabin—weathered, but intact.

His phone buzzed.

Albright

Found an old barn. Glover and I are searching now.

Ethan

Head our way as soon as you’re done. Liam and I found a

cabin. Looks occupied. Sharing coordinates.

He ducked behind his ATV, eyes fixed on the faint glow from within. A man's silhouette shifted across the window. Ethan drew his weapon, motioning for Liam to take position behind a ponderosa pine flanking the cabin.

"Scope the back," he murmured. "I'll take the front."

Liam nodded once and slipped into the shadows.

Ethan crept forward, crouching beneath the window, back pressed to the wall. Voices drifted through the boards.

"Psst." Liam appeared at his shoulder. "No exits on the back."

Ethan nodded. He risked a glance through the glass.

Aubrey. Tied to a chair, eyes closed as if bracing against a strike. His chest tightened. *Hang on, sweetheart.*

He mouthed her name to Liam—*Aubrey.* Then motioned for him to take the far side of the door.

Ethan (to group)

Found Aubrey. Hurry.

A muffled scream sliced through the night.

That was all it took.

Ethan signaled the count.

Three.

Two.

One.

Liam's booted foot slammed the door open. "US Marshals! Don't move!"

Ethan followed, his weapon raised.

Donovan stood behind Aubrey, one hand pressing a knife against her throat. Her left foot was bare and swollen, and a dark bruise bloomed across her cheek. With his other hand, Finn held a gun pointed at them. An automatic that would tear through them with a spray of bullets the second he squeezed the trigger.

Ethan's heart pounded, but he forced himself to stay calm.

Liam yelled, "Drop the weapons, Donovan. It's over."

"It's over for her. And for you," Finn said.

A deep thrum cut through the air—the distant chop of helicopter blades. Too far to help, but close enough to distract the guy. Donovan's head snapped upward. Confusion flickered across his face.

Ethan aimed over Aubrey's shoulder and squeezed the trigger. Glass exploded in the window behind Donovan. Donovan screamed, dropping the knife as the force of the hit knocked him back against the wall, blood on his shoulder.

Ethan kicked away the gun and grabbed Aubrey.

Liam lunged for Donovan, pinning him to the floor with a knee in his back. "Hands behind your head!"

Donovan thrashed, shouting, "My shoulder! You shot me!"

Liam cuffed him with efficient precision.

Ethan untied Aubrey's hands and feet, crouching in front of her. "We'll get a medic." She had cuts all over. She needed a hospital.

She flexed her fingers, wincing. Tears in her eyes. "Thank God you found me."

"I thought you were dead. Thank God," Ethan murmured, brushing her hair back gently. "I thought I might've lost you."

Liam hauled Donovan to his feet. "Glad you're okay, Aubrey."

Aubrey managed a faint smile. "Me too."

"What did that animal do to you?" Ethan asked, fingers skimming her bruised cheek.

"Nothing a little ice and rest won't fix."

Ethan raised one brow.

"And three weeks off, and six months of physical therapy. But who's counting?"

Ethan smiled. "Come on, let's get you out of here."

She looked up at him, those green eyes raw and luminous. Something in the air shifted—quiet but undeniable.

"All I could think about," she whispered, "was that I had to survive. I had to tell you how I feel."

Emotion surged in his chest, nearly undoing him. "That's a conversation for another time," he said softly. "But when that time comes . . . I'm ready." He slipped an arm around her waist. When she faltered, he lifted her easily into his arms. "Haven't we done this before?"

Aubrey smiled weakly and rested her head against his chest, then stiffened. "Roger Rousseau was here. And Supervisor Howard. He's part of all this."

Ethan nearly dropped her. "Howard?"

Aubrey nodded, tears falling from her eyes.

He spun with her and went to the door. "Montgomery!"

Rotor blades thundered overhead as the medevac helicopter settled into the clearing, pine needles and dust whipping through the air. Swallowing his words.

Ethan stepped forward, Aubrey still in his arms.

Renegade PD closed in immediately, securing Donovan and hauling him to a patrol car with Liam watching.

Two EMTs, one of them their friend Mack, jogged toward Ethan with a stretcher. "We've got her."

Ethan laid Aubrey down carefully, his hands lingering until the EMTs secured her straps and fitted an oxygen mask over her face. He stayed there, close, until they lifted her into the helicopter.

The EMT hesitated. "We can take you—"

"Go," Ethan said firmly. "Get her to the hospital. I'll be there shortly."

The doors slammed shut. The helicopter lifted, its searchlight sweeping once over the trees before disappearing into the night.

Ethan stood beside Liam, the lights from the ATVs casting long shadows across the mud.

"Well done, Ethan," Liam said, stepping up beside him.

Ethan didn't look away from the sky. "You need to head back to the office. I want eyes on Howard, now."

Liam's expression sharpened.

"Aubrey says he was here. He's the mole," Ethan said. "And I don't want him leaving that building."

"We'll handle it," Liam said. "He won't get away."

EIGHTEEN

AUBREY GLANCED DOWN AT HER ELEVATED AND bandaged ankle. A sharp stab of pain tore through her foot, and she inhaled, teeth clenched. The sterile tang of antiseptic filled her nose. This wasn't a dream. She was safe now, right? Rosy light spilled through a gap in the hospital curtains. She wanted nothing more than to go home.

She remembered Ethan's words from last night—the warmth, the safety in his voice—and let that peace wash over her.

"It's good to see you're awake."

The unexpected, yet oh so familiar, voice froze her mid-breath. Panic rippled through her veins. Slowly, she turned toward the shadow in the corner.

Supervisor Howard stood and stepped into the thin morning light.

She gasped. "What are you doing here?"

"Can't a supervisor check on his employee?"

Her heart hammered. *Where's the call button?* Under the

blanket, she fumbled for the nurse's pull string—but it was gone. He must've moved it while she slept.

Howard came closer, the fluorescent light catching the wild look in his eyes. His shirt and dress pants were rumpled, a beard shadowing his jaw. He looked unhinged.

"The nurse should be coming soon," she stammered. "They'll find you here."

He shook his head, fingers gripping the bedrail. "No, she's not. I told the nurses I needed to take your statement. Flashed the badge at them and they were happy to give us privacy." He pulled a chair close to her bed. "And the cop outside your door? Well, I told him to take a break."

He drew his service weapon and traced the cold barrel along her jaw.

Her breath hitched.

"You heard everything in that cabin," he said quietly. "But have you told anyone?"

Her pulse pounded in her ears. "You've been with the Marshals a long time," she said, hoping to stall him. "And you helped a fugitive escape from prison. How could you?"

He scowled. "I already told you. The syndicate knew I needed money. I was in deep, but I had a handle on it. I was making it work. Then your *hero*—Butler—shows up. The poster boy for perfection, and he's looking too closely. Sticking his nose where it doesn't belong."

"Ethan is good at his job. You should've known better."

He laughed—a dry, humorless sound. "That's what they all say before they stab you in the back." He dragged the chair closer, the gun steady. "You've ruined everything for me. Thanks to you not dying when you should have and Butler looking where he shouldn't, I've lost my career. But I'm not going down without a fight. You're going to testify at my trial that I had no choice. They forced me to help Donovan."

The door opened and Ethan stepped into the room, holding a massive bouquet of pink roses. Relief flared, then died the instant she followed his gaze.

The gun.

Howard swung it toward Ethan, his smile sharp and wrong. "Hold it right there, Butler. This is perfect."

Ethan tossed the flowers on a chair and stopped just inside the room. He reached for his gun. "Howard. You don't want to do this."

"Oh, I do." Howard didn't lower his gun. "Don't draw. I'll kill you."

"Let her go," Ethan said, his voice steady. "It's me you want."

Howard laughed softly. "You just couldn't leave any of it alone, could you?"

"You did this to yourself," Ethan said.

Behind Aubrey, the heart monitor spiked, its rapid beeping slicing through the room. She saw movement in the doorway. Shadows. Bodies. Liam surged in first, Adam right behind him. Then Albright and Glover with their weapons raised, filling the space so fast it stole her breath.

"Drop the gun." Liam's command was quiet but lethal.

Howard twisted, as if he wanted to drag her with him. Glass exploded around her, raining down on her bare arms. Aubrey covered her head, and Glover pulled her off the side of the bed, away from them.

She hit the floor with a yelp, Glover covering her.

On the other side of the bed, the gun flew from Howard's hand, skidding across the floor. Aubrey ducked just as Ethan slammed into Howard, driving him back into the chair. The impact rattled the room.

Shouts and yelling filled the air.

On the floor, Ethan rolled Howard over and pinned a knee to his back, then snapped the metal cuffs on him.

Aubrey sagged against the marshal next to her, and Glover patted her shoulder. "Let's get you back in bed. Thank goodness that glass was tempered."

Glover cleared as much of the pebble-like glass from the bed as she could, then helped Aubrey as she stumbled over to the bed and sat, wrapping her arms around her shaking body. Having another woman here made her wonder how Emma was doing after the accident.

Ethan straightened and hauled Howard to his feet. "Game over."

Ethan's eyes found hers immediately, and for the first time since this nightmare began, she believed that it was finally done. "Aubrey, you okay?"

Ethan handed Howard off to Liam and came over.

Aubrey nodded. "Where's Emma? And Stanton?"

"You have the right to remain silent . . ." Liam's voice receded as they disappeared out the door. The others slipped away.

Ethan extended a hand—solid, grounding. "We've got to stop meeting like this."

She laughed shakily, tears blurring her vision. "Answer my question."

"Emma was heading up to visit you. She was released earlier. Stanton . . ." He sat beside her, eyes softening. Filling with grief. "Stanton didn't make it. I'm sorry, Aubrey, but he passed away."

She let the tears flow, holding tight to Ethan for a long time.

Eventually he said, "When we get out of here"—he rested his forehead against hers—"I'm going to take you out on a proper date. Even give you a proper kiss."

"Promises, promises," she whispered.

"Oh, that's not a promise." His grin deepened. "That's a guarantee."

Ethan was bone weary, full of grief and exhaustion.

The last five days had wrung him out physically and mentally and torn him apart in ways he didn't want to examine too closely yet. But Aubrey was alive. Safe. That truth was the only thing keeping him upright.

She was still at the hospital. The doctor had insisted on keeping her overnight for observation, given the bruising and dehydration. Ethan had sat by her bed until she finally fell into a deep, exhausted sleep, and only allowed himself to leave when the nurses shooed him out.

Finn Donovan was in custody. Howard too.

That last truth still felt unreal.

As unreal as Stanton being gone.

Supervisor Howard, the man he'd trusted, worked beside, defended, had been dirty the whole time. Bugging their offices. Feeding information back to the syndicate. Playing both sides. Standing in plain sight while everything else burned.

Ethan sat in his office now, drowning in paperwork, signatures, and after-action reports. He stifled a yawn. All the caffeine in the world wouldn't clear the fog from his brain. It was hard not to notice how quickly things had shifted, how it looked like he would be in charge until someone from DC made it clear otherwise.

Acting supervisor. Maybe even permanently in the position soon.

Liam stood in the doorway, arms folded. "It's been an exciting few days around here."

"That's an understatement," Ethan said, rubbing a hand over his face. "Any word on Rousseau?"

"Nope. But we have a couple of visitors."

He closed his laptop. "Renegade PD?"

"Yep. And the FBI."

Ethan knocked on Adam's door. "Hey, Montgomery. Meeting in five minutes. Round up the rest of the team."

"You got it."

Ethan glanced at his watch. Shoot. He'd forgotten to feed Mrs. Hanover's cats last night. And the cupcakes Aubrey had baked for Liam's niece were still sitting in his office. He'd take care of the cats once he returned from this last meeting.

The team filed into the conference room and stopped to shake hands with FBI Special Agent Rudy Patterson and Detective Michael Martinelli from Renegade PD, who were already seated.

"Good trip?" Ethan asked Michael.

The guy tipped his head to the side. "Training course. I'm now bomb squad certified."

"Good to know." Ethan smiled and went to the front of the room.

After everyone was seated, Ethan stood. "I know it's been a couple of long days here in the Marshals office." He let his gaze move slowly around the room. Familiar faces. People he trusted. "Yesterday didn't just test us in the field; it tested what this badge is supposed to mean."

The room was quiet now. No one reached for their coffee.

"Our boss betrayed that trust." Ethan didn't soften it. "And I know that hits hard for us marshals. It should."

A few heads nodded.

"But what matters is what happened next," Ethan continued. "You showed up. You followed the facts, not the politics. You protected one of our own, and you did the job the right way, even when it cost us."

He paused, the room blurring for a split second as memory surged—another briefing, another pile of grief to work through.

"Deputy Marshal Stanton didn't make it." Ethan's voice tightened despite his control. "He died at the hospital. And that's a loss we all carry."

Silence closed in.

Ethan swallowed hard. This was the part that never got easier. Different faces. Same weight. Same reckoning.

"I've stood in this spot before," he continued, quieter now. "I know what it means to lose one of your own. And I know what it costs the people who stay."

He lifted his gaze, meeting theirs. Steady, present, but unmistakably affected.

Glover sniffled and dabbed away the moisture on her face.

"Stanton did his job. He protected this team every day, and he gave his life for his asset. And because of that, others get to go home."

His chest tightened as the old ghosts pressed in, names he still carried. He forced the breath through anyway.

"So I want to thank you," he said. "Every one of you. For your professionalism, your integrity—and for having each other's backs when it mattered most."

This time, he didn't look away when the silence answered him.

Ethan sat, the weight of what he'd just told them heavy on his shoulders. "I'll turn over the meeting to Special Agent Patterson."

Patterson stood at the head of the table. "As you know, all the information we and Deputy Marshal Butler have been able to gather leads to Rousseau being part of the syndicate but not the boss. We are still actively looking into Draven Frost and his involvement. The syndicate's tentacles of corruption have reached into every fiber of Renegade's society and government, and they must be stopped."

"What exactly does that mean for us?" Glover asked.

"I'm glad you asked." Agent Patterson walked to the corner of the table and leaned against it. "Because of the hard work you all have put in and the evidence we were able to collect, we now have solid leads as to who is running this operation."

The room fell silent, and suddenly everyone began talking in hushed undertones.

Ethan whistled. "Let's keep the conversation on track. What about Finn Donovan?" Because he didn't ever want to have to rescue Aubrey again. He'd do it a million times over, but until he knew that Donovan was securely behind bars, he'd watch out for her. And for every day after.

"Donovan was patched up and sent to a supermax prison out in North Dakota. He won't be making any more appearances," Special Agent Patterson said. "Well, until his new trial."

Ethan wasn't so sure. "How can we be certain? Donovan was able to escape last time."

Patterson leaned into the table, palms down. "Since you and your team exposed Rousseau and Howard, that shouldn't be a problem." He glanced around the table, assessing each member of the team. "Unless we have another marshal who's willing to break the law."

Grumbles erupted around the table.

"I'm just saying"—Agent Patterson held up his hands, his black leather jacket creaking—"it happened before, and I'm sure that won't be the last time." He looked each one in the eye. "I'm not questioning your loyalty, otherwise you would be in jail with former Supervisor Howard, waiting for your arraignment hearing."

Albright grunted and Ethan had to suppress a grin. The man was a big bear but had a soft spot for sweets—and for Aubrey. Well, they all did.

"In regard to the FBI's next steps, we're going to ramp up our investigation here in Renegade and might need the Marshals to assist us." Patterson turned to look at Ethan, one eyebrow raised.

"Absolutely. You'll have the full cooperation of the US Marshals Service should you need it."

Agent Patterson resumed his seat, and Ethan motioned to the detective from Renegade PD. "You all should know Detective Martinelli by now."

The team nodded.

Martinelli stood. "With the apprehension of Finn Donovan and Supervisor Howard, our focus is now on finding Roger Rousseau and establishing Frost's involvement."

Ethan raised his hand. "From the intel we've gathered, Roger's involvement is deeper than we originally thought."

"That's correct," Detective Martinelli said. "For the past five years, we've seen a steady uptick in criminal activity such as drug trafficking and human trafficking. Renegade isn't the sleepy town it used to be. It's grown into a city, and between the drug deals and murders, our numbers have gotten out of control. Instead of the Mob, we have the Shadow Syndicate. They threaten legitimate business owners and have them pay for protection. If they don't pay, then the business is robbed or worse. Many businesses have left downtown because they don't want to pay to keep their stores open."

"What now?" Adam asked.

"It's only a matter of time before Rousseau's caught." Martinelli's lips thinned. "We will find him and prosecute him."

"That's all well and good, but Aubrey mentioned that Roger said he was leaving," Ethan said.

"Wherever he goes, we'll find him," Patterson said with a lethal calmness.

Ethan leaned back in his chair, studying him. "You seem awfully confident, Agent Patterson."

He crossed his arms, a determined gleam in his eyes. "Because I am. I've worked cases like this before, and I've been very successful bringing fugitives in."

"One more question," Ethan said, nudging the folder away. "Do we have an arrest warrant for Rousseau?"

Patterson nodded. "Signed this morning. Federal arrest warrant. The Bureau will take point on the capture."

The shift in the room was immediate. Ethan was already reaching for his phone. "Search warrant?"

"Approved," Patterson said. "Primary residence, outbuildings, and vehicles. Digital devices included."

"Then we're green," Ethan said, rising. "We'll coordinate with your team and support the takedown. No delays."

For a beat, no one moved, the collective understanding settling in. Then chairs scraped back and radios crackled as the team sprang into motion.

Ethan cleared his throat. "That's everything on our end." He extended his hand. "Agent Patterson, it's been a pleasure working with you."

He shook it firmly. "Likewise. And something tells me this won't be the last time."

Detective Martinelli stood. "We'll stay in touch."

"Absolutely." Ethan walked them to the elevator, watching as the doors slid shut and the weight of the case finally began to ease from his shoulders.

Liam clapped a hand against his back. "I don't know about you, but after we back up Agent Patterson, I'm craving the smothered chicken at the Rocky Top Grille. Come with?"

Ethan smiled faintly, stuffing his hands into his pockets. "Can't. I've got airport duty. I'm picking up Aubrey's parents and her sister. And I promised to check on Mrs. Hanover's cats."

"Bummer."

"I'll take a rain check," Ethan said. "If that's okay."

Liam grinned. "More than okay. I think we're making this a weekly Thursday or Friday thing."

"I'm looking forward to it." And he meant it. "I'll definitely be there next time."

This, *this*, was the beginning of something new. A life that made room for people. For friendship. For love.

For the first time in a long while, Ethan trusted that God wasn't finished with him yet.

That His plan was good.

NINETEEN

THERE WAS SOMEONE IN HER HOSPITAL ROOM, and Aubrey's heart rate exploded in her chest. Voices murmured around her. Wheels clicked on the tiled hallway outside her door. Aubrey struggled to open her eyes. She was so, so tired. And she ached. All over.

"Honey? It's Mom. Wake up."

Aubrey's breath caught in her lungs, and her eyelids flew open. "Mom?"

Her throat was dry and scratchy, and tears puddled at the corners of her eyes. Her gaze darted around the room, and she tried to push herself up to a seated position. All the people she cared about most stood around her hospital bed. Mom, her sister Kristen, Jenna, Ethan . . .

"Dad?"

"Shh, now. He'll be here soon. You lie back and rest." Mom placed a hand on her shoulder and lightly pushed her back onto the mattress. "Deputy Marshal Butler here was telling us that you've had quite the exciting week."

Her mom pointed at Ethan, and his fiery gaze was like a magnet, drawing her in until she might spontaneously combust. A gentle smile turned his lips up.

"You doing okay there, Sunshine?" Ethan rested against the wall, arms crossed, and she sighed in relief. He looked so relaxed in his blue T-shirt and worn jeans.

But the name Sunshine sent a pang of grief through her.

Aubrey smoothed the thin blanket over her lap. "Yeah, I am okay. Thanks to you and the others."

Mom and Kristen shared a puzzled look before her mom looked at Ethan. "How did you know that her father's nickname for her was Sunshine?"

"I didn't." Ethan frowned and uncrossed his arms. "Stanton, one of the marshals in our office"—his voice broke—"he gave her that nickname a while ago and it stuck. It fits her perfectly."

"It really does." Her mom grabbed a tissue from the box on the table and dabbed her eyes. "I'm so glad you're safe."

Aubrey grasped her mom's hand. "Hey now, no tears." She pointed to everyone surrounding her bed, people she held close to her heart. Emma and Glover had visited earlier too. Her heart was full. "God is good."

Before she could finish, the doctor strolled in with one of the on-duty nurses. "I'm Dr.—whoa, there's a lot of people in here."

Aubrey flushed.

No one opted to leave.

"Whatever you have to say, it's fine for them to hear," Aubrey said, but she spotted Ethan and Jenna moving to the doorway. Jenna stepped out, chatting with Aubrey's sister, but Ethan stayed in the room.

The doctor cleared his throat. "I'm Dr. Burrow, and I've been in charge of your care." He was an older gentleman, around her mom's age, with gray at his temples and kind hazel eyes, a white lab coat, and a stethoscope around his neck. He checked her file. "You've had quite the adventure." He patted her good leg and checked her pupils while the nurse took her vitals.

"Temp is nine-eight point six and blood pressure is one-thirty over seventy-five." The nurse rattled off the numbers, and the doctor entered them in the chart.

The room was tense, as if everyone held their breath.

"Excuse me, Doctor. How is she? And when can she go home?" Mom inserted herself between Aubrey and the doctor.

Dr. Burrow looked up and paused. "Are you a relative?"

Mom threw back her shoulders and smiled. "I'm Emily Loftus, her mother."

Dr. Burrow's gaze returned to his tablet. "Ms. Richardson, you have a mild concussion. You're no longer dehydrated, but you sustained ligament damage to your left ankle. The surgery went well, but you'll need a few weeks of PT to help with recovery. And you'll have to wear a walking boot on your foot."

Aubrey groaned. "I hate this thing. It looks like a Frankenstein foot."

Jenna and her sister laughed from the hall, and Ethan simply frowned.

Ethan stepped toward the bed. "So there's no permanent damage?"

"Fortunately, no." The doctor turned to Aubrey. "You'll have some discomfort but should make a full recovery."

"Thank You, Lord." Mom clasped her hands and wiped away a tear.

"So, when will I be released from the hospital, Doctor Burrow?" Aubrey certainly hoped she wouldn't be stuck here any longer than necessary.

"We'll keep you overnight for observation, and then, if all looks good, we'll release you to go home tomorrow."

"That gives us time to catch up," Kristen said from the doorway.

"You should stay off your feet for two weeks, no exceptions. I'll write you a doctor's note for your boss."

Ethan said, "She can have all the time off she needs."

Aubrey exhaled. Two weeks at home. She'd go stir crazy if she was cooped up, but considering everything, she figured she could find something to do—like plan next year's Renegade Days. "That would be great. Thank you."

Doctor Burrow handed the tablet to the nurse. "You take care of yourself, young lady. Looks like you have a lot of people who care about you."

Aubrey looked at the people surrounding her bed and smiled. She wasn't going to take them for granted. "I'm blessed, that's for sure."

She was blessed. Blessed that her mom and sister were here after all the years of distance. Blessed to have a good friend in Jenna. Blessed to have Ethan standing beside her.

Doctor Burrow smiled. "I know you want to get back to work, but the two weeks' rest is a precaution. I just want to make sure you don't have any setbacks. It was nice meeting you all."

The doctor and nurse swept out of the room.

Aubrey relaxed against the pillow, the bed crinkling with her movement. "I'm so glad you're here." She focused her gaze on Ethan. "How did you know?" She sniffled.

"I checked your WITSEC file, made some calls, and got authorization to make contact."

Aubrey smiled through her tears. "I should be mad at you, but I'm glad you called them."

"Me too." Ethan blended back into the corner of the room. Standing, always watching.

Her guardian.

Always.

Mom moved closer to the bed. "It's been so long, baby, I was afraid." Mom wiped away a couple of tears and then grabbed Aubrey in a fierce hug. "Next time you leave, at least tell us where you're heading. I had no idea where you were. If you were safe . . ." Her mom's whispered confession pierced through the armor she'd clung to all these years. "The Marshals reassured us, but it wasn't the same as hearing from you."

"I had to be strong. To leave. I didn't want him to hurt you, Dad, or Kristen." Aubrey held on tighter to her mom and then eased back.

Mom tucked a strand of hair behind Aubrey's ear. "Honey, protecting you was supposed to be my job. And I'm afraid I didn't do it very well. I'm sorry. I shouldn't have pushed you away."

"We both did that. I didn't know how to express my feelings with the trial, being a witness to a murder." Aubrey waved her hands. "All of it was overwhelming."

"I'm sure it was." Mom straightened and tugged the hem of her blouse in place. "I'm sorry that I wasn't there for you. Your dad and I were in over our heads. We didn't know how to navigate the loss of Kayla and then the trial. Going into WITSEC." Mom swiped away the moisture on her face with her fingertips, a new determination in her eyes. "Dad and I are here now, and we have some catching up to do."

"I'd like that." Aubrey glanced at Ethan, smiled and held out her hand to him.

He moved into the light, grabbed her hand, and smiled back. Her face hurt from grinning. She had so much to tell her mom.

"Where's Dad?" Aubrey asked her mom.

"In the coffee shop downstairs. Said he needed something to eat," Mom said, smiling as her gaze landed on their clasped hands. "Truthfully, I think he's a little nervous to see you."

Aubrey felt tears prick her eyes and looked at Ethan. He squeezed her hand. This man had not only saved her but helped her to see herself in the light of God's grace. She was worthy. Loved. Not only by the Lord, but by this faithful man.

Aubrey stifled a yawn. "I don't know why I'm so tired."

Ethan sat on the edge of the bed. "You've had quite the week."

"Yeah, you could say that." She couldn't stop staring at Ethan. Hoping that he would choose her.

Mom glanced between her and Ethan and smiled. "I'll leave you two lovebirds alone and go find your father. Tell him it's all good." She tossed her tote over her shoulder. "Thank you, Mr. Butler, for your help. You have my number if anything changes." Mom sashayed to the door and waved.

"Yes, ma'am. I'll be sure to keep you updated."

Jenna stuck her head around the doorway. "I'll be back with a double cheeseburger and onion rings."

"Yes, please!"

Kristen lingered a moment, unsure, then grabbed Aubrey in a quick hug and whispered in her ear. "He's yummy." Her sister darted out the door, laughing.

Ethan raised one brow. "What was that about?"

"Nothing that you need to be worried about." Aubrey picked at an invisible string on the thin blanket. "Did you find Rousseau?"

Ethan stood and held out his hands. "Whoa now, slow down. One major life challenge issue at a time."

She quirked an eyebrow at him. "Challenge, or do you mean problem?"

"I'm trying to put a positive spin on all this." Ethan grinned.

A knock on the door paused their conversation, and a man Aubrey didn't recognize strode in. Ethan's face lit up. "Carlsson! Good to see you."

"Butler." The men shook hands and then turned their attention to Aubrey. She felt small, intimidated by the big men. And maybe Ethan was right about one challenge at a time. She yawned behind her hand.

"Carlsson, this Aubrey Richardson." Ethan touched her shoulder. "Aubrey, this is my old friend, Sebastian Carlsson, head of the Denver office."

"Oh!" She held out her hand. "It's nice to meet you."

"You as well." Carlsson pointed to the guest chair. "Mind if I sit?"

"Please."

After Carlsson moved the chair closer to the bed, he leaned forward, forearms resting on his thighs. "I know this is asking a lot of you, Aubrey"—he glanced over at Ethan, who nodded—"but the US attorney will need you to testify at the trials for Howard and Donovan."

It was as if someone had stuck a cold, icy blade in her heart. She inhaled sharply, the pain of betrayal and fear threatening to overwhelm her like a tsunami. She looked out the small window and shook her head.

"I don't know if I can go through that again." She swallowed back the bile rising in her throat.

"You won't be alone. I'll be there." Ethan sat on the edge of the bed. "And if I need to, I can testify as well. Add my statement."

Carlsson nodded. "You'll have to testify."

Ethan angled his body toward Aubrey and lifted her chin with two fingers. "Hey now, I'm going to be right there with you." He tipped his head toward Carlsson. "We're going to debrief you first, and then we'll discuss what we need to do next."

The icy fear running through her veins thawed. "I don't look forward to testifying. It's not high on my bucket list to go through that again. But I'm not the same person I was."

Over the years, the emotional trauma from testifying twenty years ago had affected how she saw the world and the decisions she'd made.

Aubrey looked at the window, covered with vertical blinds.

A few days ago, she hadn't thought she would be strong enough if she were ever confronted by Donovan again. She'd mourned the loss of her family's support. How could she have overlooked her coworkers at the Marshals office and Jenna? The people she loved, and who loved her, were here in Renegade, and all she had to do was ask.

They were her family.

"Aubrey." Ethan dipped his head to look in her eyes. "Hey, look at me. Please?"

She slowly turned to face him and squinted in the brilliant morning light coming through the window of her room.

"I know you've been through a lot the past couple of days. You're scared. But we need your testimony to put these guys away for good. But I'm also going to make sure that I get enough evidence so that this case is a slam dunk. Then there might be a chance you don't have to do it."

She felt her resolve slowly returning, like a phoenix rising from the ashes. "If I have to, I can."

Ethan gave her a tender smile that melted her insides. "I promise, you won't be alone. You'll be protected. You are a survivor."

She drew a shaky breath. "I'm scared," she admitted. Then she lifted her chin, just a little. "But I won't let fear control me anymore."

He gently squeezed her hand. "That's right. Besides, I don't think the Lord wants us to simply survive. He wants us to live a full and abundant life." His expression became somber. "Are you ready? For the next chapter of your life?"

She swallowed back the fear. "God's going to have to help me."

"He will." The confidence in Ethan's tone soothed her frazzled nerves. He lifted her clasped hands and kissed the backs. "I know from experience."

"I'd like that same confidence."

"It's my confidence in God, my faith. Believe me, it doesn't come easy since I'm not one to trust, but it's worth it."

She stared out the window a moment, resolve surging through her. With God's help and Ethan at her side, she could testify, overcome her fears. She looked at the men and nodded. "Okay. Let's do this."

Carlsson nodded once and hit record. Ethan held her hand while she detailed her experience on the mountain and at the cabin with Rousseau, Howard, Frost, and Donovan. She was tired of running, of not trusting. But Ethan had proven to her multiple times that he was trustworthy. And he served a God who was worthy of her faith and trust.

Faith in God. His word and promises. Yes, she would have difficult times ahead, but with Ethan by her side, she knew she didn't have to run away from God's promises but toward them.

He hated to leave Aubrey, but she was in good hands at the hospital. And he'd left Albright outside her room, just as a precaution. He wasn't taking any chances with Aubrey's life.

Ethan parked his truck in the afternoon courthouse shade. After passing through security, he scanned his Marshals badge and descended into the basement of the courthouse, where they kept holding cells.

He paused as he stepped out of the elevator and into the intake area, allowing his eyes to adjust to the dimmer lighting. Hank Green, the oldest member of the US Marshals team in Renegade, sat in front of the holding cells, feet propped up on the desk, reading a muscle car magazine.

"How is our guest tonight, Hank?" Ethan leaned against the desk, arms crossed.

Both men glanced back at the cells to the lone figure sitting on the metal bench, head cradled in his hands. "Oh, he's touchy.

Won't speak to anyone." Hank dropped his feet to the floor. "You sure you want to talk to Howard?"

"Yeah. I just have a few questions for him."

Hank buzzed Ethan through the gate and leaned in. "Watch yourself. He's shifty."

"I will." Ethan clasped Hank's shoulder and squeezed. "You're good man, Hank. We'll miss you when you retire."

Hank smiled, the deep lines around his eyes crinkling. "That means a lot."

Ethan's footsteps echoed against the concrete floor. He pulled a chair closer to the bars, sat, and stretched out his legs.

Howard looked up, frowned, and then turned his back toward Ethan. "Are you here to gloat?"

"Nope." Ethan crossed his arms. "Just have a few questions."

Howard barked out a laugh. "Right."

A tense silence fell over the small area, the buzz of a fluorescent light the only sound. Howard shifted on the metal bench, finally sitting up. The men stared at each other.

Ethan straightened and focused his attention on the defeated man. A guy who'd had a long career with the Marshals. "Tell me why, Howard. Why jeopardize your career and pension?"

"Ah, yes. The great dilemma. Always doing the right thing, Mr. By-the-Book Butler."

"Well, it works for me."

Howard let out a harsh snort. "Don't you ever get tired of it, Butler? Protecting criminals who've got more money than we'll ever see? They live like kings until they get sloppy, cut a deal, and suddenly we're risking our lives to keep their sorry hides safe." His mouth twisted. "You know what I could do with the money they move?"

"So that's it. You sold us out for their money. Integrity didn't even factor in." Ethan rose and paced in front of the bars. "Where's Rousseau?"

Howard smirked. "Wouldn't you like to know?" He stepped forward until their faces were only inches apart. "I don't know."

Ethan caught the wild look in Howard's eyes. "You don't know, or you don't want to tell me?"

Howard shrugged. "Maybe a little bit of both. Seriously, I was just doing this for the money. Roger is probably halfway around the world now, in some country that doesn't have an extradition treaty with the United States."

"When did Rousseau first contact you?"

Howard sighed. "Ages ago. Who cares? Somehow, he knew I had money troubles and used that against me."

"Money."

"My wife cleaned me out. I've got two kids in college. I'm desperate." Howard pivoted away from Ethan, paced the confines of his cell, and raked his fingers through his hair. "Rousseau and his buddy Frost offered a lot of money. Enough that I could retire from the Marshals and be comfortable the rest of my life."

"Hey, man, you could've asked for help." Ethan lightly gripped the cold bars, trying to make a connection, help Howard understand.

Howard ceased his pacing and stared at the cinderblock wall. "Oh, that's rich coming from you, Butler. You say you're a Christian, but you never once reached out to me."

The truth of Howard's statement hit Ethan squarely in his chest. Regret rolled through him, and he stepped away. "You're right. I was so caught up in my own problems that I failed to see you were going through something as well." Ethan had to make Howard understand. "I'm sorry."

"A little late for regrets now, isn't it?" Howard dropped to the bench, his tortured gaze boring into Ethan. "For both of us."

"It's never too late."

"Don't preach to me, Butler. I'm too far gone. Too caught up in the underworld." Howard sighed. "No matter what protection I'm given, I'll be dead the second I reach prison."

"No one is too far from God's love."

Howard paused a moment, looked at Ethan with something akin to hope, then it disappeared in a flash. "I wish . . ." Howard shook his head. "I wish I could believe like you."

"You can. All you have to do is—"

"Enough." Howard held up a hand and moved away to the farthest corner of the cell. "Hank! Come get my guest."

"One more thing before I leave." Ethan pulled out a business card, wrote his personal cell phone number on it, and handed it to Howard. "I know it's not much, but if you want to talk, I'll listen. And if you happen to remember where Rousseau is, call me. I'll talk to the prosecutor in charge. It might help you if you turn state's evidence."

Howard tentatively reached for the card, and Ethan held on before releasing his grip. "I mean it. I'm not saying this as a marshal but as a friend. Reach out."

"Thanks." Howard stuffed the card into his shirt pocket. "Now, if you don't mind, I think it's almost time for my chaperone to show up and take me back to DC for trial." Howard stretched out on the bench, hands pillowing his head.

"I'll be praying for you."

Howard ignored Ethan, and Ethan shook his head. If only . . . Those two words would eat him alive if he dwelled on them.

Hank buzzed Ethan out of the secure holding area.

"Hold up a sec." Hank stood, shuffled over to him, and placed a hand on Ethan's shoulder. "You did all you could, Butler. Now you just need to let God work on him." Hank pointed his chin at their former supervisor. "He listened, now it's up to Howard if he wants to accept the truth."

Ethan exited the holding cell area, taking the elevator to the main floor of the courthouse. Oh, how he wanted a do-over.

Wished he'd gotten out of his own head and been a better Christian when he was first assigned. He'd just have to leave Howard's soul in God's hands.

He pushed through the doors and into the bright afternoon sunshine and inhaled. Howard was a mess, but nothing that God couldn't redeem. Ethan was a prime example.

He rushed back to his truck and headed to the hospital, glancing over at the two dozen pink roses arranged in a fancy vase—since the previous bouquet had ended up smashed on the floor in the scuffle.

The heady aroma filled the cab of his truck, reminding him of Aubrey. Bright. Beautiful. Perfect in his eyes, even though trouble regularly found her.

Ethan cradled the vase of flowers in his arms as he reached Aubrey's room. Albright stood posted outside the door and gave him a brief nod. A couple of nurses at the station smiled and offered encouraging thumbs-ups as Ethan paused, drawing in a steadying breath.

He knocked once, and before he could enter, Kristen opened the door, her smile bright and familiar. She immediately tried to usher him in, but Ethan hesitated, his feet suddenly rooted to the floor.

He leaned closer, lowering his voice. "Is she awake? Feeling okay? Is now a good time?"

Kristen laughed, so much like her sister it caught him off guard. "Easy there, cowboy. She's fine."

She tugged him inside. "Look who's here to see you," Kristen singsonged.

Ethan stepped fully into the room.

His gaze found Aubrey instantly, where she sat propped against white pillows with her hair pulled back, color finally returned to her cheeks. Bruised, tired, but alive. The knot he'd been carrying in his chest since the mountain finally loosened, just enough for him to breathe.

For the first time in days, he let himself believe they were going to be okay.

"Hey." Ethan gave an awkward wave to Emily, Kristen, Aubrey, and an older man who had to be her father, Bill. He hadn't felt this nervous in, well, a long, long time.

"I, uh, brought these for you." He shoved the vase toward Aubrey, and she caught it with a laugh.

"They're gorgeous." She buried her nose in the fragrant blooms and inhaled. "How did you know I like pink roses?" she asked as she smiled at him over the bouquet.

"Just a hunch. You wear a lot of pink."

They stared at each other for a long moment. All he could see was Aubrey. Her light. Her personality that filled a room and made you feel welcomed.

"Well, I guess we'll be leaving now." Emily tugged her purse over her shoulder and looped her arm through her husband's. "Let's go grab some dinner. Kristen, you coming?" Emily glared at Kristen. "I'm sure Aubrey would like to rest."

"Fine." A smile lit Kristen's face as she flounced toward the door. She pivoted in the doorway and winked. "Just don't do anything I wouldn't do." Her laughter faded as the door closed.

Aubrey's face turned an adorable shade of pink, and she muttered something about talking to Jenna. "I'm sorry about my sister."

"It's fine."

"She's always been a tease. It's great to have her back after all this time, even if she is annoying." Aubrey cleared her throat and ran a finger over some of the delicate blooms. "Would you mind setting this on the window ledge?"

"Sure."

Ethan resumed his seat, an awkward tension settling over them.

"So—"

"I wanted to tell you—"

"You go first." They spoke at the same time, looked at each other, and then burst out laughing.

Ethan shook his head. "Please, ladies first."

She glanced down at her clasped hands. "I'm grateful for your help. For finding me and saving me from Donovan. The situation could've ended a lot differently." She exhaled, and when she looked at him, tears shimmered in her eyes. "If it wasn't for you, I could've died."

Seeing her near tears about ripped his heart in two. "Hey now, it's okay. You're safe." *With me.*

He sat on the edge of her bed, and she curled into him, her arms wrapped around his waist.

This was heaven. He wanted this. *Her.*

She sobbed into his chest, and he hugged her close. He never wanted to let go.

One last shudder wracked her body, and she leaned back, a beautiful smile on her lips. "Thank you." Her face was blotchy and tear-stained, but to him, Aubrey was the most beautiful woman in the world.

"For what?" He cupped her cheeks with his hands, his thumbs swiping away the last of her tears.

"For being you."

He smiled. "Isn't the man supposed to say that?"

She leaned back and then gave him a playful swat. "You're quite the comedian."

"I have many talents." Ethan leaned closer, cupping the back of her neck with one hand. He tucked a strand of hair behind her ear. He gently tugged her closer until their lips were a fraction apart. Aubrey's minty breath fanned his cheek, and her eyes were almost closed.

"I do have one question for you."

"Hmm? What's that?" Her voice was a low hum, warmed by the afternoon sunshine.

"Finish our date?"

"What date?"

"The one from Renegade Days." He pressed a kiss to her temple, then her cheek. All the tension left his body as he headed for her lips.

Her eyes flew open, and she leaned away from him. "That was a date?"

He tapped her nose. "Of course it was. I don't cosplay for just anyone."

"Well then." She pressed a light kiss to his cheek. "I accept."

"Good." Ethan closed the distance and kissed her as he'd wanted to for a long time. The kiss was full of heat and a promise for their future. She melted into his arms, and he never wanted to let her go.

He'd been so caught up in his own grief, his own survival, that he hadn't seen the gift God had placed in front of him this entire time.

They would navigate this life together, the highs and the lows, and lean not only on each other but on the goodness of God to pilot them on their journey.

THANK YOU!

Thank you so much for reading *Guardian*. We hope you enjoyed the story. If you did, would you be willing to do us a favor and leave a review? It doesn't have to be long—just a few words to help other readers know what they're getting. (But no spoilers! We don't want to wreck the fun!) Thank you again for reading!

We'd love to hear from you- not only about this story, but about any characters or stories you'd like to read in the future. Contact us at www.sunrisepublishing.com/contact.

Don't miss what happens next with the Heroes of Renegade in *Rescuer*!

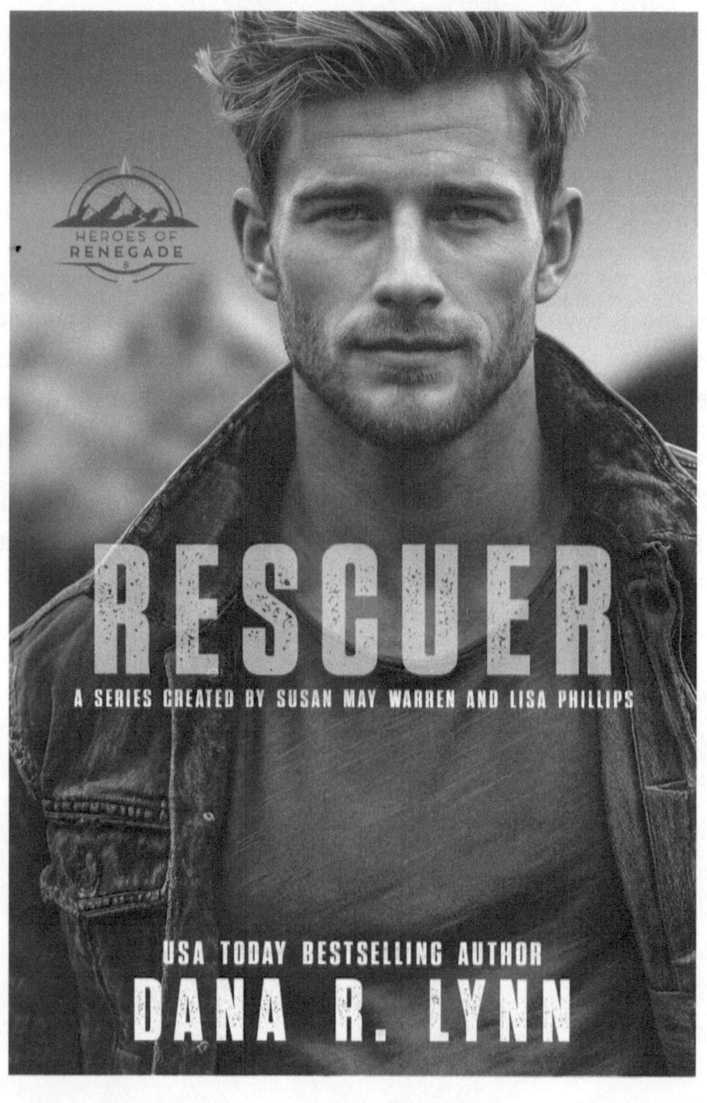

Some rescues require risking everything—including your heart.

Special education teacher Mia Turner never wanted to return to Renegade, especially not to face Jackson Stewart—the man who shattered her heart and abandoned her in her darkest hour. But when her students start disappearing and a shadowy foundation's "youth camp" becomes ground zero for a dangerous plot, she has no choice but to trust the one man she swore she'd never forgive.

When the past collides with a deadly present, survival depends on forgiveness.

Paramedic Jackson Stewart will do anything to find his missing brother Dylan, even work with the woman who decimated his heart. But as dangerous secrets surface in Renegade, Jackson must face the possibility that finding his brother means confronting not just his painful past with Mia, but a conspiracy that could destroy everything he's fought to protect.

Get it early from the Sunrise Shop, or order from your favorite retailer.

Keep reading for a sneak peek...

ONE

JACKSON STEWART TORE UP THE STEPS AND INTO the courthouse, dirty and smelling of blood and sweat. Gavin, the guard inside the courthouse, shot up from his chair, his eyes locked on the dark blood stains that smeared Jackson's light-gray uniform shirt.

"Not mine, Gavin," Jackson ground out. "I was on a call before I came here. Motorcycle versus pickup. It was bad." That was an understatement. Jackson dumped the contents of his pockets into a bin. His hands shook. His brother's entire future hinged on this court appearance, and he reeked of death.

Gavin set the bin on the conveyor belt. He frowned. "You couldn't take ten minutes to go home and change? This isn't a good look. Judge Fields is on the bench today."

Jackson grimaced. "I know. But I didn't have ten minutes. The hearing got moved up. It wasn't supposed to be for another two weeks. The letter was sent to the wrong address. I only found out twenty minutes ago."

He and Gavin exchanged glances. He'd known Gavin Weldon

since high school. They'd been on the track team together. They both knew that this particular judge held a grudge against Jackson.

Gavin waved his wand over Jackson. "All right, you're clear. They're in courtroom two. Good luck."

Jackson swallowed. "Thanks, Gavin. I'm going to need it."

"For what it's worth, I don't think Kevin blames you," Gavin murmured in a low voice.

Jackson barked a short laugh, the bitter sound echoing in the high-ceilinged room. "Then why hasn't he talked to me since I returned from active duty? Last time I saw him, he told me, in very colorful language, that I had ruined his life. He hates me, and so does his old man. But I will go in there and be kind and respectful. Whatever it takes to get custody of my kid brother."

They belonged together. He and Dylan both wanted this. Jackson had jumped through hoops, done everything the system demanded. Background checks. Home inspections. Supplying solid proof of longstanding employment and financial security. He'd even missed several search and rescue trainings because he needed to be available.

His boss had been interviewed and so had the sergeant he'd reported to in the Army. This custody hearing should be the last box to check off so his fifteen-year-old brother could finally leave the foster system and move in with him.

The only roadblock left was the man on the bench.

Jackson sent up a silent prayer for guidance and control. The guard at the entrance of the courtroom opened the heavy door. Jackson slipped into the room, shoulders tight, and trod as quietly as possible to the front. Cynthia Reese, Dylan's foster mom, caught his eye and nodded discreetly toward the seat in front of her. Dylan sat beside the court-appointed attorney. Jackson slid into the seat next to his brother, heart aching when Dylan's pale face turned toward him with a shaky smile. His brother sat on his hands, rocking slightly.

The kid was terrified but desperate not to let it show.

"Mr. Stewart," Judge Fields called out, ice dripping from his tone. Jackson jerked his face toward the front and met the hard eyes of the man who would decide Dylan's fate. "This hearing began half an hour ago."

Jackson rose to his feet and held up the notice. "Yes, sir. My apologies. The notice of the hearing date change was sent to my previous address. I only found out today."

Judge Fields's glance bored into Jackson, slowly moving down over his ruined uniform. "And yet you still made it. I am appalled at your lack of respect for this court! Your attire is not acceptable. You're filthy. I can smell you from here. Is this how you show yourself capable of caring for a minor?"

Jackson's knees shook. He forced himself to remain calm, while inside, his heart pounded like a jackhammer. "I have a lot of respect. I found out twenty minutes before I arrived. I was at a fatal motorcycle crash when my chief drove this notice over. The woman who lives in my old apartment brought it to the station. When he saw the return address, he figured it was important. I came here straight from the scene."

He held his breath.

He noticed a few people wince. At least he had some sympathy in this room.

"Hmmm." Judge Fields's jaw moved back and forth. His gaze touched each person in the room and his nostrils flared.

Jackson kept his silence, unwilling to encourage the man's internal anger to spill out. He had no doubt the man had correctly read the room. While Jackson couldn't prove that the letter had been deliberately sent to the wrong address, the date on it told its own story. The trial date had been moved forward with very little notice.

"Jackson Stewart, you already abandoned your brother."

Jackson blinked. “Sir, I went into the military. He was living with my grandfather.”

“You didn’t try to get custody until your grandfather had been dead for eighteen months.”

“I had to finish my tour. I didn’t reenlist even though I wanted to make the military my career. I came home. Got a job. Bought a house so he’d have his own room, just like I was told to do.” He held on to control but bit off each word as heat flooded his body.

“I’m ready to rule,” Judge Fields announced, his voice overly loud in the courtroom.

Shocked whispers rippled through the room.

“Your Honor.” Darcy Faust, their attorney, jumped to her feet. “We haven’t presented the case y—”

“Save it, Counselor,” the judge interrupted her. “Jackson Stewart is an adrenaline junkie. He craves violence. I’ve known him for years. And then to enter my courtroom covered in blood? I refuse to continue this farce with that man dressed this way. He’s making a mockery of our system.”

“Your Honor, Mr. Stewart has explained his attire. He didn’t have time—”

The judge glared at her. Her words stuttered to a halt.

Jackson clenched his jaw. The anger brewing inside threatened to erupt. He clamped his lips shut to keep it in. If he let it go, all hope would be lost.

“Careful, Counselor. Arguing with me could land you in contempt.” Judge Fields shook his head. “I don’t buy his lame excuse.”

Dylan opened his mouth. Jackson gripped his brother’s shoulder, and Dylan’s mouth snapped closed. He shot Jackson a hurt look. Tears swam in his eyes.

“Don’t give him a reason,” Jackson breathed, his mouth barely moving.

“Custody denied.” The gavel slammed down. Dylan flinched.

Denied.

"Your Honor!"

"Keep it for the appeal." The judge threw one final glare at Jackson, then swept from the room.

And it was over. A strangled sob escaped Dylan before the youth's face tightened. Angry words filled Jackson's mouth. He had no recourse. He couldn't tell Judge Fields what he really thought of him.

"We can file an appeal in thirty days," Darcy told him. "Then wait for the paperwork. With luck, we'll be back here in three months."

"Three months," Dylan whispered, his voice breaking.

Jackson opened his arms. His younger brother, despite being fifteen, fell into them and allowed Jackson to support him. Dylan had grown taller over the summer. He'd let his light-brown hair grow longer so it flopped over his hazel eyes. His head rested on Jackson's shoulder. It wasn't hard to imagine him topping Jackson's height of five eleven.

The teenager tensed a moment before he shrugged out of Jackson's embrace. He was at that awkward stage where his clothes never seemed to fit right. He had dressed in khaki pants, a short-sleeved button-up blue shirt with a collar and a tie. The same outfit he wore to away wrestling events. The tie looked tight enough to choke him. And it was too long. He'd probably watched a video on how to put it on. If he got custody of Dylan, Jackson would make sure his brother knew how to do simple things like putting on a tie.

Now he'd have to wait another three months to plead for custody again.

Darcy shuffled her papers and dropped them into her briefcase. She moved away from the table and joined them briefly. "I know this isn't what you wanted to hear today. But it could have been worse. At least we can appeal this decision. What did you do to get on his bad side?"

Jackson stiffened at the implication. He wanted to ask if the judge had a good side, but he knew that wouldn't go over well. Instead, he shrugged. He didn't know her that well. Even if he did, there were too many people around to go into his dark history with Kevin Fields and the events that had turned the judge against him.

Darcy pursed her lips and gave him a look that said they'd be talking about it later. "I'll be in touch. We have three months."

He watched her stalk from the room, aware of the voices buzzing excitedly around them. Jackson caught more than one person staring at them. He ignored them. Only Dylan mattered.

"I'm sorry, Jackson." Cynthia played with her bracelet while she talked. Next to the dark clothes most people wore at the courthouse, she stood out in her royal-blue summer dress with its complementary floral jacket. The highlights in her short, fluffy brown hair glowed under the lights. "If I'd known you were unaware of the change, I would have told you about it. It never occurred to me that you didn't know."

"It's not your fault, Cynthia." The words tasted like ash. If she had asked him about it, he would have made sure he had today off. But he couldn't blame her. Dylan had been shuffled through several foster homes. Cynthia's was the best by a mile.

But her home still wasn't his.

He turned to Dylan and placed a hand on the fifteen-year-old's shoulder. "Are you okay, buddy?"

Dylan stuffed his fisted hands into his pockets. "It's not fair. Why can't we live together? You're my brother. Doesn't he get that? We're family!"

Jackson ruffled Dylan's hair. "We are. Nothing can change that. It's not the way we planned it, but you know you're my number-one priority, right? Even if I don't have custody today, nothing matters more to me than you do."

"Yeah, I know. But . . . but . . . he didn't even let you talk. You were helping people, and all he talked about was how messy your uniform was."

"I know. We'll talk about it later."

"Three months, Jack! Three months!" Dylan's voice rose, then broke again. The court reporter glanced their way.

Jackson held out a hand to stop the tirade before his brother started crying or got really fired up. His kid brother looked ready to go into a full-blown meltdown. Jackson didn't want it on display for anyone to see, especially not the judge or anyone who might report back to him.

"I know, Dylan. We can talk about this later, when we're not out in public. For now, let's move outside."

"Sorry," Dylan muttered, ducking his head.

"You did nothing wrong. I just think this might be a longer conversation. I want to talk about it though. It's important." Jackson's eyes stung. He blinked. He hadn't lied. Dylan was all the family he had left.

"Come on, Dylan." Cynthia prompted Dylan to move toward the door. "Let's head home. It's been a long day."

She gave Jackson a sympathetic smile as she and Dylan moved past him.

"I'll call you, Dylan. I need to head back to the station. I left in the middle of my shift."

Dylan nodded, but Jackson could tell his brother wasn't happy. Not that he blamed him. He wished he'd taken the rest of the day off, but he'd promised the chief he'd be back as soon as the hearing ended.

Discouraged, he made his way out to his truck. He caught his reflection in the window and grimaced. His short dark-blond hair had blood in it. Blue eyes peered out of a grimy face. No wonder Gavin had looked so shocked to see him.

It had never occurred to him that he'd be returning feeling like there was a hole in his heart.

Maria Turner, known as Mia to her friends, drove past the Renegade School District sign, hands clenched on the wheel and a mission in her heart. When she rounded the corner that passed the high school, she slowed. A lone figure trudged toward the street in threadbare jeans, a T-shirt, and sneakers so old that the back half of the soles flopped every time she lifted her feet.

She knew this girl. Emma Stacy. Mia had never had her in class, but she'd seen her in the halls. Emma's smile had always lit up the room. Now, however, tears tracked down her pale cheeks.

Making a split-second decision, Mia pulled the car to the edge of the drive and hopped out. "Emma? Emma!"

The sophomore spun toward her, rubbing the tears off her cheeks. "Miss Turner. Hi."

Awkwardly, Emma ducked her head and shoved her hands in her pocket.

"Is there something wrong, Emma? Something I can help you with?"

"No, ma'am. I'm fine."

Mia stepped closer and kept her voice low and calm. "I can see that you aren't. You were crying. Is there anyone I can call for you?"

The girl's eyes flooded again. "Nobody'd come. My stepmom doesn't have time for me, and Xavier just dumped me. Like I was nothing. And he said he loved me." Emma sniffed and touched her stomach.

Mia's breath caught in her throat. Oh no. She knew what had happened. Better than most, she knew the situation. The shame. And the despair. "Emma. Are you pregnant?"

Emma's eyes flared wide, and her mouth fell open in a surprised O. But she didn't deny it. "Yeah. Xavier told me to get an abortion. But I don't want to, so he left me here. It's two miles to my house. And I don't know what my stepmom will say."

It was like living her past mistakes all over again.

"Look, let me drive you home." Mia had never let a student into her car. She couldn't abandon her on the side of the road though. Docile as a pet dog, Emma trotted after her, back to her car. She got in and buckled when Mia told her to. "Would you be willing to talk to Mrs. King?"

"The school nurse?"

"That's right. She's an old friend of mine."

Emma shrugged one shoulder. "I guess."

Mia tried to ask a few more questions, but Emma seemed to have shut down. Mia sighed and gave up. "Where do you live?"

Emma stared out the window and mumbled the address in a hopeless voice. Mia knew the street. She drove without attempting to engage again so she wouldn't alienate the teenager to the point where she'd refuse to confide in Mia in the future.

When they arrived at the house, there were no cars in the driveway.

"Oh, good. She's not home."

Mia didn't share Emma's relief. Two young children, no older than seven or eight, sat on the front porch, playing. "Do you have a babysitter?"

"What?" Emma's eyes flashed to her siblings. "Oh, nah. I guess she knew I'd be home sometime."

Mia stiffened. The casual excuse informed Mia that seeing the children home alone was a normal thing. She didn't trust herself to speak, so she confined her response to a nod.

Emma opened the door and slid out of the vehicle. Mia waited until the teenager had taken her brothers into the house before reversing out of the driveway. She headed back to the school, seething.

She wanted to help Emma. But what could she do? She wasn't a counselor. This was a delicate situation, and she had to step carefully. If only there were a pregnancy center in Renegade to recommend. The wish to help and the inability to do so tore at her frayed nerves.

No matter how hard she tried, she was never enough.

She needed that money from her summer job if she was going to make a difference.

At the intersection, she headed toward the school district campus. She recalled her promise to call Shannon King, the school nurse, who happened to be Mia's best friend since college. Shannon had been the one to inform Mia when the position for a learning support teacher had opened up at Renegade South High School.

She punched Shannon's button on the dashboard, then drummed her fingers and waited for her one and only friend to pick up the phone. Mia had tried to keep her distance when she'd walked into her dorm room for the first time to see the perky blonde hanging posters on the wall. Shannon seemed to see that as a challenge. After a month of resisting, Mia had given in. When she'd left Renegade after college, they'd maintained contact.

Shannon still didn't know why Mia kept to herself and had no other friends, or why she had ghosted her parents for years. That was one reason Mia loved her. She didn't try to force her way past the invisible boundaries Mia had drawn.

"Mia! What's up?" Shannon's bubbly voice oozed down the line. "Did you get your money?"

"Not yet. I got distracted—"

"Mia! You need to get paid! Didn't you tell me that's the only way you can afford to finish your counseling degree and open the pregnancy center? Girl, you've been talking about that for *years*!"

Shannon knew Mia's dreams. Just not why they meant so much.

"Trust me, I realize that. Look, I called because I need your help." She quickly described Emma's situation. "Shan, the poor kid. And to have no one at home? I feel so helpless. I know we can't help everyone, but we should be able to help her. Right?"

Shannon bit off what could only be described as a growl. "I thought something was up with Emma's family situation, but I could never prove it. Are you sure there was no one at the house?"

"I'm sure. Those littles, they were just hanging out on the porch, waiting. I have no idea how long. According to Emma, her mom just 'figured' she'd be home at some point."

Heat simmered in her gut. Anything could have happened to them.

"I'm going to have to ChildLine this, you know that." The bubbly tones had molded into steel.

"Yeah. I know. I just hate that she's suffering."

"I get it. Look, I'll keep you informed. At least, I'll tell you what I can. You know I can't break confidentiality."

"I do. I appreciate it." It was on the tip of her tongue to explain why she felt so strongly about Emma's situation, but she couldn't bring herself to say it. "I'm back at the district office. I need to go see if they can help me get my paycheck."

"I'll let you go. I'll say a prayer."

"Um, bye." Mia hung up. "That was a jerk move, Mia. Shannon was trying to be supportive. But she should know I'm not into that God stuff anymore."

Shannon had grown up in a Christian home, vibrant with love and faith. The only thing vibrant in Mia's home had been the facade her parents put on when they were in public. Both Mia's parents had been cold guardians.

Sometimes she envied Shannon.

She parked her car and turned it off. Sucked in a deep, bracing breath, held it, then slowly released it. She could do this.

She opened her door, then marched up the walkway leading to the district office and pushed the buzzer. When the door clicked, she opened it and walked into the main office. Instantly, cool air whooshed over her, hitting the sweat dotting her neck. She shivered.

Casually, she glanced around, her gaze taking in the closed door to the superintendent's office. It looked dark beyond the frosted glass.

Blaine Turner, her father, wasn't in.

Tension leaked from her shoulders.

"Hey, Helen." Mia smiled at the administrative assistant at the front desk.

For the millionth time, she wondered why she'd agreed to take a teaching job in the same district where Blaine Turner was the superintendent. But she knew why. When her aunt had gotten sick, she'd needed to move to Renegade fast. The teaching job had been the only job with benefits she could find on such short notice.

"Yes, Maria. What can I do for you? Are you having an issue with your classroom?" Helen flashed a cool, professional smile, one that didn't touch the smooth skin around her eyes. Her eyes flashed to the calendar on the wall. Clearly, someone didn't appreciate being interrupted.

That was fine. Mia wasn't here to make friends. She'd learned the hard way that letting people get too close meant giving them permission to rip your heart out and stomp on it. No, thank you. She'd focus on her students, teaching them to advocate for themselves so they could live a good life. They were her heart.

"I wondered if you could help me. I worked over the summer with that teen camp. You know, the one sponsored by the Youth of the Future Foundation? I haven't been paid, and I need the number to contact them. I tried the number I had, but it didn't go through."

Helen's smile morphed into a frown. Her brow furrowed. "I don't recognize the name of that foundation."

Mia opened her purse and pulled out the letter and the contract she'd signed. She handed them over to Helen, who perused them, shaking her head, before handing them back. "Sorry. This has nothing to do with the district. You'd better contact the foundation directly."

What did she think Mia had been trying to do the last few weeks?

Smiling through clenched teeth, she thanked Helen and stalked from the office, out to the parking lot. Her pulse pounded in her ears. The midafternoon heat slammed into her, robbing her of breath for a moment. Construction workers pounded on the roof of the high school. The roof repairs were scheduled to be completed at the end of the week. Several sleek SUVs and a newer-model hybrid lined the administration building. In contrast, a handful of older sedans, SUVs, and pickup trucks sat scattered in the lot by the high school.

She walked back toward her car, passing a row of scraggly cottonwoods. They didn't provide that much shade. While she walked, a faded van pulled in and parked. Lisa Fuller, the seventh-grade language arts teacher, got out and carried a box of supplies into the middle school wing of the high school.

Mia would have to track down the foundation people herself. She was surprised that Helen didn't know about the foundation, but a little extra work never intimidated her. Mia had been on her own for a long time. She knew the value of hard work. Going to the school district for help had been out of her comfort zone. She was independent and capable and preferred to act on her own. That's the way she liked it.

Then why did she suddenly feel so alone?

She blinked rapidly and pulled her sunglasses over her eyes. She wouldn't cry. She hadn't allowed herself that luxury in a long time. It never helped, only made her appear weak. Like a victim.

She might have been a fool, but she was no victim.

A truck rolled past the parking lot. She glanced at the driver and blinked.

Jackson Stewart.

Twelve years had passed since she'd seen him, but she'd recognize him anywhere. He was harder, his profile like granite. His head started to turn in her direction. She sucked in a breath. Her hands trembled at her side, and she ducked behind a tree.

In her mind, memories flowed like a movie. Jackson laughing at a joke she'd made. His lips moving close for a kiss. His hands caressing her face.

His face, rigid in shock and anger when she'd told him he was going to be a father.

She pushed the memories aside. Jackson had been her world. She'd trusted him with everything. Her heart. Her secrets. Her body.

When she'd lost the baby, she'd been devastated. And he'd betrayed her, ripping her life to shreds, destroying her reputation in a single day. To him, the child had been a disaster. To her, it was someone she could love unconditionally.

All the dreams she'd created about him had been a lie. Only she could make her dreams happen.

She waited another ten seconds to be sure his vehicle had taken him out of sight, then she strode to her car and jumped in. Once inside, she folded her arms across the steering wheel and dropped her head onto them. She only had until June next year to complete her master's degree, or she'd have to start all over again. She couldn't afford to do that. She only had two classes left to take. Two! Unfortunately, one of the courses was only offered in the fall. She had to enroll now, or it would be too late.

The problem was, she didn't have the money to pay for the courses she would be doing during the school year on top of her demanding job. She'd had money saved up, but then Aunt Augusta had gotten sick. Gus had no retirement money saved. No pension. Her insurance barely covered her medical bills. Mia had left her comfy apartment in Denver nearly two years ago and moved in with Gus, back in Renegade—the last place she wanted to be.

In the past two years, she'd paid the medical bills and caught up on the mortgage. Her job as a learning support teacher would cover the day-to-day bills, but the money she'd saved for her college classes was gone.

The summer stint as a camp counselor had seemed like a great opportunity to bring in some extra cash. Once she got her master's in counseling, she could finally become a full-time counselor and open a pregnancy center for those without support. Not in Renegade, of course.

Mia would have to go after the money herself.

Sighing, she pulled herself up and started the car. She needed to get the AC on before she suffocated. Glancing down, she saw she'd missed a call while she was in the office. She tapped the voicemail.

"Hi, Maria," a young female voice said. Obviously someone who didn't know her well, if she was calling her Maria. "You don't know me. I'm, well, I'm . . . It's too hard to explain over the phone. Listen. I have some information you need. Please call me back."

Mia scoffed. "Uh-huh. Right. Like I'm really going to call some stranger back without any more info than that?"

Her finger hovered over the delete icon, but something kept her from tapping it. What if this wasn't some kind of hoax? Or what if it related to the money the foundation owed her? She pressed the dial button.

"The number you are trying to call has not set up voicemail. Goodbye."

"Huh." She ended the call and pulled out of the parking lot.

What had she accomplished today? She still had no money to sign up for her classes. Her counseling degree was still out of reach. And her palms were still sweaty after seeing Jackson Stewart from a distance. She'd managed to teach his brother for a whole two years without a single glimpse of him.

Looked like her luck was changing. And not for the better.

Mia had one more stop to make, and then she could return home. She dialed her cousin Anne Marie's phone. It went to voicemail.

She frowned, uneasy. "Anne Marie, it's me, Mia. I'm going to get

Gus's medication now, then I'll be home. How has she been today? Call me if I need to pick up something else before I head home."

Call me so I know you're actually taking care of her.

The temptation to steer toward Gus's house was strong. But Gus needed her heart medication refilled, and the pharmacy closed at six. She wouldn't have a chance to come back into town.

Her cousin was a grown woman. She was popular, beautiful, and educated.

And Mia didn't trust her one bit.

NOTE FROM AUTHOR

This manuscript saw many changes over the past year. But isn't that what editing is for? There are many people I should name, but I won't for fear that I might forget someone. If you've encouraged me over this past year, thank you. I've received lots of encouragement from my previous launch teams as well as family, friends, and social media friends. Your kind words have inspired me to keep going, not give up on my writing journey.

This book would not have been possible without the love, prayers, and support of my family, specifically my mom and my husband, Ronnie. They've been my cheerleaders as I've struggled with deadlines and been my sounding boards as I talked out ideas.

To my ACFW Charlotte Chapter fellow authors—you are my tribe! You all have inspired me with your grace and patience this past year. You've lifted me up in prayer many times while I was writing this story. Your acceptance, love, encouragement, and prayers have helped me press on even when the road was tough and I didn't think I'd make my deadlines.

To my first editor, Kara Leigh Miller, who started me on this journey to write romantic suspense. Your encouragement made all the difference.

Finally, a huge shout-out to Lisa Phillips. To say that I was shocked when you first contacted me is an understatement. I kept asking myself, "Why me?" But you saw something in me and my writing. I am grateful for that first email correspondence. Your encouragement as well as availability over the past year have been invaluable, and it's something I don't take lightly. Thank you for your investment and faith in a new author.

Jennifer Chastain has been devouring books since her small-town childhood, when she dreamed of epic adventures, brave heroes, and love stories worth staying up for. Today, she writes suspense-filled romances threaded with danger, devotion, and hope that carries her characters through the darkest moments.

A northern transplant, Jennifer fell in love with the charm of the South—and with a Charlotte native she's been married to for more than thirty years. By day, she works at a research center at UNC Charlotte. By night and weekends, she writes, fueled by dark chocolate, Diet Coke, and determination. Jennifer enjoys rom-coms, long conversations about books, and being thoroughly supervised by a very opinionated cat who believes all keyboards exist solely for napping.

For more information, visit her at jenniferchastain.com.

HEROES OF
RENEGADE

Another epic series created by

SUSAN MAY WARREN

and **LISA PHILLIPS**

We solve the problem of what to read next.

WE THINK YOU'LL ALSO LOVE...

Infiltrating a dangerous militia to save her troubled brother, Jamie Winters finds herself kidnapped. Only Logan Crawford, the man she once broke, can rescue her—but he demands a promise in return. As they navigate peril in the Alaskan wilderness, their unresolved feelings spark a chance for love and redemption.

***Burning Hearts* by Lisa Phillips**

Stunt double Vienna Foxcroft's stunt team are the only ones she trusts. Then in walks Sergeant Crew Gatlin and his tough-as-nails military dog, Havoc. When an attack on a film set sends them fleeing into the streets of Turkey, Vienna must face the demons of her past or be devoured by them. And Crew and Havoc will be tested like never before.

Havoc by Ronie Kendig

When an attempt is made on Grey Parker's life and dead bodies begin piling up, suddenly bodyguard Christina Sherman is tasked with keeping both a soldier and his dog safe... and with them, the secrets that could stop a terrorist attack.

Driving Force by Lynette Eason and Kate Angelo

We solve the problem of what to read next.

www.ingramcontent.com/pod-product-compliance
Lightning Source LLC
Chambersburg PA
CBHW020912060726
47591CB00004B/1208
9781966463801